More From Meta Mad Books!

It was written first, but *The Campbell Club* is the sequel to *Saint Susan* (in terms of chronology of the point of view character). In *Saint Susan*, Sutra is a teenager going to boarding school, and the time period is 1978-1981. You can read either book first.

Saint Susan:
Mesa My Heart
David R. Smith
978-1763853959

The Campbell Club

An Historical Romance, 1985

David R. Smith
Meta Mad Books

ISBN: 978-1-7637262-7-7
Cover artwork by the author.
5 x 8 inches
Typeset in California FB 10/11pt.

Second Edition (Author's Preface, changes to Part 1).

For Lachlan

Author's Preface

初春まづ
酒に梅売る
匂ひかな

Early Spring. The first plums are sold for sake.
I can smell them.

—Matsuo Bashō (1644-1694)

The period of this 'historical' novel is right smack in the middle of the "Greed is Good" Reagan years, and can be fixed more precisely by saying that Oregon had just recently cut out the cancer of the Rajneesh cult—I think September 1985 is about right—and similarly where we will end the narrative, somewhat arbitrarily, is with the rediscovery of the Fender's Blue butterfly, *Icaricia icarioides fenderi*, which was formerly believed extinct but turned up unexpectedly, like a ray of light in a garden of joy, during the Spring of 1987, right there in the Willamette Valley.

The setting is in and around Eugene, Oregon, a beautiful location for a love story, and also for the birth of the Green Revolution. Eugene sits in the Northwest corner of the United States, just tucked under Washington State like a left armpit where California is the arm.

People used to come to Oregon, settlers, by way of the Oregon Trail. They came for the land, more specifically for the rich black soil. The native people, who were somewhat less than enthused by the new arrivals, were called the *Kalapuya*. They were peaceful hunter gatherers. These locals were soon infected with smallpox, and then later forcibly "relocated" to concentration camps in far eastern Oregon, so that beautiful black soil west of the Cascade Range was just lying there ready to be ravished, after a kind of forcibly instigated Terra Nullius.

Ah, that lovely, lovely, fertile soil! Dogs rolled in it; but perhaps they were wiser than men. Wildflowers grew, bees hummed, butterflies flitted freely feeding on abundant wildflowers, and mule deer foraged for juicy stems from sagebrush and mountain-mahogany. It must have been a paradise. There is even a river, a great and wonderful river that here has not yet become impassable on foot. You can wade across it all year around. Beavers dammed up its many seeping streams and tributaries, trout and chinook and coho swam in the vigorous, living water. Yes, the great Willamette, now somewhat reduced by our civilization's hatred of nature, but still, it flows on. By the time it reaches the Columbia up near Portland, and merges into it like a woman joining with a man, it is a mighty river.

Those settlers who claimed the land in and around Eugene—and they did just that, they simply "staked a claim" —typically between 320 and 640 *acres* per family, as per the Donation Land Claim Act of 1850—yes, they claimed the land. And they and their descendants eventually got around to building a University, once the ploughing had produced enough to support ideas like higher education. That was in 1876. Naturally the students needed places to live. So they built fraternities and sororities, and invented ways of hazing, and, just a bit later, they built the place that would become the Campbell Club. That was around 1925.

So our general environs is a big, amazing house filled with the sons and daughters of Americans going to University: a positive, uplifting experience for most. The whole concept of a student cooperative association that owned its own buildings and assets and was run democratically as a not-for-profit corporation—that was mind blowing; and obviously worthy of recording in a narrative about the dark years of the Reagan Presidency. Good things can happen even in the darkness. That is one theme of the novel.

Just to be clear, The Campbell Club was a real place; you can google it. It does not exist anymore in the exact form that I have described, but I have been in touch with the current inhabitants. They are apparently socialists or communists, working people, and not students. They are, at least in my definition, squatters (because SCA was always a student house). However, who am I to say what they are doing is wrong? My confidant in the house said she had just joined a polycule and also that she recently earned $500 for 10 minutes of work in the sex trade. So I guess more than a few things have changed. But they still have a cooperative house there, and they still have shared meals and so on. The kitchen looks much the same, and I imagine the carpet in the great main room is still the same and stinks just as much as it used to.

This novel is a work of fiction, and any resemblance to real persons, living or dead, is purely coincidental; however, the co-op and its values from that time in the 1980s were very real. Those values actually would serve contemporary Americans quite well, which is one of the reasons for writing the novel in the first place.

With respect to the protagonist, I know some readers will feel the need of more backstory. That cannot be helped. Robbie Gray's, aka Sutra's, backstory is told in considerable detail in *Saint Susan* (ISBN: 9781763853959, also from Meta Mad Books). So I will have to refer you to that work.

I hope you enjoy the story and that it inspires you to begin your own Green Revolution.

DRS
Avoca Beach, April 2026

The Campbell Club

An Historical Romance, 1985

David R. Smith
(2024)

Contents

Part One. How Things Started. I Practice Shock Buddhism and Make Some New Friends. Oh, and I Go to College.

"Fallen petals returning to the branch? —No, they are butterflies!"
—Arakida Moritake (1473–1549)

Connor glared at me through the open door. He knocked, I guess just to check if he was in the right spot, possibly hoping he was not. I said, "Welcome, earthling." And he just took one look at me and involuntarily shook his head. Just a smidge. "I'm Robert," I said. "But most people call me Sutra. You must be Connor?"

"Yeah. I'm Connor," he said. "Most people usually just call me Connor." He rallied quickly, after the shock of my appearance, and entered the room, beginning the business of checking it out, poking into the closet, seeing my few things in there, trying the adjacent bed to mine (which looked too short for his long 19-year-old frame), and, perhaps without being consciously aware, took in a few experimental breaths to experience the air of the room. He eventually relaxed onto the bare mattress for a few minutes and just grokked. It was natural, he had come a long way and finally was at the destination. It is like a small death to do that. I let him be. Meanwhile I was busy doing roughly the same exact things as he did, only I had a few hours lead time. I was ahead of him in all the physiological and emotional stages. I had even figured out where East was and had also helpfully reorganized the furnishings to maximize the Feng shui in the room. Not that he needed to know about that.

He started unpacking, then. Finally he said, not really looking in my direction except to glance, "Am I going to have to look at that all year? And why are you wearing that get up?"

"What? This little thing? It's just something I threw on." Yes, I was letting my freak flag fly that day and wearing my Sannyasin robe intentionally to get that all out in the open. I called it Shock Buddhism: if you hit people with *difference* hard enough, with the fact that there is another way, or perhaps even a myriad of other ways, potentially better ways, then they have to either take offence and risk being accused of bigotry, to cling to their smallness (in which case they were lost souls) or else accept you and feel righteous about it. I had hit Connor hard and I was sorry; but it had had to be done. My robe was saffron-coloured and quite comfortable. Yes, there was underwear. If someone said something silly I would usually just explain how comfortable the robe was. Actually a lot of women got that and didn't even take it as a put on, which it most certainly was.

The picture he was complaining about was a very small black-and-white picture of Osho aka the Bhagwan Shri Rajneesh, which I had cut out of a newspaper article from that morning. The article accused him of being a con-man and terrorist and so on. Of course, that was all true. By this point he had been deported. But still, the newspapers needed to rehash the story. For those who might have been under a rock for, you know, six or seven years. There was something poisonous in that kind of continuous replay, especially of the salacious; a lot of details were even invented for effect; something which suggested that underneath the condemnation of the blown con-man, was the essential truth that most of what was going on (such as in the newspaper business) was itself a con not yet blown. And that they were working over-hard to avoid it.

Be that as it may, I could not say things like that out loud. I had to keep driving within the lines. At least, if I was going to be accepted as a fellow student and co-op member. Which I badly needed. Right now (after all the shenanigans of being in a cult) going back to school meant a lot to me.

"It's not like a portrait of Chairman Mao or something. It's just by my bed. Is it a problem? I can take it down if, you know, you can't deal with it. The other option might be a blindfold. We could blindfold you when you come into the room so you don't have to see it."

He laughed. "Yeah, Good one. That's OK dude. You do you. And I guess I'll do me."

"I hope not too frequently, and please try to do it in the bathroom. Otherwise your sheets may become a biohazard."

He laughed again. "Good one. But what's up with the robe?"

"The robe is to remind me that I took a vow to myself, to be on The Path. Have you heard of The Path?"

"No," he said. "But I have a feeling I'm about to."

It was my turn to laugh. I was starting to like this Connor.

"The Path is the way of truth. Like on *Kung Fu*."

"Dude! At last we're on the same page. I like *Kung Fu*."

"Who the heck doesn't? Anyway, this picture is here to remind me that con-men exist and distractions and it's easy to go down the wrong rabbit hole. There's a lot of opposite of truth-telling going on. It's hard to know who God will use to speak through at any given moment."

"Whatever, my dude. We're cool. For now."

***

He got up from where he had been lying on the naked bed and went about unpacking his case. His handful of paperbacks went into a stack on the windowsill; I suppressed the urge to read the titles. He readied the small wooden desk for study-service by clamping a mechanical lamp fixture onto the side. Then he went out and came back a few minutes later with more boxes, and busied himself setting up a stereo, complete with turntable and speakers, over near his dresser. A crate of records rested in paper sleeves nearby. I wanted to ask about music, but I figured that it might be too soon. 'We'll get to that,' I thought. 'No use blowing things up right away.' So I asked a less monumental question.

"What's your major, Connor?"

"Fine Art."

"Wow. That's cool. What uh—what medium?"

"Ceramics."

"Ah! That sounds interesting," I said. Actually at that time I had no interest in it at all, I was just trying to make conversation. But now Connor's eyes were glowing.

"According to the professor who I interviewed with for the program, it's actually the art of *materials and techniques*. Ceramics is just a word. It doesn't tell you anything. But the actual thing itself, I love it."

"The 'art of materials and techniques' does sound better. I'll give you that."

"It's just more accurate. Ceramics is all about the elementals, about the four elements. Earth, Air, Fire, and Water. It connects to the total man, the Vitruvian man, that Da Vinci talks about."

I pricked up my ears at that. "Wow. Actually that *does* sound very cool. Better than what I'm doing."

"And what's that?"

"English Lit."

He laughed again. "Yeah. That would suck."

"But I plan to get into Creative Writing! I'm a shoo-in!"

"Sure dude, that's what all the English majors say."

***

Besides my dude Connor, were Maggie and Raven and Napoleon. There were other kids in the hall, but those were some of the first co-opers we hung with in those first few days of Fall Term, September 1985. This was the second floor, and it was no doubt very cool indeed.

Everyone seemed to have their own idea of what a good Campbell Club room looked like; but I liked the one Connor and I had, with the gabled window and the sunlight entering like a tide at particularly auspicious times of day. The Rasta threesome seemed to love their room too. It was huge, for one thing. In the beginning Connor used to go and sit in their room sometimes, learning how to smoke pot and talk about Bob Marley and things like that. I would usually hang back but drop in after the weed had progressed (as I was trying hard to be pure for spiritual reasons). Plus I just thought stoners were hilarious and they loved me when they were all stoned. I was a kind of hilarity maker—they laughed and laughed at whatever I said. But I won't try to reproduce it, because:

"Hey Sutra, you got underwear under that robe?" (Laughter.)

"Uh, sure. Lots of it."

"So you're not going commando?" (Laughter.)

"I would, but who would believe me?"

(Laughter.) "Come on, let's see!"

"But Raven might be frightened." (Laughter.)

"It's just too big, huh?"

"Too thick, actually. It's one inch long and six inches wide. That's a new record as far as I am aware." (Laughter.)

Dialog like this is to no point. It's just the Ganga talking.

***

Magda Slater, who we all called Maggie, was a Sociology and Communications double-major originally from Chicago's Far North Side. Like Connor, she grew up in Evanston. Her piercing blue eyes reminded me of the small clearies from my childhood marble bag. Her nose was eventually obliterated by rhinoplasty, but at the time of this story it was glorious, like the hood ornament on a Chevrolet. Wild brown hair frizzed into an afro if she did not take special steps to constrain it.

Magda was social in the positive way, social perhaps even to the definition of sociology, as a way to see and conceptualize the world. Her deep people-perceptions and uncanny intuitions turned out to be critical to the success of the whole co-op (as I will explain later).

Her admired and respected beau was Napoleon Brown Jr, late of Kingston, Jamaica. He looked a bit like Peter Tosh, but lanky to the point that his pants sometimes slipped down catastrophically under the force of gravity when his belt was not tight enough. And was very deep into Rastafari. They both were. It's not strange, this was 1985 after all. Bob Marley's smiling face looked down on their room from a huge poster, guru-like.

Napoleon claimed to have seen the great man *on the street* in Kingston, which was not entirely unbelievable; just imagine seeing a Bob Marley show *in Jamaica*. Now, everyone in those days claimed to have seen a Bob Marley show. Death magnifies and focuses the public attention, creating wannabes and a desire to claim a part of the legacy; while in life, the great man is often hated and despised.

But for Magda and Nappy, 'The Lion of Judah' was everything, and I believed them. All true gurus are, perhaps, one, in their aim. Jah is Love. Napoleon instructed me on these things, and many others, standing half-dressed in hallways, even as I taught him about Buddhism as we sat at our ease on the house porch, he gently toking under blue skies, me stoically enjoying the smell. He borrowed *The Way of Zen* by Alan Watts and never gave it back.

Did I mention the pot? There was an omnipresent scent of it in that room of theirs, and I often imagined an atmospheric effect of condensation not unlike the effect which causes a thunderstorm, might proceed from it. Weed and patchouli, a kind of perfumed miasma, yes, the sweet Ganga smoke mixed with the other gasses and smells of youth, female and male bodies in a yin and yang harmony, passive and active, in stillness and in movement.

And of course the music. The smooched articulation of it. It was not like the crass sonic emanations of a typical dorm room, like those on campus. And it was not the blare of MTV one experienced while walking by a frat house. More like an omnipresent vibe of love and joyful dance, as dancing often broke out. It was good times. Their triple was adjacent to the toilets, so one had to brave that doorway going down the hall to the john and it was always there, the music, softly emanating, vibrating in the coolness of the old house. A sound-current of magical movement.

Raven was the third wheel. I don't know how that worked, but apparently it did. It was no polycule, to be sure. They all lived in that room in close quarters for three consecutive terms in a state of boyfriend-girlfriend-platonic-third-wheel-friend until the whole thing blew up spectacularly. Everything works until it doesn't.

***

One night Magda and Napoleon walked down to the 7-Eleven for a Slurpee. They both had cottonmouth and their eyes were bloodshot, but not unduly so. This was an early evening in the Fall term. As I have said, the school year was only just getting going. Napoleon thought it was all so exciting to be in a new place in glorious America and have so many new experiences. He thought Oregon's climate was freezing, but it was worth it—he now had his squeeze to keep him warm. Magda had happened only a few weeks before at a music festival. Everything was going so well for them; he couldn't get the thought out of his head. *Jah*. It was meant to be.

Magda thought much the same. Her mother might not be thrilled, but Napoleon was certainly a charming black prince in tri-colored armor. Magda's mother assumed it was just a phase, a black boy phase. But Magda was hooked deep. She thought she had found a real Lion of Judah. She was seriously considering dreads but had not made the commitment.

The 7-Eleven was down Alder Street, which was our street. It's a one-way street, something that Johan (an Architecture major that I will speak more about later) always found inappropriate. He said traffic flowed poorly on a one-way street; that it was a bad use of public space. And there was never a lot of traffic, that much is true. I suppose it is still underutilized to this day and Johan is probably still distressed by this lack of good design. I can clearly hear his voice in my mind, discussing it in his baritone German-accent, as Connor and Leo listened on, eagerly learning from him, because he had lived abroad, and knew many interesting things, and had seen much of Europe. "That type of urban design is an anti-pattern. This city is in real need of a revamp. Preferably along the lines of a well-designed European city like Freiburg or Barcelona."

It was a pleasant evening to be out and about. And Magda was not even self-conscious about going without a bra, as she sometimes did around the co-op, but never out on the street. She felt safe with her man, walking in this mellow little college town, grooving along. She smiled a stoned smile and looked over at him, and he looked back at her in wonder and perceived the sagging in a delightful way that Napoleon interpreted as holy.

***

The frat boys who were in the 7-Eleven that evening were trying to buy malt liquor. They were already aroused that night by the excitement of using a fake ID and the feeling of power, and also of the forbidden, that it brings to have the all-important access-token to underage alcohol.

Probably they had done some minor moral outrages already that evening and now wanted to continue with their fun. I don't know if they were buzzed or what— it's quite possible. Anyway, things turned from uncouth laughter to outright derision pretty fast.

"Oh, look," one of them said, "a Jew and a nigger out for a stroll." It was the tall one, apparently the lead dickhead, and he was carrying a cardboard case full of Colt 45 towards the counter like Conan the Barbarian hefting a princess from Shadizar.

I will call this dickhead Frank, which is what was on his fake ID (more on that in a minute). Frank was dressed in preppy attire, salmon-colored shorts with a thin brown leather belt under a blue plaid button down that was half tucked in. What I mean is, one flap was in, and one flap was out. His uniformly proportioned face smiled at the world; his mop of brown hair stood at attention under gel; the skin on his hands, face, and arms, was silky and smooth, like baby skin. His friends were similarly dressed although with different shades of pastel. These were the guys who might have applied to Stanford with high hopes but only got into the University of Colorado at Boulder and the University of Oregon, Eugene, and chose Eugene because Dad had heard Boulder was too much of a party school. Dad wouldn't help pay for Boulder. Well, they partied anyway.

Napoleon didn't even look in their direction. He was focused on operating the slushy machine in an effective, even artistic, manner. He worked the controls like a dancer. But when she heard what Frank said, Magda drew a startled breath as if tased. Their laughter hurt. Her face, normally pleasantly round, almost rotund, contracted longitudinally into an elongated grimace, like the Grinch looking aghast; and it also flattened, her eyes becoming two angry beads, like pinpoints of lava. "*WHAT? What the hell*...what the *HELL* did you say?"

The frat boys tittered but quickly turned back to their task of buying the brew. They grinned their big boyish grins. The store clerk, an older guy, looked at the frat boys when Frank put the beer on the counter, but said nothing. Frank boldly presented his ID, slapping it down on the worn Formica countertop as if he were making some form of political statement. The clerk frowned—he was no idiot—but he had deniability, I guess. He nodded at the brown mop head.

"So you're 24, are you then, uh, Frank?"

"Yeah, that's right."

Magda had taken a step closer, working on adrenaline and sheer hate, interjecting herself into the conversation. She pointed a thin finger at him like a claw. "Yeah, that's 'Frank' alright. Frankenstein. He flunked a few classes and was sent back. That's pretty obvious. Otherwise everyone knows what an underage kid looks like."

The frat boys were no longer smiling. Frank couldn't keep himself under control. "Hey, bitch, we're trying to make a transaction here."

"Skank," said another, eying Napoleon.

That worthy had now completed drawing the cold, reddish slushie substance from the dispenser into two paper cups, had applied lids and straws, and was casually waiting to approach the counter once the frat boys had cleared the area. His eyes grazed the top of their heads, not looking at their faces at all.

However they misinterpreted his casual glance. "What are you looking at, boy?" said the flabby one with baby blue shorts.

Napoleon was still silent, although he now made eye contact. His eyes, which formerly were oriented above their heads, in a completely peaceful mode, now slowly, gradually, drifted down onto their faces, connecting eyeball to eyeball. His face, according to Magda, began to take on "a definitely harder demeanor," like a rat terrier at a pig farm.

Meanwhile the frat boys, having had their fun, wanted to rush on to their next happening—the beer was not getting any colder—their gayety must migrate, chaos was their style, and having paid with a $20 and receiving a few coins in return, the herd trippingly exited the store.

Napoleon sighed and then took his position at the counter. He hated confrontation. "Dos guys," he said. His corduroy Rasta cap, which was unsnapped and overladen, trembled as he shook his head back and forth.

The clerk pushed buttons on the cash register. "Yeah. Frat boys," he said, as if this explained everything.

Magda and her man had got about a block back up Alder Street when Frank and the boys pounced.

"Rasta nigger!"

"Kike! Big-titted kike!"

They knocked Magda over from behind and her Slurpee splashed violently onto the ground, the cup somersaulting and then flying into the dirt. Napoleon was a bit quicker and tossed his drink onto the chest of one the frat-boy squad but got hit in the face with a water balloon in return. A few more balloons pelted down from the dark surrounds.

"Skanks! Get out the fuck out of town!"

"We don't want you here!"

The frat contingent—there were at least ten of them in all, at this point, their numbers had swelled—scattered gleefully, pathetically high-fiving and slapping each other on the back as they disappeared into the darkness.

Napoleon helped Magda up. She was shaking with rage, her chest heaving. Then she stopped and began to cry. Because she was suddenly sad. They had called her a bad word. It was mean. The kids cleaned themselves up as best they could.

***

Back at the co-op, the story was told and retold, and then once more at breakfast. There was general agitation, and word travels pretty fast. But it did not make its way to Terry Bradman and Mike Dix until later in the week.

Bradman was something of an enigma, at least to those who did not understand his way of thinking and being. He was a junior, a Human Physiology (Sports Medicine) major. He, Bradman, had given up a promising football scholarship to pursue his dream of one day playing Ultimate Frisbee on a professional level. Tough, physically and mentally hardened by the Wisconsin football mentality of his tiny hometown of Green Bay, he was very much everything one would expect from a guy with the exceptional agility of a wide receiver. He probably could have played any position he set his mind to in the college game format. And yet, he passed.

"I want to play the Gentleman's Game, Dad," he had said to his father. "It's called Ultimate. It's a kind of frisbee game like football and soccer all in one. They're starting to play it professionally."

As I imagine it, the old man was grim and stood weepy-eyed, just stunned, dazed and confused. He knew very well what Ultimate was. Ultimate was for pussies.

"There's no referees in Ultimate, Dad. If there's a disagreement, the two captains work it out. Civilized like. It's so cool."

His father, who we will allege worked many tedious hours in a department store in downtown Green Bay, had long ago accepted that his son was *different*. He even worried his son might be gay. But when he started playing sports, much of that worry vanished. Everything was good, the boy was no faggot. But now, things began to go off the rails once more.

"Son, this is your big opportunity!"

"Ah, Dad."

"But a football scholarship! Think of the money. It's a golden ticket, for Christ's sake. I already told Ted next door!"

"Please, Dad...don't do this to me..."

That's how I imagine it. I don't personally think he was 'different' at all; and I know for a fact he wasn't gay, because we talked about all that. Bradman always struck me as an ordinary guy with ordinary tools put into the extraordinary situation of being called upon to be heroic. (Or what passes for that in our time). In another time, he would be going off to war to kill Nazis; but now it was the sublimation of war, the substitute for war, which is football, that he had been called upon to accept as his destiny. And he pissed on it. Sorry, I should say, he passed on it.

Perhaps he was more than anyone knew, and he didn't like the bullshit we as a nation were swimming in. He was attracted to the counterculture, certainly, to weird ideas and conspiracy theories, exactly because the authentic world of the times was so fake. This was America in the "Greed is Good" 1980s. What a mess.

Reagan was well on the way to senility and who knew who was really calling the shots. We were literally afraid of nuclear annihilation, and the Big Ronnie was making jokes about it. So, yes, it was admirable what Bradman did in passing on a football scholarship. We all thought so.

And then there was Mike Dix. Dix was Patroclus to Bradman's Achilles: smaller, more maneuverable in some ways, but still athletic, he was a tiny little dude, and prone to bouts of hysterical laughter mixed with sputtering coughing fits. He was asthmatic. Or something. The guy was always there with his buddy, listening, laughing, and dosing right alongside of him, all-in. They would take their shirts off and do push ups while the ecstasy was coming on. They were considering matching tattoos, but Bradman didn't want to have to explain one to his mother.

So, that Wednesday they heard about what happened. Terry went to get more details from Napoleon, perhaps a description, or some Greek letters on a jacket, something to trace them back. He then listened closely to Maggie's hysterical story, which was still fresh in her mind even if there had been slight exaggerations and conflation of detail with each telling. In the main, it was as I have narrated. "Are you OK?" he said. He was full of sympathy, like a knight errant who must now kill a beast to save a maiden.

"I am OK," she said bravely. "It's so hard to face this kind of thing. It's just not fair. We didn't do anything wrong."

He patted her on the shoulder. "You are right, you did not. And I *really* do hate Nazis with a passion. I really, really do."

"And so do I," put in Dix.

"These frat boys are bad enough," he continued. "They pollute the very air by their presence. But antisemitic slurs? Calling our dear friend Napoleon the n-word? Don't worry Maggie. This will not stand!" He said it loudly, and to the room at large, for they stood in the dining room and many were present. They could hear him even in the kitchen through the swinging doors.

Magda now looked up at him from below, that is, she looked up at him due to her short stature. I suppose many women spend their entire lives doing that to men, and it seems if we could just cut men off at the knee or else give women higher lifts, a lot might change. But anyway, what she said was, "What will you do? Are you going to do something to them? I don't want you to get in any trouble."

Bradman Achilles crossed his arms. It was as if the heavy shield of Hephaestus was already strapped to his back.

"You'll see," said Mike Dix.

***

But retribution, like an unstoppable plot point in a heroic ancient narrative, perhaps by Aeschylus or Homer, had to wait until the weekend. Three long days. Magda's eyes bled. Nappy? Well, he'd already got past it. Being an outsider, he was used to such things. Jah was his Protector. "Dat is di truth, man! In Jah!"

***

I have not said much about Mike Dix. He was a Chemistry major, an undergrad. He had friends in that Department, grad students, really sharp cookies, one in particular who no longer attended classes, but was still busy with chemistry at home. In his basement. Mike was in the inner circle of chemistry lab knowledge, which is like a tribe specializing in materials and techniques, but not for art, but rather for industry.

He went over to this guy's place that Friday night. In those days MDMA had only just become illegal. There was a clampdown, but all the old ways and means of getting the stuff were still working. The lab was still in operation. In fact, it had never been busier. And the market for MDMA was about to explode.

That Friday night Terry and Mike suited up for battle and dosed in their room, downing the little capsules with Gatorade. They called it 'E.' It is a drug that I am ashamed to say I eventually took myself.

After about twenty minutes they started to rush. They went down to the 7-Eleven, then, and hung around outside in the parking lot, doing push ups, Dix goading his friend on to greater efforts.

There was music outside the 7-Eleven, and perhaps surprisingly, it was classical music that blasted from the loud-speakers, not rock or country. The selection at the moment was Bach, a cantata, and the purpose of the music was to keep homeless people and hooligans from loitering. It's true, music has the power to repel as well as attract. I'm not making this up; 7-Eleven did this experiment and classical music kept the homeless away when other music did not. I don't know if it was just Bach; perhaps Beethoven would have worked as well. But Terry and Mike loved working out to a good basso continuo. They found it calming.

After a while the frat boys showed up looking for malt liquor. It was the same squad, Bradman even thought he recognized 'Frank' from the gym. It's a small world, the U of O Athletics Department. Bradman was known and respected. And probably, feared. They had seen him lifting, sweat pouring off his back, or in the shower, like a side of raw beef, or later in a towel. Frank certainly eyed him as they went in, sensing trouble. Yes. The frat boys went into the shop and tried to ignore Achilles, who apparently had decided to work out to *Wie schön leuchtet der Morgenstern* in a parking lot.

Achilles watched them go into the shop and then cruised in, shirtless, his pectoral muscles quivering, eyes dilated; he brought death and destruction. And Dix-Patroclus walked behind, sniffing, and grimly looking out for his friend. The frat boys moved toward the counter with a box of beer just as they had that other night, but Bradman got in their way, pushing through them. One of them foolishly said, "Hey, what's your problem?"

Bradman stopped, slowly, he turned around. Stared him down. "Oh, so we've got a frat boy. Actually a whole pack of them. Come on over here, Mike, and have a look at these pussies." He took Patroclus in his arms and gave him a big kiss on the lips. There was tongue. Then he turned to the frat boy. "You got a problem with that?"

The frat boy didn't say anything. His buddies hovered around the counter, wanting to move on, and 'Frank,' the one with fake ID, hurriedly tried to pay. But

Bradman stepped forward, brusquely pushing through to the counter and interrupting the transaction. "We were here first. You're going to have to wait, frat boy. Hey, wait a minute." Speaking to the clerk, he said "that ID of his—that's fake, isn't it? Don't you know there's a lot of that going around? This guy's name isn't frank."

The clerk—this guy was himself younger— mumbled.

Bradman's deep voice was like fate itself, it rolled on inexorably. "You could lose your liquor license for that, you know? I don't like seeing these punks in here breaking the law. It upsets my sensibilities. What about you, Mike?"

"I got a mind to call this in, bro. My uncle is a cop. Get that ID!"

Bradman lunged, and Frank the frat boy tried to retrieve the precious ID. But Bradman's grip on the flabby wrist gradually tightened like a vice.

"Let go! Let go, dammit! Ouch! That hurts!"

This was enough for the other frat boys, they charged towards and through the store doors, banging and jangling their way outside, leaving their prize of beer behind on the counter. I can see them in my mind's eye clumsily making their way out into the darkness, mouthing obscenities. Bradman let go, then, and Dix laughed as the unfortunate Frank rubbed his arm. For a moment it looked like he was going to cry.

"Oh look," said Bradman. "I made him tear up."

Frank the frat boy left, angry now, cursing under his breath about getting even.

Bradman eyed the store clerk. "Well, well, well. It looks like young 'Frank' left his ID. I think I'll keep this for him. I wouldn't want him to get into any more trouble with it. Right? Don't you agree?"

The store clerk continued to mumble about 'no shirt no shoes no service' as Terry, still laughing, pushed the door open for his friend. He held up the ID. "That's OK, we got what we came for, friend. Now, you didn't see us steal this, did you? He left it, right? We'll return it to him someday, maybe."

They blew outside like a saffron cloud. A glowing mist, perhaps the radiance of an ancient god, surrounded them and the night applauded as they strolled unconcerned up the street, laughing. That's the way I picture things.

The next morning, with much fanfare and many flourishes, Bradman presented the ID to Magda at a late breakfast/brunch that was well attended. Napoleon bowed. It was a happy Saturday. I was in the kitchen that morning and had cooked the Greek Camp Stew, which is fried potatoes and spinach and then eggs cracked on top, and finally feta cheese. It made for a very satisfying meal. People crowded around; plates were filled. Sounds of laughter and much back slapping could be heard. "Here's a trophy for you, my dear," said Bradman. "Courtesy of Mr. 'Frank Boffin' of the Alpha Beta Gamma House."

***

Moving Day was in late September, and it was a ritual immediately preceding the Fall term, when housing all came available and everyone was coming back. It was a time of joy and plenty. I met Leo then, because he asked me specifically if I wanted to go with him. I had an idea of who he was, but this was our first outing. He spotted me in the dining hall reading at breakfast.

"What are you up to?" he said.

"Nothing much. Just waiting for Godot while I eat this incredible yogurt."

"Our secret recipe. Why don't you come with me dumpster-diving today? Sometimes I need an extra pair of hands."

"Why not."

***

Leo and I set out on foot. We each had a pack; I had borrowed Connor's, which was robust and made of canvas. Leo wasn't saying much, but I didn't care. We headed generally towards the dorms, roaming the streets outside the residence halls like ragged bandits, scouring the sidewalks, scanning for useful cast offs. College kids are of course notorious for throwing things away. I once scored a full, unopened bottle of liquid laundry detergent—a ten-dollar value—that someone just didn't want to pack.

Amidst reeking, urine-stained castoffs and piles of sour beer cans we found oak tables, very serviceable upholstered chairs, random stainless steel forks and spoons of all kinds: everything in quite good condition, and perfect for our little housing co-op. But the pickings were sometimes much better and more diverse than sundries.

Leo Johansen—I should introduce him properly; he was Campbell Club's house president. And eventually my friend—Leo rounded the corner down on Kincaid Street—the whole block was *Chi Omega Mu, Delta Delta*

Delta, Kappa something something or other—when he saw it.

"Sutra," he said. "Look. My God!"

"What? What?"

"That!"

His thick stubby finger pointed at a wooden assemblage of ancient origin. It was a piano. A huge piano.

"It's a grand by the looks of things!" Leo was almost dancing. But inwardly I groaned.

A group of girls were gamely pushing the huge instrument out the door of their house, struggling and grunting and groaning. They had opened the large double doors at the front of their stately Sorority house, all brick and glass and white paint. The manicured yard, serviced no doubt by their 'Jap gardener' every Thursday, was immaculate.

Always the gentleman, Leo joyfully came forward from the sidewalk, his arms outstretched like a welcoming family member—perhaps a second cousin, just extended family, but still—a guest who has been invited to Thanksgiving dinner. "Ladies, ladies! May we be of any assistance?"

One of the sorority sisters, a pretty one, designed for maximum self-sufficiency, smiled at him. "Of course big guy, get your ass over here."

Yes, Leo was physically quite tall and well built, an attractive specimen. "Thickness," someone said. He was an Alaskan and always talked up his physicality as being required for the harsh existence of his home state. (Of course, he hailed from Anchorage, where life is much like it is anywhere in the lower 48).

We proceeded to heave and lift along with the sorority sisters. There were uglies and beauties among them. I had noticed this effect before—an ugly and a beautiful will often team up. The pattern held good here as well, among the four females. Understand—I had no bias towards them, either for being sorority sisters or being female. To me, they were merely souls in need of emancipation. Leo smoothly gleaned their names. Babs was the pretty one pulling at the front, and Taffy was her ugly alternate. They were assisted by two more sisters who were pushing from the rear. Sadly, I no longer remember their names, or I would report them here for posterity.

"So you're trying to transport this great old beauty to a new location, is that it? What an amazing instrument!" said Leo.

"We're trying to get rid of it if that's what you mean." Babs stopped and flexed her arms, as if in pain, causing the whole crew to come momentarily to a halt. "We just want to get this old junk out onto the street for pickup. Can't stand looking at it any longer."

"What?" Leo feigned shock. "But, what's wrong with it?"

The sisters had a variety of complaints.

"It's just old, I guess."

"And it's terribly out of tune."

"People just pound on it like a toy."

"It's got to go!"

"Yes, it really has to go."

Yes, the sister-consensus was clear. Leo put his fingers together into a steeple and the tips of each of his fingers bounced off one another—one of his signature gestures—and cogitated. "So, this means if I and Sutra here wanted it...for the Campbell Club?"

"Obviously," said Babs.

"The Campbell Club?"

"Over by Kappa Delta!"

"That used to be a sorority house, didn't it?"

"Like 100 years ago!"

The sisters chattered and twittered like little chirping birds. They eyed me as if I were a freak of nature, which of course was probably true. I was wearing a robe and beads, and my head was shaved at that point. I was still in my intimidation phase, where I tried to shock people into submission by being different. I was like the black kid on the block, the one with the weird vibe. They had to deal with it and wake up; or else crash out. Shock Buddhism was like open mic poetry. You never knew exactly what the day would bring. The girls were certainly tripping, but they were interested—not scared. I had a sense that if time permitted we could have had a sorority piano orgy. Like *Animal House*. But no. The "Babs" sister in particular had a lot of what ever it is that every college guy is after; and Leo was lit like a 4th of July sparkler. But my fantasy assignation was not to be.

***

We had now made progress, got most of the way down the yard towards the sidewalk, a distance of some thirty feet. Gradually as we got closer to the sidewalk the sisters had dropped off, until it was just me and Leo doing the pushing. Suddenly I was pushing on my own, the mad monk, and Leo was standing with the sisters chatting up a storm. His arms were on his waist, the left arm occasionally raised to allow his large, meaty hand to gesture, and the sisters were smiling and laughing, almost giggling, staring at the ample hair on his partly exposed chest. He seemed to engage as easily with the uglies as with the pretties. I thought it was pathetic; but then I rarely even feel human. I understood, this was a thing humans did. It was mating, the mating ritual of the *Homo Economicus*. The dominant species, but likely soon to be extinct.

I was perspiring heavily now and stopped, having attained the sidewalk like a hard-won realization. My robe was drenched; my beads drooped in exhaustion.

"We'll be back soon, ladies!" Leo was saying. "Just got to organize for transport. Don't let anyone walk off with this beauty, now, will you please?"

"Don't worry, big guy!" This from Babs, who had a big smile.

"Bye-bye," said the sisters, who laughed and waved.

***

Walking back towards the co-op, Leo pondered the question of transport.

"Will it fit in the van do you think?"

"I doubt it," I said. "That thing is huge. And how will we get it up onto the porch?" At that point in time we had no wheelchair ramp: Thomas Pincheon III, our first disabled co-op member, had not yet moved in. One still had to navigate steps up to the great wooden front door of the house that was now our shared home away from home.

Leo snapped his fingers, an idea having penetrated into his prominent, even over-sized, brow. "I think this is a job for Stan Harmon."

***

And so, that afternoon a grungy step-van motored down Alder Street and turned, creaking slowly to a halt in the alley next to the co-op. I didn't know Stan, this was my first taste. But everyone talked about him.

Stan Harmon, who we called Wig for obvious reasons, was a tall, wiry *mensch* with a wicked goatee and hair that, like a Thing wanting to begin a wild rumpus, demanded to be set free. He stepped down from the driver's side and pulled out a packet of Camel Straights, igniting one in a blaze of glory with a Ronson lighter. Riding shotgun was Larry Caputo wearing his usual leather cap, filthy jeans, and stolen letterman jacket.

Leo greeted them warmly and then introduced me. They were both co-op veterans. We began moving the stuff that was currently in the step van—lots of it, the thing was packed with heavy objects—onto the back porch and entry-way of the co-op, to make room for our cargo.

Tools, mostly, and objects that seemed to be made of iron. Paint cans. Orange cones. Signage. An entire machine shop, apparently, from the looks of it. Of course, Stan and Larry both had lift belts. They laughed when I cried out while trying to budge a huge metal toolbox down to the ground.

"You shouldn't really be lifting without a belt, you know, Sutra." This from Larry, as he easily hefted the toolbox with a powerlift to his shoulder.

"Safety first, my boy!" laughed Harmon.

"But—I don't have one."

"Then maybe you should sit this out. We don't want you to bust a nut or get that nice saffron robe of yours too dirty. You can say a prayer for us instead. It's frat boy row—enemy territory, if you know what I mean."

But Leo quickly came to my defence. "We need him for sure. Lifting that monster is going to take at least six people. Maybe eight."

Stan said, "It's going to be a family affair? That's fine. The more the merrier. Sutra, why don't you go and see who you can find inside to help with the move. We'll get the van ready."

I walked through the empty kitchen into the dining hall and spotted a girl who I initially found to be quite intimidating. Rachael Day was her name.

"Um...Hi," I said. "I'm Sutra."

"Hi there," she said. "What can I do for you?"

"I'm out back with Leo and Stan Harmon? We're doing a dumpster dive caper and I need to find some guys to help. But I don't know anybody yet. Can you suggest some people? Maybe help me to find some strong bodies?"

"But—what about me? I want to help too."

"You? But it's heavy lifting..."

She shook her head in disgust. "You're such a dinosaur," she said. "Didn't Osho ever teach you anything about women's liberation? I'll get Raven from upstairs. Or maybe Carrie Anne is around. She can probably bench press more than you can." (That was true enough as I learnt later. Carrie Anne was another Alaskan and was training for the winter Olympics. She only appears once more in this book, but it is at a critical moment.)

"Well, OK," I said. "But it's a piano."

She laughed. "A piano? Tell me this isn't Leo's idea. Well, I guess a piano would look nice in the living room."

So Rachael left to get some more volunteer labourers to assist in the cause. She came back in a few minutes with hiking boots on and a blue bandana around her neck, good to go—not with Carrie Anne, alongside her was another rather intimidating girl named Eva. Eva Redbone. Eva was shorter in stature than Rachael, but looked quite strong, which made sense, I soon learned she was a Dance major. I followed them out the back, and we all climbed into the step van.

Then Harmon addressed the assembled group: "All right boys and girls. Strap yourself down or hang on as best you can! Next stop, frat boy row."

The cranky old step van started up and Harmon moved the clutch to put the rig into gear.

"We're moving!" said Eva. "Woohoo!"

Eva Redbone had a southern drawl that might have been originally from Alabama. "You'all boys drive real careful now. You got precious cargo back here." It was like her nose was perennially stuffed up. A deviated septum, perhaps. Secretly I thought she might be intentionally exaggerating her southern drawl for effect.

When she was present in a room or came into a situation, to make an entrance, strike a pose, somehow it always quickly became Eva Hour—she was the center of attention or tried to make herself so. She smelled like a patchouli nose gay.

Rachael Day was a completely different cup of tea. Very laid back, "grounded." Later in response to my query, Leo explained she was from Bozeman, Montana. Her accent was neutral—clean—but the timbre of her voice was high and musical. There was a tang about it. Her golden-sectioned face was put together like a Greek marble, the nose aquiline, chin jutting forth just a little, Picasso-esque. Her sturdy frame was well-developed, almost voluptuous in its proportions; and yet her typical outfits, what she found most comfortable to wear, usually included hiking boots and wool socks and the inevitable Pendleton plaid shirt. She was perfectly at home in these forested Eugene environs, like a goddess of the woods, a goddess of the Weyerhaeuser Corporation, good to go for a hike or a skinny-dip in the cold Willamette on a warm spring day.

I watched as Leo positioned himself strategically next to Rachael. Of course he did. They seemed to be chatting softly and she was smiling. I was just busy trying to hang on as there was no hand grip near my position. The van crept along at variable speed in low gear, and we took a bump that tossed me with a jolt into Eva's arms. I could suddenly down-blouse her ridiculous spaghetti-strapped top. She grinned and we had a moment of shared patchouli before she popped me upright like a dancer popping up from a fandango. Yes, she had some strength in that slight frame.

Eventually we pulled up to the Sorority and piled out. Suddenly Leo's face contorted. He had not been able to see out the front window as we rolled in. Larry gave out a low whistle, and Stan scowled. "See, I told you—enemy territory."

The piano had had visitors while we were gone. There was spray paint on the black polished wooden top and rim with the words, "CO-OP SCUM!!!" There were additional touches, a penis or two, and other obscenities. I could see some guffawing frat boys over at the next house, but when Leo approached them, they thought discretion was the better part of valour and bugged out.

"I'm going to scrub all that off," he muttered, "don't you guys worry." But our immediate task was clear: to get the thing loaded into the step van. Luckily Stan had the situation well under control. It seemed the mechanical business I had hardly noticed near the back door was a winch. Harmon busied himself setting it up, and Caputo got us moving to position the monster. He produced straps, such as a professional mover might use to move a large object, and directed us to wrap them around the bulk of the beast.

Leo was glowing again as if irradiated. "Oh my lord, it's a Steinway!"

"A Steinway? Well I declare!" Shouted Eva.

"Not so loud!" Leo and I looked at each other and shared a telepathic thought: we both realized at the same time if the sisters knew what it was they had pushed out onto the street they might want it back. He spoke in a low voice. "This is a Model M. It's a smaller model, and has been abused, but come on guys! We've got to get going! This is a treasure we must retrieve, and to quote Ulysses S. Grant, we must stand our ground *at all hazards*."

"We're almost ready," said Harmon.

"Good to go back here," said Rachael.

We pushed the great black beast until it was directly under the hook of the winch. Caputo moved into action, attaching the winch to the tackle and giving a quick thumbs up.

Harmon pulled the lever. "Here we go, kids!"

The piano slowly rose off the ground, its three legs dangling wildly as Leo tried to stabilize it, the winch straining terrifically under the load. When it reached the necessary height, Caputo pulled one of the straps gently into the van with a rope. He gave a quick thumbs up, and we cheered. It was in!

Just as we were finishing up, I noticed Babs, the sorority sister, looking out the window of the shiny brick and white paint Kappa house. She seemed to be speaking with some concern into the telephone, listening, and speaking again. I motioned to Leo, and he immediately got the drift.

"Oh Lord. We're out of time. We've got to go."

"But we're not entirely strapped down back here," said Caputo.

Leo was red-faced. "Go!"

Babs had now hung up the phone and was moving towards the door. She soon opened it and stood there waving, beautiful in her concern and confusion, trying to get Leo's attention.

"Don't stop whatever you do," he said to Harmon.

"Who's that?" Rachael had taken notice. "She looks like Farrah Fawcett-Majors!"

"Just a damsel in distress," I said.

Formerly so happy to socialize, Leo suddenly went all stone-faced and ignored Babs, turning quickly away as she came outside and began to run towards the van. We were rolling. Stan pressed on the gas.

***

Back at the co-op, and flushed with triumph, Harmon gently backed the step van off the road and between two trees, moving slowly over the lawn, and as far as he could towards CC's deck and huge front door.

There remained a few feet of steps which must be transited by heavy manual labor. Indeed, it took an additional four bodies to accomplish it beyond the current step van raiding complement. Miraculously the piano legs did not have to be removed, although it was necessary to bring the majestic instrument in on its side.

***

I should now explain a little bit about the interior of the co-op house. The Campbell Club possessed a very large living room, or front room space, carpeted, and for most of the time I lived there, mostly clear of furniture—a couch or two, picked up from previously successful dumpster dives, but that was all. And at the far-end was a working brick fireplace, now cold and dark, but useful on winter nights. Windows with brass hooks and clasps stood mostly closed or slightly ajar, letting in a bit of freshness that helped make the dusty, positively filthy carpet more bearable. Leo now directed, like an empresario, as the piano was moved into what he called a perfect position near to both the fireplace and an outside window.

"It's perfect! Better than perfect!" He trumpeted.

"So...now then...can anyone play?"

No one put up their hand. After a moment I cleared my throat and stepped forward.

Leo seemed surprised. "Sutra?"

"What?" I said. I took a seat using an improvised chair from the kitchen—we had failed to recover the piano bench—and played a few test notes. "This thing is horribly out of tune." Then I plucked out a melody— the famous melodic line from *Casablanca*, the one Sam plays for Ingrid Bergman. My mother had a piano. It seemed to surprise people that I could play. I guess they had never seen a guy wearing a saffron robe and beads playing a piano.

"Sing!" Eva called out.

"Don't be silly," I said.

***

We heard later that several calls were placed from audibly upset callers—probably parental units—to the SCA corporate office, which is basically a closet situated in the sister co-op, the Janet Smith house. It's a few blocks down the street. Abigail, the ancient bookkeeper, fielded those calls. Bravely, she fronted for us. Or perhaps more specifically for Leo. Abigail had survived the wreck of Rajneeshpuram (as indeed I had). Leo 'rescued' her and gave her a job when no one else would. But as she honestly knew nothing about the piano—I can see her in my mind's eye, answering, thinking *oh my what have the kids done*—she could honestly report nothing.

Yes, we had pulled off the dumpster-diving caper of the century. No scrounging dorm-dweller could be more impressed than we were with ourselves that day. A special dinner, perhaps even pizza, was in order. The Steinway is a little worse for wear but still a beautiful instrument and we hope someday someone here will play it in earnest.

***

A few more basic facts about the Campbell Club: it's a three-story building, brick and wood, with beautiful wood floors that could seriously use refinishing, and an enormous wooden stairwell with a real banister, like in the movies. It's a structure that indeed started out as a sorority house—all the way back in 1925. Those of us who have lived there know this is true because of the ghost. Yes, there's a ghost in the Campbell Club.

When I moved in, that first term, I wanted to paint the walls in our room. They needed it, to be honest. The Feng Shui was all wrong; icy blue cooled the room when what we needed was more heat and energy. Connor didn't care, but I looked into it. I found plenty of paint stuff in the basement and started scraping into the paint coating the ancient radiator. Layer after layer of paint—maybe 20 layers revealed themselves. Multi-colored, variegated, even whimsical, but buried deep.

I stopped scraping then, in part because—what's the point—but also because I understood many other people had come before me. I could no more erase their spiritual presence from that room than I could change the past. What was past was done, but it lingered. People call it "history," but what does that word mean?

History is a slaughter-bench, said Hegel. Well then, it is also an interpenetration of the dead into the world of the living.

The ghost was something like that, I think. A trace energy, a past remembering. And sadly a remembering of someone who suffered.

She first appeared to Foster the Stoner. I know what you're thinking, but Foster had no reason to make up a story. He was a quiet, studious stoner, a Mathematics major (of all things) and his calm round face with bloodshot red eyes and a ginger mop was a common sight on the landing of the second floor, where his room was situated across from mine. He was located across the hallway and just slightly down from the triple where Magda and Company lived. So, that worked. No doubt, there was flow of bud and conversation and Napoleon Brown Jr had stories of sunny Jamaica to share—wonderful fare for the stoned imagination. And what did Foster bring? Well, Foster had the power of abstraction. When he was high—which admittedly was often—he could speak to the power of abstract thought, could spin it out for hours. It was like having Hegel on tap. The abstract properties of reality, in particular the mathematical unwinding of the attributes of the Zeitgeist, both the inner man and outer, were his specialty.

All that one had to do to enjoy this splendor, to taste this wonder, would be to knock on the door armed with a bowl. If he was in, and not yet engaged in his schoolwork, then he was game.

Now, it happened that one night, very late, Foster had succumbed to his interests in experimentation and had dropped acid. I know what you're thinking, he was just tripping. But that was not the case. He was on the downward slope, all the primary experience and the high had left him. He was alone, which was not good, for Foster was a somewhat lonely and melancholy fellow. It was good that he didn't like alcohol: one imagines his type quickly falling into the trap of alcoholism. As it was, he was standing in the darkened hallway. His initial intention had been to visit the toilet. But passing into reverie, he stood still, listening for the sounds of the house. Every house has night sounds, and the Campbell Club was no exception. It was deep night, the time when the morning is far off, and many forms of life awaken and move about, the nocturnal crowd.

It seemed to him as he stood in the hall, that time began to pass more slowly, and yes, slower still, until finally it stopped entirely. He looked at his watch; the second hand did not move. The world was completely silent and motionless. A mist appeared then, creeping into the hallway, filling the space with cold and damp. He began to feel mildly afraid. "*Am I dying?*" he wondered?

And then *she* came. A face appeared in the mist, a young woman, teary eyed, sad, and as his heart opened to her, her face exploded into a face of rage, terrifying to look upon.

In a panic he burst into the shared bathroom, moving in the dark by feel, and pushed his way into a stall, hitting his head, closing the stall door, jamming it closed, frightened. But time was still frozen. The water in the toilet bowl was still as glass. As he looked blankly at the darkened stall door, a face materialized there.

The next morning he reported on this most terrifying incident to those at the breakfast who were up early. But the general consensus—yes, for this was Foster after all—was that he had had a bad trip. LSD was known to sometimes react badly with certain personalities. He would do well to stick with weed. And so on and so on. Nor was he revisited by the apparition.

Some time later, Eva Redbone, who I have mentioned, and who lived in a single at the far end of the third floor, had come in late after a particularly bad night. She came up the stairs in the middle of the night in her army boots—clomp, clomp, clomp. Noises of people being woken up and groaning or yelling, 'God damn it. Eva!' came from behind closed doors. She took off her boots then, sad and disordered, and accidentally went into the second-floor hall, not the third. It's a mistake one can easily make late at night. She suddenly realized everything seemed unfamiliar, the walls and doors were similar but wrong; an alternate reality. And she looked down the hall to see the ghost down at the far end.

It was slowly rising from the floor, like a mist. Eva stood looking at it, distraught, and then screamed at the top of her lungs when it swooped past her.

There was a phone closet in the corner of the hallway—I know it sounds strange, but in those days we had rotary phones and the phone lived on a cord in a phone 'booth' which to us just meant a closet—and Eva ran and hid, sobbing, in there. A few people got up and someone turned on the hall light. It was Karen Tamlen. She found Eva and helped her to her room, as others looked on, concerned. In the morning, the story was discussed around one of the tables in the dining room. Karen was the first to bring it up.

"So, what can we do about this ghost? This is beginning to be a thing."

"Maybe Sutra can do something," said Rachael.

"Sutra? That religious guy? What can he do?"

"Well, maybe he can say a prayer, or invite a priest to come to the house, or something like that."

"He's not even a real monk." This from Rob, who was also fairly new. Most people called Rob a troll. "He's a 'sannyasin.' A Rajneeshi. He's a fake. He just pretends to be a spiritual person to get attention."

At that time Rachael and the others didn't know me very well yet. I moved into the co-op that term. I was the new guy. Leo liked me; we were fast friends. But the others were yet to really get acquainted.

***

When Leo heard about the ghost, he thought this notion of Rachael's was an excellent idea. I saw him the next day standing in the back hallway as I was coming out of the bathroom. "I told everyone you'd be glad to help," he said.

"Oh did you?"

Leo was smiling and holding his flute. He was a Music Performance major, and his instrument was the 'Boehm flute' (that's the metal one they use in orchestras, not the shakuhachi or anything a Kwai Chang Caine would have played). "Don't worry," he said. "If you can't do anything practical it doesn't matter. Maybe you can meditate in the hallway? Say some chants? I feel like we need to do something on the spiritual level."

"You guys have a totally corrupted view of Sannyasins," I said. "We were just ordinary people who wanted to make a better world."

"But you're religious, or something, right? You were at that thing?"

I didn't really want to admit to Leo I had been at Rajneeshpuram. Besides, a lot of people in Oregon had a bad taste in their mouths over that and probably with good reason. Maybe he was one. But there *was* actually a real Buddhism, a real Dharma. I was convinced of that. And I was still trying to find that Way and exist inside of it...I told myself I had just made a wrong turn for a while. "It's not like we lay people have any special powers," I said. "Of course there are hungry ghosts in the world, I thought everyone knew that."

"Hungry ghosts!" exclaimed Leo.

"Yes. They exist in their own plane, but that world interpenetrates this one. Surely you've seen them."

"What do they look like?"

"They sometimes enter into the speed freaks, you've seen those guys walking down on Alder Street in the middle of the night, gesticulating wildly and muttering to themselves? Those are most likely hungry ghosts who have entered a human being."

"Hmmm." He played for a while in the hallway. And I went over and kind of listened, because it seemed like the polite thing to do, and because he seemed to want to be my friend.

Finally, he stopped playing and said, "So how did you learn about this stuff?"

"Well, I read a lot."

"But what about the place?"

"Yeah, probably some hungry ghosts there, too."

"No, I mean, I thought it was a cult."

"Probably."

"So...are you still into all that?"

"No. I decided, you know, an ordinary religion would be sufficiently cultish. I did not need the real thing."

He laughed.

"I'm just into Eastern things. I watched *Kung Fu* as a kid. I wanted to experience something. You know what I mean? Something spiritual. So I tried it. But I tried a lot of other things after high school, too. I was a regular Jack Kerouac."

"I see. So...did you experience?"

"Oh, I learned a thing or two."

"That's fair enough." He blew a few notes and then curiosity seemed to get the better of him. "Uh, but what I mean is—"

"Yes?"

"Was there any *weird sex* going on?"

"Not really that much," I said. "It was mostly just ordinary boring sex."

He laughed again.

"Anyway, what are you doing back here?"

Leo had been sounding his flute, sort of experimentally, scales and single pitches, all the time as we talked. "I'm looking for the sonic sweet spot back here. I thought maybe, if I play something soulful back here, it will help clear the bad mojo."

"Yes," I said. "Not a bad plan. Look, about some kind of prayer, I'll see what I can do. All right? That's the best I can commit to."

***

That night I put on my beads and saffron robe again, but only because it seemed that's what they wanted from me. I had pretty much stopped wearing it, by this point, because I didn't want to attract undue attention to myself anymore. My days of Shock Buddhism were winding down. Besides, my life now was a humble student life, with simple, wholesome student concerns. All that Rajneeshi stuff was behind me. Still, I was elated to be asked to help with a hungry ghost. I did not have the heart to explain to Leo that almost everyone in America was more or less infected with hungry ghosts, that the world was overflowing with them. It was a sign of the times. We live in the Kali Yuga, the age of darkness.

I asked Leo and Rachael to gather Eva and Foster, and anyone else who wanted to participate, and have them come to the second floor back stairwell landing at 10pm. Rob and a few others wanted to participate, which surprised me. Rob was not exactly friendly but we had met in an interesting way; I will say more about him a little later.

Once everyone had gathered I made them sit on the stairs a little above me. I lit a few candles and sat cross-legged on the landing.

"It's crowded back here, all of us together, isn't it?" I said.

"Are you going to do some chanting or something?" said Rob. He seemed very sarcastic. It occurred to me he had come simply to make fun of me.

"Not a chant, exactly. Just a heart-to-heart talk. You see how we're all sitting close here, how we are sitting together. As friends. Listen, you can hear your own breathing. You can hear the wind outside; the wider world reaches in to touch us. But regardless of what is going on out there, even if it's a storm or a natural disaster, we are together. Now, that closeness, that love and kindness, was denied to someone who lived here a long time ago."

Rob was still not settled. "You're just making that up!" But Foster hit him in the shin. "Shut up, Rob."

I waited for a minute to settle myself and let the sounds of the house gather around us again. Then I said, "No. I'm not making it up. This house was originally a sorority. It became a frat after a few years, and eventually the co-op. But originally, it was the Delta Zeta House. That was in 1925. There was a girl, from a well-to-do family, who lived here. But she wasn't liked. She was shunned, for whatever reason, hazed, I suppose, and apparently she was miserable. But in 1929, after the stock market crash, her parents lost all their money. The father committed suicide. She asked to stay on, but the sorority sisters rejected her. On the night that she was supposed to leave the house, she drank methanol. This was during Prohibition. It's not clear if she was just trying to get drunk, or if she intentionally drank poison. But I suspect the latter."

"And how do you know all this, Sherlock?" said Rob. "Did you learn about it while meditating?"

"No, I learned about it at the University library in the local history section. There was an article about the girl's death in the precursor to the *Register Guard*, called the *Eugene Daily Guard*. They have it on microfiche."

"What was her name?" said Foster.

"What?" I said.

"What was the girl's name?" He seemed deeply shaken.

"Caroline A. Murry. I think the A. was for Alice. Her father was some kind of industrialist. Glen Murry was his name. He gave a lot of money to the University. There's a plaque somewhere. And there's a street out by College Hill that was eventually named after him."

"Are you sayin' she died, right here in this building?" It was Eva, and she seemed scared.

I held out my arms and mapped out an area on the floor. "I'm saying she was found dead, just about here, right where we're sitting."

"Oh my god!" cried Rachael.

"I've got to get out of here!" shouted Rob.

"Now WAIT," I said. "Just wait. I have a plan."

They all looked at me.

"There's a grave down in Pioneer Cemetery. It's labelled Caroline Alice Murry, 1910-1929. It's not very well kept. There were no flowers, just trash here and there. I could barely read the inscription. In fact, it was difficult for me to find it, so I had to ask for some help."

"What do you think we should do, Sutra?" said Eva fearfully.

"I think we should go down there and hold a vigil. Think good thoughts. Send some good energy her way."

***

Rob was unwilling to go, but the others put on a brave face. Eva was the most fearful. But she held hands with Rachael and soldiered on like Scarlett O'Hara in a crossfire hurricane. We put on some shoes and jackets and a few people had flashlights. It wasn't that cold, just very dark. There was no moon.

"Let's do this," said Leo.

The Pioneer Cemetery is the oldest cemetery in Eugene, and contains the graves of civil war veterans, amongst others. It was actually quite close to the house. As we walked I spoke to Foster, who was shuffling slowly beside me. "The land in the cemetery is worth a lot of money," I said, "and so over time people have made efforts to move the graves elsewhere and bulldoze all of this down—turn it into apartment complexes.... But those efforts failed."

"That seems good," he said. "Fuck 'em."

"Yes. It's a historic landmark now. I don't think anyone will be able to muck with it going forward."

Suddenly we were there. We looked out in the darkness at stones and stones, propped up against the ravages of time and student late night partying. "The grave is down a bit, I think. Follow me."

Finally we came to the spot and Leo pointed his flashlight at the marker. "Caroline A. Murry," he slowly read out. "You're right, Sutra, the stone can barely be read."

"It stinks like piss around here," Foster said. "This is terrible. Unacceptable. And look at the trash. Fucking frat boys no doubt."

He was right, there was a fair amount of detritus, some of it had probably blown in and had collected simply out of neglect; but some of it was also deliberate litter: beer cans and broken glass from bottles, and the paper wrapper remains of Hostess products: Twinkies, in this case.

Immediately Rachael said what everyone was thinking: "We've got to clean this up."

I asked if I should say something to the spirit of the girl, but Foster wanted to do that. "Dear Caroline, I don't know if you can hear me, but I promise you I am going to clean this up. And maybe a few other people will help me."

We sat for a while and held a sort of vigil, and eventually people had to leave—it was getting late. Walking back, I asked Foster if he felt better. "Yeah, I do. I feel much better. Thank-you so much, Sutra."

"I'm glad I could help."

"You are all right by me. You need any tutoring in higher math, just let me know." A little bit later he said, almost to himself, "For myself, I have a job to do."

And he did it. The grave was cleaned up and he approached the task of maintaining it with a certain zeal that surprised me. For Eva, things were different. She could not bring herself to take part in the business of cleaning and maintaining a grave. But she did integrate the story and her feelings into an interpretive dance, and we were all invited to her performance. The others who were there at the grave site that night each seemed changed in some way, except perhaps for Rob. Rob was, in a sense, a Hungry Ghost himself, so his lack of interest was not really much of a surprise.

***

Leo and I spent a lot of time together that first term. He was interested in everything and not afraid to embrace what he found useful, or good, in the wide world, and discount the popular opinion. That was a great gift.

Very few men are so openhearted. In the time of our friendship I knew Leo to wear kilts. Our conversations ranged from the political to the contemporary art world, to world history, the causes of war, poverty, famine. He seemed to appreciate my weird, spiritual orientation as coming out of left field, something to laugh at; but also to consider. I remember impressing him one day.

We rode bikes down to the 5th Street Public Market, perhaps with the intention of buying a lunch, and Leo ran into a busker he knew from the music department. It was Brian Lawson, a keyboardist or pianist, and he had got himself setup in a high traffic corner back behind the food stalls. Leo chatted him up a bit and then he started playing. We stood nearby and listened, just hanging out. People walked by, time passed, and then I looked down and saw something on the ground; it was a hundred dollar bill folded small. I showed it to Leo and then immediately said, "Huh, I guess this must belong in here," motioning to Brian's tip jar. Brian, who had observed the whole affair and continued to play, but spasmodically, now played momentarily with one hand, stride piano, and quickly recovered the hundred from the jar. Into his pocket it went, like a clownfish darting into the dark safety of a coral reef. He wasn't about to allow time for someone to come back looking for it. But Leo was astounded that I cared nothing about the cash. We neither of us were exactly rich. One hundred dollars in 1985 was a lot of buying power. I could have bought a bike like Connor's or maybe three of them. I can still remember Leo's face when I impulsively put the money into the tip jar as if my hand was shot from a bow drawn by Eugen Herrigel. Leo's jaw dropped and eyes widened. He looked like a man who has seen a miracle virgin birth.

"Was that Buddhism?" he said.

"Nah," I said. "I'm just a big tipper."

***

Earlier I promised to say more about Rob Meister. I met Rob in the University Bookstore early on. I wasn't even in the co-op yet. I was looking at books in the 'Spirituality' section and as he walked past, he casually but quite directly—he was looking right at me—said "you won't find much in there, friend."

I looked up and said "No? Why not?" My Shock Buddhism was working—it had attracted him and he had taken the bait and was now hooked.

He stopped and smiled. "Because if you want to find answers about life, you have to create those answers yourself."

"So you don't think religion can help there?"

He shook his head.

"Well, what then?"

"Revolution. We have to end Capitalism and create a just society."

"Ah. I see. Out with the old, in with the new. But what is the new, exactly?"

"Well, Marxism for starters."

"Marxism. Hm. Not sure how that worked out in the Soviet Union."

"Or Cuba. Or China. I know. But maybe things just broke down in the implementation. But the basic idea is great."

"Really?"

"Sure. Eat the rich."

He seemed like an intelligent, affable kind of person. I thought maybe he was gay and trying to pick me up.

"I already have a girlfriend, by the way," I said. "I'm not looking for that special someone. You know, if that was where this was going."

He laughed then and held out his hand. "No. Not at all. Rob." We shook hands. His grip was like that of an arm wrestler.

"Sutra, they call me. Nice to meet you."

"Sutra? You're pulling my leg."

"Nope."

"So what's your major, Sutra? The Pali Canon?"

"No," I said. "Although I wouldn't knock the Pali Canon."

"Why not?"

"Because I think you might be a Buddhist at heart."

He laughed. "What makes you say that?"

"There's a fine line between Buddhism and nihilism. You strike me as being a nihilist."

"Only a part timer. My regular job is being a Communist."

"You know, you might be a good fit for the co-op. The Campbell Club. I am going to live there this term."

We talked about that, and he smiled and grinned like I was an idiot. About two weeks after I moved in, I saw him again and suggested he come over for dinner. He was non-committal. I didn't really expect him to show up.

***

But that night Rob arrived promptly at 6 p.m. and I met him out on the front porch. After we loaded up plates of brown rice and potato and bean Tarkari I led him over to one of the tables in the dining room.

"Leo? Meet Rob Meister. He—what are you, maybe a Rugby scholarship?"

Rob laughed. "Actually, I'm working on my master's in political philosophy. I've never touched a football in my life." Nevertheless, he was stout, as wide as Leo but not as tall. Rob had a pencil-thin moustache that made him look a little bit like a young John Waters. He was dressed in slacks with a collared button-down shirt and a brown sports coat that made him look more business-world bourgeoisie than anyone else in the room.

"A man of letters. Fantastic." Leo held out his hand. "Leo Johansen, damn glad to meet you!"

I told Leo a bit about my earlier conversation with Rob.

"Right," said Leo. "Well, the SCA is first of all a 501(c)(3) non-profit. We're set up with a charter that says the members own the buildings. They pay fees, not rent."

"So you're a corporation then? Yuck!"

"I'm not sure you understand the advantages. First of all, there's no landlord. Sutra here, and myself, and, well, all these people, who currently live here—we own the house. That means *full control*."

Rob's mind seemed to be clicking. "So—you're saying if you wanted paint the walls—"

"We're currently planning to put in a ramp to become wheelchair accessible. It's all about equality. Fairness. Diversity, too."

"But you're probably deep in debt, having mortgaged the place to the hilt—"

"Actually, no. The place has been paid for, oh, for about 50 years. This house was built in 1924. It was originally a sorority, then a frat house for a few years, and it became a housing co-op. Initially it was all male. It became co-ed, I think in the 1970s."

"And, so, what, you cook and do chores, this vegetarian business—"

"Vegetarian food is cheap and wholesome. Meat is ecologically unsound." He looked Rob up and down. "I suppose you are, what, a Young Republican?"

Rob laughed. "No. I'm not part of the current shift to the Right."

"So you understand ecology?"

"I understand hunger. To me, food is food. But I like to feel full. If I don't eat meat, I don't feel like I have eaten."

Leo smiled. "Merely a matter of getting used to something new."

"It's not bad," Rob said, as he took another mouthful on his fork. "So, you guys align with the counterculture? Hippies? Druggies? What goes on here?"

"We like to have fun. We work hard and play hard. But freedom is a very important concept here. Also minding one's own business. But the co-operative movement started far back before our time. It goes back to the Labor movements of the turn of the century..."

And so on and so on. I won't bore you with the details. Leo went on and on, as I had hoped. Eventually

I became a third wheel and left the two of them to their animated discussion.

***

It seemed that Rob was now spending more time at the co-op, and I can't say I was too thrilled by it—the time I would normally be spending with Leo, was sucked up by his long droning conversations with "the Meister." I was positively man-jealous. But things cooled down after a while and I thought maybe Rob had found something new. Then one day, suddenly, Rob was moving in. He scored a single up on the third floor—ironically those were the most expensive rooms in terms of fees in the whole house. Obviously, Rob wasn't broke. He was a contradiction to me: he spoke constantly about the evils of Capitalism but dressed that part better than anyone. Still, I liked having him in the house. At least in the beginning.

Each term we had an all-house meeting, which basically meant all the members over at Janet Smith came to Campbell Club and gathered with us in the living room. It was the only space that was big enough, but it also gave the Campbell Clubbers a bit of an advantage. We also had an advantage in the sense that the Campbell Club had room for 38, while the Janet Smith House only had 18 rooms, all of them singles. It was a completely different vibe over there, and most of the Janet Smith crew were grad students—quiet, just trying to get their studies in—and the place was dead at night. Meanwhile the Campbell Club was a bit livelier (as perhaps I have suggested already).

The meeting got underway, and Leo read the agenda and started off with an update on the two houses and their financials, and also a bit about the goings on in the Campbell Club. He told the story of the Hungry Ghost extraction, and I seemed to figure prominently in the story, which was very kind of him. He then asked Stuart Longfellow, the house president from Janet Smith, to give his update. It seemed the blond, bowl-cut Stuart had overseen the final construction work on the new kitchen over the break. Everyone was pleased with the result.

Then things moved on to the new business.

"We will be holding SCA elections today. As you all probably know, the SCA board is responsible for making decisions on expenditure and also for handling incidental business during the term that doesn't rise to the level of requiring an all-house vote. There are five officers: SCA President, SCA Treasurer, Membership Coordinator, and the SCA Secretary. The SCA Bookkeeper is also on the Board and advises on financial matters. Finally, there are two House Representative positions which are sent to represent the opinions of the members in each house. Sort of like delegates. They also organise house parties and things in that vein."

There were some scattered cheers at this point. Shouts of "Party!" could be heard here and there.

"Indeed," said Leo. "Alright, and now to the election. Those interested in a position should put themselves forward by coming up to the front here when I call for the candidates for that particular office. The candidates will then each have three to five minutes to explain why they would be good for a position."

"First up is the office of SCA President. The job involves using *Robert's Rules of Order* to run the weekly Corporate meeting, and also sometimes being the advocate for the co-op. To the wider community." At this point Stuart Longfellow, who had been at Janet Smith almost as long as Leo had been at the Campbell Club, stepped up.

But so did Rob.

Leo spoke first and gave a short speech about why his experience in the role and encyclopaedic knowledge of the principles of the co-op made him the best candidate.

Stuart spoke glowingly of his idea about raising fees to fund replacing the buried water mains, which he maintained were made of lead and probably posed a serious health risk.

But Rob gave the most interesting speech, at least from my point of view. "Friends, I know I'm new around here. My name is Robert Meister, and I'm working on my master's degree in political philosophy. I don't know about you, but I think we live on an island of good will amidst a river of greed. This is the "Greed is Good" decade, although some people don't realize it yet. Reaganomics is just another way to steal from the poor. We need to fight back..."

Rob was really just getting up to speed when Leo had to remind him of time. He didn't get elected, but everyone including Leo could see he was a formidable guy.

The Membership coordinator spot easily went to Magda Slater (as everyone expected). And Raven decided she would make a good SCA Secretary. The group seemed to assent, although the office almost went to one of the Janet Smith crew. Finally the voting came up for the two House Representatives, one for each house. I plucked up my courage and put my hand up for Campbell Club House Rep. And as it happened, Rob did too.

Leo signalled to Rob to go first. He started out by saying he was old enough to buy beer and even knew where to source kegs at a discount, which seemed to go over well. But then he launched into a diatribe about economics—he seemed to think house fees were too high, and we were not getting enough for our money. But he ended in a way that seemed out of line to some of the membership, but perhaps not to all. "Look, I didn't want to say this, but since I'm in competition with our friend," —here he pointed at me— "I have to say I'm not sure someone who lived at Rajneeshpuram is a good person to have represent us. I'm not even convinced we should have, you know, cult members, living here. Maybe we should talk about the requirements for membership in that light."

I was looking at the faces, and it seemed some of them were stunned, but no one said anything. "Are you done, Rob?" I asked. I was trying to keep my voice very calm.

"Uh, yes, I'm done."

"Well, friends, for those who don't know me, I am Robert Gray. Most people call me Sutra. I would like to be the house representative for Campbell Club because, firstly, I think this place is really amazing and I feel so blessed to be here. It's about the people, you know, everyone here is really cool. And so I want to bring their problems and issues to the SCA Board."

Leo, who was officiating, then took the bull by the horns. "As far as what Rob just said, which I think is totally inappropriate—"

"I need to cut you off right there, Leo," I said. "It's perfectly fine. It's true, I did live up at Rajneeshpuram for a year. I was looking for a religious experience. And, actually, I did have an experience, and I learned a lot— just not exactly what I expected." Addressing Rob directly, I said, "Rob, I did want to respond directly to what you said. Do you mind if I do that?"

Rob raised his arms and spread his hands. "Be my guest."

"Some years back—I think in 1960—Chairman Mao instituted what he called the "Four Evils" campaign. The idea was to kill off the "four evils" or "four pests:" rats, flies, mosquitos, and sparrows. The first three might seem obvious, but the last one maybe needs some explanation. You see, Mao thought, and made people believe, that sparrows were evil: he said they were eating up the grain that the peasants were growing. So the whole countryside was put on a programme of exterminating sparrows. And that program was largely successful. Most of the sparrows were exterminated in various ways until none were left.

"Problem was that sparrows don't eat grain. They actually eat insects, particularly the ones that were eating the grain. So killing the sparrows caused an ecological crisis. Several million people starved as a result of this mistake. In fact, it was the largest famine in human history.

"The point of the story is that if you're going to make an enemy out of someone or something, it's important to make sure that someone is really your enemy. You may be stabbing a friend in the back."

It seemed that a number of the people who were listening got the point of the story; there was general laughter. Rob was a bit sullen. "I suppose you learned that from Rajneesh?"

"No," I said. "I learnt it from the *Wall Street Journal.*"

Leo now interrupted. "Thanks very much, both of you. We're out of time so we need to vote for the House Rep for Campbell Club. Please only vote in this contest if you are a Campbell Club resident."

I had a feeling that I would win the vote, but I was wrong about that. People overwhelmingly voted for Rob. I only got 6 votes.

"Don't feel too bad, Sutra," said Rachael, later. "We love you. You have friends here now."

That was a very strong vote of confidence and did a lot to cheer me up. But Foster probably clarified things the most when he said, "I think people voted for Rob simply because he can buy kegs. That is, after all, a major part of the House Rep job. Don't let it get to you, Sutra."

It was true. I didn't have ID. I stupidly burned my ID when I was at the Rajneeshpuram. I also thought the alcohol culture on campus was destructive and divisive. So I did not have either the capability or the desire to 'buy kegs.' It just shows how out of it I was. What kind of loser was I? But I just had no interest in beer and keg parties. It just wasn't me. My lack of alcoholism was a depressing failure as far as I was concerned.

***

The Fall term was winding down and all in all, my impression of school was that it was a waste of time. The books I cared about, like *On The Road*, or *The Once and Future King*, or *Setting Free the Bears*, were nowhere in sight. In their place was the complete tedium of parsing historical fiction and placid, dated prose. Garbage like Emily Dickinson. Even Shakespeare, at that time, was of little consequence to me. Besides, the entire act of reading no longer satisfied me. I needed to be more active creatively; to be modern or even post-modern. I wanted to be violently strange and aggressively mod. I had heard of Salman Rushdie but not read him; ditto to Margaret Atwood, who had just released *The Handmaid's Tale* to great controversy. I had not read their books, but I loved the idea of them, of being controversial in the sphere of literature.

Also (although I did not say it to myself) it was a question of ego. I associated writing with high art or at least low art; whatever it was, it was art; I wanted to cut myself a big heaping slice of it and drink it down like Coke; it was the Real Thing. To bleed on the page; to impress people with my many semicolons and flashing trash lamps.

***

The next day I set out to the Creative Writing Department office to see if the acceptance list for next term's writing classes had been posted. The building was just down the street. I realized I was trembling a little as I walked. *It's just getting cold*, I told myself. *There's not going to be an issue.* At that time I was probably even cocky. Perhaps I was used to easy success. I was a prep school kid after all, my father had money (although we were estranged at this time due to the whole cult thing, and I got nothing from him). But I had told everyone, probably ad nauseum, about my ambitious creative plans and how I was going to take the novel by storm.

Climbing the stairs up to the landing of the large house converted into an office space that was now a University property, I could see a number of people milling about. It seemed that the list of next term's admitted had been posted only a short time before. I moved forward, none too happy to make this a public process.

As I scanned the posted sheet, my heart sank. I couldn't find my name. But then I saw one that I recognized. And it wasn't mine.

Just at that moment, Karen Tamlen tapped me on the shoulder. I jumped.

"Sutra?" What are you doing here? I thought you were already in the...oh my God! I got in! I got in!"

The round-faced roly-poly of a girl began to dance and sing and jump up and down. She looked like an insane jack in the box. I had to make a quick exit. I really didn't feel like talking to her anymore. I didn't even do the right thing and congratulate her or do any of the things a normal human being is supposed to do in that situation. I just stomped out.

What I remember is walking and talking to myself, probably gesticulating wildly like a methedrine addict, exactly like a hungry ghost, not caring where I was going, but somehow inevitably tracing a path down to the Willamette. It was like the wind pushed me there.

I walked through the buildings and grounds unseeing and unthinking, like a sick migratory bird.

There was an 'Urban Farm' class held down there across Franklin Boulevard, a place where students learn about ecology by gardening, and the ceramics and painting and sculpture studios were all down there, too. I didn't know much about it at the time, except that from what I could see the grounds looked very hip. Very "1970s."

I realized this *locus delicti* was where Connor had class most days. It was a very pleasant place, perfect, at least, for a certain kind of soul.

I looked for Connor for a while through the windows of one of the buildings, watching kids do ridiculous things on potter's wheels, but eventually gave up. It was just an idle, confused thought that he might be there. I stood for a while staring dejectedly at the sluggish mill race. The putrid water percolated slowly forward. My brain was full of mush.

After that I wandered out into the Urban Farm garden space, looking at the dejected flowers and watching bees buzzing in sadness at the unfairness of life, and all the while the wind moved mysteriously through the fruit trees standing sentinel at the entrance to higher knowledge. It was back there, I was sure, in those Quonset huts. The garden was so glorious and beautiful that I wanted to cry.

"Hey Sutra!" said a girl's voice.

It was Rachael Day. She was absolutely resplendent, kneeling like a young mermaid in a harvest field of undersea wonders. Well, I was in no mood for company. But I had to respond. I just needed to be human momentarily. I said, "Hey, you." I tried to put on a better face and move along.

"So you know about this place, too?" She was wearing gardening gloves and a straw sun hat that her blond curls fell out of in a delightful way. I won't deny it, she was beautiful in that moment, stunning, and I suddenly loved her the way a lost dog is grateful towards a familiar piss stain.

"Yeah," I said. "I heard about it from Connor. He says it's a very special place."

"It is. I had the class last year but I still like to come down here and monitor the raspberries and strawberries. There's a big wildflower garden here. One the largest anywhere on campus."

"That's very cool."

"You want to help?"

She was trying to be nice, and I was about to say something stupid or whine like a dog, but miraculously I held those words back. It was like swallowing acrid vomit. "Uh...yeah. I mean, I want to. But I'm not much of a gardener."

Seeing that I was a complete ignoramus, Rachael pointed me in the direction of some gloves back in the shed and put me on weed patrol. Suddenly we were doing something together. It was just us two at that moment, there was occasionally a passerby or three on the footpath, but otherwise it was just us.

I tried not to stare at her butt when she leaned over. It wasn't easy. She had the habit of taking exercise purely for the joy of being active—something I could not even comprehend—but I could see the results of that lifestyle. Her body was strong and well conditioned. She loved to walk, hike, bike, and whatever else she and Leo were getting up to in his corner third-floor room. Her gloved hands moved carefully as she passed a secateur over the vines of the raspberries, removing dead vines. Sometimes she put straw down that she worked free from a nearby bale.

I kept pulling weeds and tried to be useful. Occasionally I'd say something foolish, like "so this is a weed?" And she'd be like, "no, that's a zucchini plant. Try over on the other side of the path."

She eventually turned to me, half looking, and asked the obvious question. "So how are things going? Did you get in?"

I didn't immediately answer. Finally I said, "I like this place. It has the feeling of the Garden of Eden, don't you think?"

"Well, there's certainly something sacred about, you know, the Earth."

After a while, I said, "Karen Tamlen got in."

"Really?" She was bending over again.

"Yes. She did. But I did not."

"Ah." She didn't say anything for a while. "But...I thought you were a shoo-in."

"Yeah, I know. I said that."

"I see. You're a bit of bullshitter, aren't you?" She was smiling, not exactly looking in my direction, but not exactly looking away, either, her eyes down. After a while she was doing the Greek statue thing again. "So...English major it is?"

I sighed. "Yes. It's absurd, isn't it. About the dumbest major imaginable."

"I don't know...it doesn't seem so bad if you like books."

"Yeah, I like books. Hey, wait a minute, what are you studying, Rachael?" I realized I didn't even know.

"Ecology."

"Wow. A scientist. That's very impressive."

"Nah." She shrugged, but she was also smiling. I could tell she was pleased.

"So what do you want to do with that fancy Ecology degree? Start a green revolution?"

"Absolutely."

"I'm so envious. That's like, a real career that matters. Sometimes I forget why I'm even here."

She paused and sat on that beautiful butt of hers, her legs kind of spread apart with her gloved hands dangling between them. "Can't you still just, you know, be a writer? I mean, what do you need school for to write?"

"Yes! Exactly!" I cried. "That's what I think. But a friend of mine thinks I belong in school, that school is somehow critical to my future. She was very persuasive."

Rachael laughed. "Ah. I see. Now I'm beginning to understand. That's funny. So you listen to what girls tell you? You do what they say?"

"Not always."

"Was it because of a girl that you—"

"What, joined a cult? No, that was my own idea."

"So you really did that? You're one of them?"

I laughed. "Yeah. I was. Do you think that's a bad thing?"

She didn't say anything for a while. "No, I guess I don't see how it matters. Who's business is it, anyway? But was it weird?"

"No. We didn't do anything bad. At least I didn't."

"Well then?"

"But it did take up time that a normal person my age would be in school. I never went to University. After high school I just gave up on, you know. I wanted something else, I guess. I was a seeker."

We kept working for a while. I moved closer to her. "You see, I think the world speaks to us."

"What does that mean?"

"Well, I believe people are actually God. Everyone. They just don't know it. Even the birds and bugs and insects—those little butterflies over there—are all God."

"God, God, God?" she said.

"Yeah. Pretty much."

"I'm sure there a word for that."

"Yeah. There is."

"Well, go on, Sutra. I interrupted you. I'm listening."

"That's kind of you. OK, well, generally, they don't know this truth and in fact cannot know it. But once in a while, something happens and the curtain is pulled up for a minute, and then they say something that actually matters. Like, for example, someone suddenly has an idea, maybe that is not very likely for them to have, a powerful idea that changes the world. Or maybe they make an unusual decision, or sacrifice everything, or do something incredibly surprising and brave. Things like that come from a higher place. The only explanation is that, inside, they are more than they know."

She looked at me, puzzled. Slowly, her expression changed. "Ah. Now I see. This person—I'll bet it was a really hot girl—the one who told you to go back to school, she told you something that you took as a message—"

I smiled. "Yeah. I guess. She even mentioned the Campbell Club, too, that I would love it. And I do."

She laughed. "OK."

We kept working for a while. "So here's a question, how do you know? I mean, if I told you to do something, like be my slave, would you do it?"

I laughed. "In your case, yeah probably. I find you to be kind of intimidating. But there's a difference between a message from the gods and, you know, someone messing with you."

She stood up. "Well, Sutra. I have to say, that is the most insane pickup line I've heard in a long while. I'm going up to the restrooms over by the Art Department. I'll be right back."

***

I continued to pull weeds. The sky was a beautiful azure and the wind had begun to pick up. The fruit trees I had seen earlier were all awake, their branches rocking in a satisfying motion. My frustration and irritation seemed to have melted. Of course, I was now totally rudderless. My 'educational goals' were in tatters. But in that moment, things seemed fine. I had an inner sense of calm which I recognized as the sign of an impending change. Something was going to happen, maybe something with Rachael, or the Campbell Club, but I wasn't sure what. It seemed just possibly related to the Green Revolution.

***

After a while Rachael came back to the garden field and put her gloves back on. I was turned the other way working in the strawberry patch.

"I'm back!" she said.

"I'm glad," I said.

"Any message yet from God?"

"Nah. Just the sky and the clouds."

She laughed. "You know, I get a lot of lines. Sometimes guys can be very inventive. But they always want the same thing. Always. You know how many guys have come onto me in the last year?"

"Probably a lot. Naturally, you're totally a babe. I get it. I guess I should be trying to come on to you as well. I mean, you know. Just out of proper respect for your big—"

"Oh my god, Sutra. Do not say things like that to me. Do not tease me. Sometimes guys are really a problem."

"Yeah, I'm sorry about that. We're all pretty bad. If I had the ability to change that, I would."

After a while she said, "Did you have a girlfriend when you were—when you were in the cult?"

"No. We were mostly trying to be pure."

"You mean like, sexually, you didn't do it?"

I laughed. "That was the general idea. But some people did. There were some situations where I could have got into a relationship, but I was pretty serious about the whole thing. I wanted a higher life. You know, the whole idea was to have an intentional community. That doesn't sound so bad? We wanted a Green Revolution, too. It kind of sucked that it didn't turn out that way. Just more bullshit."

"I see."

"But these days I'm just trying to return to, you know, normality."

"Normality?"

"Well, yeah."

"So you aren't—you know—"

"No, I'm not really practicing chastity. I have not even taken a vow. I'm just a douchebag English Major now, sniffing for chicks. Like the rest of the assholes on your tail."

She laughed then, kind of a girlish laugh, and shook her tasselled head. We kept working and then Rachael got up and took off her gloves. She stretched in the sunshine. For some reason it made me think of the last line in *The Metamorphosis*, where the daughter "stretches her young body," as a sign of hope.

"It's getting hot. Don't you think?" She pointed further back into the garden. "There's an old farmhouse around the back and it has the most amazing grape arbor. The grape vines are like, 100 years old. I don't know if there's any grapes yet. You want to go and take a look?"

"Uh...sure," I said. "Why not?" It was a stupid response but the best I could do in the moment. I suddenly had a sense now of the direction things were going—like a spider sense, but it was down in my Sacral Chakra, a dull pounding in the base of my pelvis that made my asshole pucker.

We walked down the path together and I could not help noticing how my entire day, the whole mood and vibe, had changed as if by magic. Then she reached over and took my hand. It felt warm. We held hands as we walked and she smiled at me like a forest maiden. Suddenly in my mind we were nude and I could see her entire form clearly. Her touch was becoming electric and I almost stumbled and would have fallen over but for her hand.

So, yeah, then I understood. It was indeed a sort of intimidating magic spell that I was under because of Rachael, her yin power, the magnetic field of her body, a field I was now inside. Yes, Rachael was magic in the sense of old-school Renaissance thinking, Da Vinci, Michaelangelo: it was like being in the presence of the statue of the Venus de Milo come to life (and with arms, obviously) or, better, one of the women from a painting by Botticelli, maybe the *Primavera* or the *Annunciation*, moving true to life in ancient Italian garb, padding on soft feet through a pleasant garden scene. Her power seemed to pollinate the surrounding air with glitter, like Arwen on a hilltop in the Tolkien saga. I was completely lost, ready to submit to her will.

***

But as we walked back towards the broken old farmhouse, I saw a blue butterfly. It flitted across the garden bed in front of the gate.

"Whoa. Look at that," I said.

Rachael was impressed. "That's cool. I don't know that one. Did you know, blue is a rather rare color in nature."

"No. I did not know that."

We saw another butterfly or two and I suddenly felt transported. It was a moment frozen in time and for me, it seemed to go on and on. The energy was completely different and not erotic at all. A feeling of the eternal now, or renewal. And a story came into my head.

The moment was very brief and then we returned to normal consciousness; or rather, to the normal Rachael vibe, which was all ecological and woodsy and down to earth, pure pussy power. I looked over at Rachael and she had not seemed to notice the time dilation. For her, nothing had changed. I let go her hand.

"Rachael, I was just wondering—"

She smiled and put her hands on her hips, arching her back. "Oh you were, were you?"

"No, no, no, hear me out. I was wondering, have you ever read a book called *The Man Who Planted Trees?*"

"I don't think so."

We were now close under the huge old grape arbor—unfortunately there were no grapes, it was too early in the season, but the sheer size of the arbor made it seem ancient, and it was covered in beautiful grape leaves, some brown from last year, but mostly new growth. We where alone with the sun and the wind and all the life around us.

"I think I'm supposed to tell you that story," I said.

"This is a message, is it?"

"Maybe. It's just possible. Because you have inspired me. Should I tell it?"

"Yeah. I had another idea, but this sounds good, too."

"But this is serious."

She laughed. "OK. I get it. Go on then."

She was smiling and relaxed and I think feeling in total control, this was not new to her, I was sure she thought I was trying to begin a mating ritual, maybe not understanding that words were no longer required. All systems were go, from her point of view. It was like the female bower bird who is now ready, but I was going to show her my plumage and do a dance anyway. But that wasn't where I was at. At least, that wasn't the only thing going on.

"So, in *The Man Who Planted Trees*, there's a hiker who decides to take a tour through some French countryside, it's near the Alps, very remote. There's not much to see, it's barren land and wilderness, dry, windy, and desolate. All the trees had been cut down to burn for charcoal at some time in the past, and the people who lived in that area are all gone. In fact, they all more or less destroyed themselves through alcohol and greed and madness.

"The hiker comes upon a solitary shack and knocks and asks to spend the night. The owner of the shack is named Elzéard Bouffier, he's a shepherd. He lives alone there with his dog. The visitor can see he's a very conscientious man; his clothes are carefully mended; the place is clean and tidy. But of course he has almost nothing. They eat a frugal meal, and then before bed, Bouffier starts sorting acorns."

"Acorns?"

"Yes, he has a big sack of acorns, you know, from oak trees."

"Yes, Sutra," she said, eyeing me. "I know what those are."

"He observes the man examining and sorting the acorns and asks Bouffier if he would like help. But Bouffier responds no, it is his work. He discards any acorns that are not perfect and makes rows of ten. When he has ten rows of ten perfect acorns, then he puts the hundred acorns into a sack. The hiker asks what the acorns are for, and Bouffier explains that he believes the countryside is ruined due to lack of trees. So, having nothing better to do, he is planting them."

Rachael seemed to be a little more interested now in the story. She leaned on one of the old farmhouse supports. "He's planting. Planting acorns... He does this every day?"

"Yes," I said. "The hiker goes out with him in the morning and observes him planting. After he has got his sheep looked after, Bouffier goes and plants the acorns along a hillside. And the hiker notices there are some areas nearby where little trees are growing, two, three year old trees. He says good-bye to the man, and keeps walking on his journey, but he continues to think about this lone man, every day going out and planting more and more trees."

"And he keeps doing that?"

"Yes, after a period ten or fifteen years, the trees are growing and there are news stories about the spontaneous growth of a new forest near the Alps. Scientists go out and observe what they think is a natural reforestation, a miracle, really. But meanwhile, Bouffier is still alive, still planting trees each day, over on other hills. Eventually, something happens."

"Yes?" Rachael was looking at me intently now.

"The land rejuvenates. The whole region. Springs start to run again, and animals and plants and even people, families, come back into the area. Even the climate is radically changed by the presence of the forest, the area becomes habitable again. People begin to have hope."

"All due to that one man."

"Yes."

"I want to read about this forest!" she said.

"Well, you can't do that exactly."

"What do you mean?"

"It's fiction, Rachael."

"WHAT?" She seemed mortified.

"I know. I'm sorry. When I read the story, I was 100% convinced it was real. The story feels so very convincing. But it is fiction. The author is Jean Giono. He's, you know, a novelist."

"But—but that is so depressing. I was getting excited. Now I feel cheated. It wasn't real."

"But don't you see, Rachael, that is what I want to achieve. That's what my idea of good writing is. Don't be sad." I was a little worried because I thought she might cry. "It made me react the same way. I read the story when I was about 12. When I found out years later it was fiction, I couldn't believe it. I grieved about it. That never happens with me."

She crossed her arms and thought about all that. Finally she said, "No, I get it. I just want to do something, you know. I want a Green Revolution. I want things to change. I want a better world. Not a shitshow of politics and money and Republican church-going bullshit. Planting trees...that seems so natural, so powerful. I could, you know, be like that man, live like that in a cabin and tend sheep and plant trees. That would be alright."

"I can relate."

She sighed. "That was a good message, Sutra. You, you are more serious than I thought. What you said before, I thought it was just total bullshit to get you laid. But now. I don't know how you did that. I feel weak inside. You did something. I need to sit down."

There was an old rotting wooden bench underneath the arbor. I said something about it being weak and crumbly, to which she dissented, and so we both sat down at once. It abruptly fell apart into a pile of shattered wormwood and we collapsed into a heap, laughing. We both rolled onto the grass, the smell of freshness invading my nostrils, and I found myself on top of her, chest to chest, her face a few inches from mine, her breath on me. It was girl breath, and it was entirely intoxicating. She smiled at me and cosied herself, pulling me in, so that we were at action stations. My free hand grazed her Levi-covered thigh.

"Message received," she said.

But then a bad thing happened. I remembered how, in the movie *Animal House*, the guys go on a road trip and Otter tries to get sympathy sex by pretending to be the boyfriend of a girl recently deceased. I didn't want my "pickup line" to have worked, because it wasn't a pickup line. I just wanted this to be a higher thing.

Worse, I couldn't stop thinking Rachael was suddenly being "nice" to me out of sympathy for my failure. You see, my failure was still there. I was a lousy piece of shit English Major. It was a poisonous thought, filled with ego. I thought about Leo, who was my friend, and how this beautiful girl was in some sense his (that was completely wrong, and my misunderstanding, but that's how I imagined things to be. In those days I still had a lot of things to unlearn). I rolled over and pounded my fists on the grass in frustration. "Damn it! Damn it!"

"What is it?" she said, concerned.

"I've got to go, Rachael. I'm sorry. I'm such an idiot."

She looked at me, incredulous, and then lifted herself, supporting her de Milo head with her newly grown statue arm, white marble elbow pushing into the soft dark earth. She shook her head gently and her blond marble tresses vibrated. I got up and walked away.

Obviously it was one of the stupidest things I've ever done in my life. One does not get the chance to make out with the Venus de Milo—then just recently having grown arms—every day.

But it turned out that more serious business had been transacted. Rachael thought about *The Man Who Planted Trees* for a long time after that. She got that book and read it and told other people about it. Years later she still had it on her bookshelf. So regardless of what happened later, I had helped the Green Revolution to begin. It is one heart at a time, as we all know.

***

I had not gone 300 yards when Connor's head popped up around the corner and I saw him walking in my direction, his face phasing in and out between friendly and sardonic. He greeted me from a distance: "Hey dude! What are you doing out my way?"

"Oh nothing. Actually I was looking for you. Or maybe just, thinking, you know, thinking and walking, and I was blown in this direction."

"Yeah. I get you dude. A gust in the God. Well, you want to come out to the shop? It's pretty good times."

I didn't feel like going back to the co-op just yet. Karen Tamlen would probably be there blowing her own horn. So I said "Sure, dude, let's go."

We walked back past the urban farm, and for some reason I didn't want to see Rachael again so soon, but it turned out there was no reason for me to be concerned, she wasn't anywhere in sight. We passed by the huge Quonset hut where the painters all had class and went into the ceramic's studio next door. It was another huge Quonset hut. There was something very cool about these, something about craft and making things with your hands in this amazing space of creativity—and the roof was curved! Imagine, a building with a curved roof—so organic. I couldn't conceptualize it adequately. I pushed on the door, and it clicked but did not give. "It's locked," I said.

"No problem, dude," said Connor. We walked around to the back of the building and he had me give him a boost at the last window in the long row of windows running along the outside wall. It was cracked just a little by an intentionally placed stick, to keep it ajar. In he went like a slithering snake, pushing the window open as he went. It snapped shut as he passed in.

"I'm in," said his muffled voice. "Go around to the back door."

I followed instructions and he let me in.

The back end of the enormous Quonset hut was where the kilns were. There were some that seemed to be electric and others that looked like they might be gas powered. Several seemed to be active, and one glowed with inner fire.

"Are you sure it's cool to be down here?" I said.

"Sure. This is my kingdom!"

We went into the large main room with tables topped with canvas and potter's wheels, both kick and electric, and a set of large sinks positioned in the center and clustered around one of the huge supporting beams. Above and to the right I could see an upper area with tables.

"Give me a minute," he said. I sat back to just hang out for a while. I was thinking about the day I met him. There was no system for pairing or grouping roomies in the co-op, but Magda had an eye for who might work out in a double or triple room. It must have been her who chose the pairing. I wasn't capable of thanking her, however. That thought didn't even enter my mind.

At any rate, Connor and I were fast friends after the Shock Buddhism wore off and he accepted I was just a regular guy. At first, I found him to be irritating, because his manner is so ironic, bordering on the sarcastic and rude when the mood took him. He was constantly responding with, "Oh really?" Or "Oh yeah, sure." And he said "dude" a lot. Everybody was a dude.[1]

But after a few days, I had to wake him up in the middle of the night—I think it was a late night phone call, maybe his parents, I was downstairs, someone asked me to go up, and when I woke him up, he answered in the same weird sardonic, laconic way: "yeah, sure, dude" and he rolled over and ignored me. He could care less about a phone call. "I'm sleeping, dude." I realized that this was his real personality— that was him warts and all. After that, I began to appreciate his sardonic nature. The second thing was his taste in music. He was a Joni Mitchell fan. It was impossible to think there was not a sensitive soul hiding in there when he put on an album like *Blue* or

---

[1] This was twelve years before the *Big Lebowski* (1998).

Court and Spark. It was Connor who taught me how to keep warm, how wool was necessary on all parts of the body if you are going to work in the woods or do something serious outdoors where you get wet. He cared about things. I know he did. He just didn't want anyone to know that. I privately began to see him as a character in my novel—a novel I was certain would make me famous, or at least fabulously well to do. And we had many points of mutual interest besides my brilliant future career in literature.

He was interested in things Eastern, certainly. We both agreed all the great pottery, the great tradition of ceramics, was from the East—from Japan, Korea, and China. So we had that in common. He taught me about the Western revival, the arts and crafts movement in England, about Bernard Leach and Michael Cardew.

He was also a reader, at least to some extent, more than most. Not so big into science fiction, which was more my thing, he was obsessively into horror. Connor was an absolute Lovecraft freak and we talked about that sometimes. I said, "You know Lovecraft was in the KKK, right?"

He was incredulous. "What? Are you putting me on, dude?"

"Now would I do that?" I said.

"It seems like you might."

"No seriously, there's plenty of evidence. He wrote a poem about how much he hated 'niggers,' you know that?"

"Well, colour me sceptical. ...See what I did there?" After a while he said, "So, what is this poem called?"

"It's called, *'On the creation of Niggers.'*"

"No way."

"I'm not making this up. It's a thing."

He seemed staggered but rallied. "Maybe he was young and foolish. I think single-handedly reviving the Elder Gods makes up for a lot of foolishness in one's youth."

"Maybe," I said.

He stewed for a while and then said, "You know very well everyone in 1920s America was a racist."

"You're probably right. Woodrow Wilson was probably in the KKK."

"And Henry Ford!"

We laughed. It was nice to know someone who understood the core facts of American history and how fucked up everything was, contrary to the fanciful lies we had all learnt in elementary school.

***

The fact that I didn't get into the Creative Writing program and my hopes there had been dashed—just completely crushed—and kind of the whole point of my University plan—did not destroy my attitude forever or send me into a depression of glum looks and sarcastic remarks. I am more resilient than that. At least, I like to think so. There might have been one or two dark stares...a few unkind words...Because unfortunately it seemed almost every day, Karen Tamlen crowed and cawed like a rooster about her success in getting into the program. She stood in the hallway and raved about how much fun it was, and how she was learning so much, and on and on.

Anyway, due to my continued agitation and resentment that Rachael described as a funk, I decided

I needed to push back. I made the journey back to the Creative Writing office and looked for the Head of the Department.

Her name was Dr. Mandy Reamer, and she had posted office hours from 4 p.m. to 5 p.m. on Tuesdays; that was what the little card said on her door. When I came by, her door was already open; so I was in luck. "Dr. Reamer?" I said.

Before me was a pair of horn rims mounted on a round head as old as President Eisenhower and mottled like a camembert cheese wheel. The cheese spoke. Or rather, words were emitted from it:

"Hello, how may I help you?"

"Yes, my name is Robert Gray. People call me Sutra. I wondered if we could have a quick chat."

"Sure. What would you like to talk about, Mr. Sutra?"

"It's just Sutra. One word."

"Ok."

"Well, I applied for the Creative Writing program, and I wasn't accepted...I wondered if you could give me some insight into what I should work on. You know, to be better prepared for next time. If there can be a next time"

"Sure. Unfortunately the program is swamped with applicants. So you are right, we may not necessarily want to reconsider an applicant once they've been rejected. Places in the program open only rarely."

"Of course. And yet a friend of mine, Karen Tamlen, just got in recently."

"Ah yes, Miss Tamlen. I remember her short story. Such a charming entry."

"Really."

"Oh yes...she wrote a wonderful story about a dog."

"A dog?" I was puzzled.

"Yes. *A Dog With Fleas*. I would show it to you but actually, it's a much better idea for you to work with Karen. I'm sure she would consider letting you read her piece if you asked nicely. You could learn a lot from her."

"I see. But...well, I thought I had submitted something that was pretty good."

"Oh? What was your piece called?"

"*Antelope Agonistes*"

"Ah yes...what did you say your name was?"

"Robert. But people call me Sutra."

"Sutra...yes...Oh, I do remember this piece." She pulled out a few pages that I recognized from across her desk. Her face had changed. It was not an imperceptible underlying personality; I could see a different entity had surfaced. "Well, this was all very nice, of course. Everyone tries so very hard. But there's a *lot* to do to improve this. Tons."

"Yes. Uh—that's why I wanted to take a Creative Writing class. To get better."

She ventured a small laugh, like a cough coming from a dying gopher. "Of course. But we can only take the most talented. Or at least, we have to take those worth saving."

"Sounds like the Nazi selection process."

She frowned, but it was as if she did not get the reference. "There are other factors, too," she went on, "like making sure the class is reflective of the community and well-balanced as to overall equity of opportunity."

"I see."

She looked over her spectacles at me like an evil librarian. "Yes? You see? Good. I'm afraid your work just did not stack up. It happens."

I nodded. "Fair enough. Is there anything about my story that you liked?"

"I can't recall. But I do remember a section that made me very angry." She paged through my story and then read out loud:

I hitchhiked up to Rajneeshpuram and joined the community of sannyasins there who had gathered around an Indian guru named the Bhagwan Shri Rajneesh—

At this point she stopped. "You see, this business of going to Rajneesh-whatever. Perhaps you understand how hurtful all that was to the people of Oregon? How disgusting your behavior was—and still is? I mean, look at you," and she pointed at my robe. "Don't you see how that would have to be a big strike against you?"

"No," I said. "I don't see that."

"Well, it does. It most certainly has to be."

I guess my Shock Buddhism had found a lost soul.

She was red in the face, but I was not sure why. I tried to maneuver very gently. "I sense that you have some personal feelings about this? Were you molested by a Buddhist monk as a child?"

She leaned back in her chair and rocked once, then twice, as if to dissipate the negative energy that was fast rising inside her body. "What is going on in my personal life is no business of yours! And what you just said is very impertinent, young man!"

"Oh, I'm sorry."

"You're sorry? Sorry?" she had raised her voice now.

"Yes. I'm sorry if I offended you. You are right. I'm a bit of a smart ass." I raised my hand. "I'm sorry. For real."

"You have no idea what I've been through. My partner, my best friend, Abigail, went up there and disappeared for two whole years! I couldn't contact her. She wouldn't even speak to me..."

I just sat and listened, nodding occasionally as she blathered on. I wondered if this "Abigail" might be our Abigail West, the SCA bookkeeper. *So that was where I had seen her*, I thought.

After a while, Dr. Reamer's anger seemed to wind down, like a child becoming tired, and I tried to stay calm and reflect compassion. I was actually considering laughing in her face and walking out, but that was not from my higher self, that was definitely a negative impulse. I reflected that this Dr. Reamer was a normal person, that is, a soul, but covered in a shroud of body and mind. Instead of being mean, I tried to think of this soul, this Mandy Reamer, as a songbird. I listened to her voice change in my mind into that of an older, but kind and sad, American Robin. She warbled away in sadness, like a worm had been stolen or one of her eggs had precipitately fallen out of the nest: there was a lot to say about all that, all of it sad.

When she finally paused, I waited, and then very calmly said, "I'm so sorry. You have suffered terribly. The thing that happened up in Antelope was horrible. I know. Of course, I know. If only things could have been different. We didn't understand how bad he was. Honestly, we didn't know. But you have been hurt, terribly hurt, and for that I am sorry."

"Well then. That is very kind of you."

"But Dr. Reamer, if you don't like that story, for obvious and very reasonable reasons, please let me have another try at something more socially acceptable. I'm trying to readjust into society, you see. Like I'm sure your friend is doing. I've just moved into a housing co-op, all kinds of interesting things to write about going on there—" I stopped.

But she seemed to stiffen again. "A 'housing co-op?" She seemed to draw a blade. "Which one?"

"It's called The Campbell Club."

Dr. Reamer seemed to have expected this answer. "The Campbell Club. Yes. I've heard all about that."

"So you're a fan?"

"No. No, I am not."

I sighed. It seemed I had walked into another minefield.

"Have you heard bad things then, I take it?"

"They say it's run by communists!"

"They do?"

"Yes!"

"Well, I'm only aware of one communist," I said, "and I think he's just a part timer. He's probably going to become a very successful stock broker one day."

"I was also told, by someone very well informed," she went on, "that there is a lot of sex and drugs. Students living together in moral depravity. Places like that should be shut down."

"I'm celibate, myself, and I haven't done any hard drugs yet, but you never know. Unless you consider Greek Camp Stew a drug. It's pretty good on a Sunday morning."

"I'm not interested in your drug stew. I think this conversation is over, Mr. Whoever you are."

As I walked out I realized I'd have to think of a new major. Or something. My time at UO might end up being a lot shorter than I had planned.

***

For those who are wondering, Greek Camp Stew is fried potatoes made on the grill with eggs, spinach, and feta cheese liberally applied on top. - DRS

Part Two. In Which I Meet Cindy Sterling, and Get an Education in Love—From Someone Else.

"Am I human", he thought,
"dreaming I was a butterfly?
Or am I butterfly, dreaming
that I am a human being?"
—Chuang-Tzu, Warring States period (457 BC)

The coming of Cindy Sterling, who I sometimes called "Hot Water Cindy," was long heralded. I started hearing her name being discussed all the way back in the Fall of '85, and then the Winter came and went, filled with occasional name dropping, and finally in the Spring, it seemed that Magda (who was the Membership Coordinator after all) had fully confirmed Cindy's intentions to return to the Campbell Club. Her application had been received and fees paid. It was official.

The chief architect of this intermittent wave of gossip and constant build-up was little Karen Tamlen. She was that short and round English major with a patchy red complexion and sandy blond hair who always seemed to stand a bit too close for comfort, that I have been telling you about.

I liked Karen, actually. Her bright blue eyes seemed to sparkle or twinkle with delight. Those eyes had the tendency to stare off into space above and to the left, as if witnessing some angelic scenery that was going on above, at a great height. Yes, her eyes were mounted on an ever-smiling face, round like a tank turret, mounted under heavy bangs. Like Eva Redbone, she was a hirsute blond; the skin on her face and much of her body was covered in soft blond fuzz, and her pubis (I was made to understand) was golden brown, like a toaster waffle. But unlike Eva, Karen spoke with the crisp twang of the Midwest. She was from Iowa or somewhere ridiculous like that.

Karen lived in the co-op in the year before my own arrival and so had much familiarity with the "previous crop" of co-opers. Cindy Sterling was one of those; and it seemed that Cindy had made a big impression. A few others from that crop also stood out in Karen Tamlen's feverish imagination: she was particularly infatuated with Stan Harmon. She would stand and talk about him in that funny gently hysterical way that she had about her, eyes darting from side to side as she paused and smiled, gesticulated and smiled. If she were to travel anywhere, on Christmas Day, or up to Portland, or just on a day trip to the Oregon coastline (which was a mere 50 miles to the West) she would always stop and buy a postcard and send it off immediately to Stan Harmon. These cards never had any writing on them; they were, perhaps, a mute testament to a hidden love. For love is dumb; it cannot speak. (Later I learned that Harmon kept them. He put them up on his elite third-floor room wall with thumbtacks in a little area above the non-functional radiator, like the alcove in a 12th century monk's cell. When he left the co-op to move into a place with his girlfriend, Tamlen continued her practice; and in turn, Stan Harmon continued to thumbtack the cards. By this stage he had bought a pin board dedicated to this exact purpose).

Karen was always bursting into the kitchen—a place I have so far spoken of very little, but in fact it was the emotional and spiritual heart chakra of the whole house—she would burst into this huge almost restaurant-scale kitchen and announce some juicy gossip, whatever might be the dish du jour, to whomever or whatever was washing dishes or cooking, or merely sitting quietly in one of the many stools that ran along the immensely long Formica breakfast counter.

On this day, I was sitting on said stools eating some cereal out of a badly misshapen ceramic bowl; I don't think it was one of Connor's. (OK, it was a hideous creation of mine). Karen bounded into the room like a basketball through the swinging double door and said, "Cindy's coming! Cindy Sterling will be coming in later today. Maggie said so."

I nodded, focusing on my cereal.

"It's true! It's so exciting...I can't wait. She's so fun. Really, just a fun person! She's Australian on her father's side, her mom is from the Midwest somewhere, maybe Michigan. She loves the whole Co-op concept, is very into it. And she's a Dance major."

"What's her room assignment?" I asked.

"I think she's on the third floor. You would expect that. In Chad Smith's old room."

"That's a nice room. Excellent Feng shui."

"It's a single," she said, with a sly look, as if this fact had a hidden meaning.

"Well. Yes. Of course it is a single," I said.

"She always needed a single, you know. Because—privacy—" She left this hanging but could not help herself. "You can ask Leo about that!"

She quickly made her exit up and out of the other side of the kitchen, through the door that always reminded me of an escape hatch, the door that went towards the back hallway stairs.

Later when I asked Leo about this cryptic comment, he seemed reticent to talk about it.

I pressed him, and he said, "You will have to form your own impressions of Cindy Sterling. She's a unique person. But she did get into some trouble. She slept with a guy who used to live here, and he sort of went bonkers over her—wouldn't leave her alone. That's why she had to move out. She actually had to go back home and flee all the way to Sydney to get away from that dude."

But it turned out that Cindy the Australian *femme fatale* and human drop bear had had carnal knowledge not just with 'that dude,' but also with Leo and Stan as well. There had also been a girl from Norway named Elsa—Cindy was bisexual.

In fact, it seemed based on Karen's fantasy melodrama intel that Cindy had slept with many of the "last batch" of co-opers. Not all at once, of course, and not in any way that would draw undue attention or embarrassment to any one of them. 'And not Larry Caputo,' who was 'too weird' (she told me much later).

So Karen ran up the back stairs, laughing, joyful even, and this burst of energetic yin metabolism suggested that Cindy—sexual Cindy, the goddess of lust—must indeed be inbound.

I could not visualize her, however. The fetid information I had been subjected to did not lead to any precise image; and I tended to write off the claims of sexual depravity (or sexual freedom) as tedious gossip, regardless of how titillating those jaw movements and tongue clicks must have been to others. I was a spiritual being, after all. Or wanted to be. I had not taken vows, but, well, I was at least hopefully on The Path.

***

I must now say a bit more about that Campbell Club kitchen, for reasons to become clear in a moment. The kitchen was the abdomen of the whole co-op. Many important organs could be found there: the heart, the spleen, the liver, perhaps, at least one kidney, and certainly the intestines, both small and large. Even the house asshole was sometimes present (sorry, Rob).

It was a huge kitchen, like something out of a cooking fever dream if you happen to be the kind of person who likes kitchens. Which I am. There was a six-burner Wolf stove with a full-sized grill, the grease trap overflowing with the residue of endless breakfasts, and a hood fan above that, which made a tremendous racket; an enormous oven below that could be cranked up to inferno for pizza; a functional dish machine; two large stainless steel fridges, and then two smaller ones in the back hall for personal food. No walk-in, but still. Impressive.

My favourite part of the kitchen was the cooking island; it dominated the room with sullen girth, like something out of a Stephen King novel. Above it hung myriad pots and dangling utensils. A legendary wooden knife block stood to one side, with many strange legacy knives, of dubious sharpness; and cutting boards of even more dubious sanitation lay stained pale green and orange on its stainless-steel countertop. Malodorous piles of onions and garlic heaped ready for use, as did the eggs in cardboard flats until someone incorrectly concluded they required refrigeration; and bananas mouldered endlessly in a sodden fruit carafe that hung from above like a wire gibbet.

I have a memory also of much house-made yogurt and granola on hand in that kitchen, too. This was before the era of plant milks; all the yogurt was entirely traditional and plain, almost proletarian. It was so creamy that people asked about how it was made; but the secret, which was adding powdered milk, stayed hidden for a long while.

I think I have described the breakfast nook/barstool arrangement already; these ancient bar stools originally went all the way around a breakfasting area constructed in the original house design from the early Greco-Roman period. The Formica counter stood interlaced with sturdy white pillars that supported the ceiling while allowing full frontal view of the cooking action within.

Thus, it stood adjacent to the kitchen proper; but some of the counter had been removed at an earlier stage in the long evolution of the space, and now large bins of flour and rice and other staples and dry goods in bags stood where some of the ancient stools had been; and considerable shelving had been installed above to better meet the requirements of bulk storage and supply.

That shelving was so heavily laden with pantry that it bowed, and I had the distinct impression it would crash down at any minute; but nothing like that ever happened, and so my anxiety was for naught.

There were also cupboards with all the dishes and bowls and odd service, and drawers with silverware of many mixed patterns, like a fantasy sampling of a hundred bride's decisions, festooning either side of the double doors.

The interface to it all hung on megalithic swinging hinges. These endlessly creaking double doors allowed a steady flow of traffic in and out of the space binding the big dining area to the kitchen in an endless kiss. The dining room itself was filled with folding tables, like from a primary school, durable and probably indestructible except by atomic blast. Perhaps ten or twelve of them stood open and ready, with a smattering of similarly Enduro chairs. The flooring in there was solid oak that begged for attention, for polish, but never got it.

So that was the kitchen. It was, shall we say, a proper scene for the seduction of the senses. For my spiritual downfall—yes, my long drawn-out fall into the dreaded waffle iron of love.

***

Perhaps you can now see why I thought it was symbolic that the first time I met Cindy Sterling was in that kitchen. She came through those double doors as if they were a bathroom window, protected by many silver or at least stainless-steel spoons. And of course by Connor's Zen tea bowls.

It happened like this: the day before, as I sat in the living room watching the piano tuner try to get the contraband Steinway into shape, there was a commotion. I should say the piano was still not in use but Leo had put considerable effort into scrubbing off the spray-painted penises; the results were not great, but it looked better. And it took a few months to get the money to have the piano tuned. We went through the usual money-getting processes in the co-op. There was an agenda item, discussion, even a vote. But in due course—perhaps a good five months had passed since our daring caper down in fraternity row—it was time.

The piano tuner, an old wayfarer, probably a Jew, who said his father had left Poland after the wreck of World War I, seemed immensely pleased to be alive. Every time he turned a peg, or pressed a key, he let out a small sigh of satisfaction. Sometimes he repeated this action again and again, seeming to question. A note as a question. A note as a message? Perhaps from a shambling god of music? But eventually he found that feeling of aural satisfaction in that particular pitch, a subtlety of the frequency perhaps, which he craved, something completely beyond my ears, and then he sighed, smiled, and moved on.

I listened to him work from a discreet distance—no point in distracting the maestro. I was sitting cross-legged with my eyes closed near the fireplace, not really meditating, but just sitting, deep in my own thoughts, when there was a ruckus from the far side of the great room. The huge green wooden door had opened and people seemed to be gathering, bounding down the stairs in that direction. A general alarm of some kind—Karen Tamlen was there, laughing and giggling; and Leo had turned out; and standing dangerously close to Leo was Rachael Day, all smiles, looking very blousy as if she had just returned all sweaty from a vigorous hike, even as Leo's face was flushed. And his fly was undone. So, yes, they were now a couple. Very much so, it seemed.

Of course, the signs were obvious for a few weeks now, it had been entirely superfluous for Karen Tamlen to burst into the kitchen a few nights before to announce this new and very juicy titbit to anyone who would listen.

I myself did not feel like joining the throng. I didn't know Cindy and besides, there is not much of the social butterfly in me. I figured I'd meet the new girl in due course. Perhaps that was why I didn't bother to get up. They say first impressions are important; well, I was a shit for first impressions almost all the time. This was no exception. If Cindy had looked over she would have seen nothing but a dirty saffron-coloured lump and an apparently bald, eyebrowed pinhead.

***

The next morning I was up fairly early and had retrieved the *Register Guard* from the porch—we had a house subscription—it was not as good a paper as the *Oregonian*, but it was something to read. I was just keeping a bar stool warm, I guess. The door swung open behind me and I heard a new voice.

"Where'd all these ceramics come from?" the voice said. That voice had a distinctive tinge of the foreign.

At the time I found it to be amusing, an affectation. But eventually I longed to hear it, just a word or two, a hint, spoken in that accent. I think this is true of many men and I am not ashamed about that anymore. Sometimes, predictably, it is the French language inducing this narcotic effect on the male of the species. But this was not French.

I didn't even bother to look up. "Uh...those are mostly from Connor. He's in the double on the second floor, the one near the back stairwell." I turned to look and it was the new girl. Cindy.

"These are great! It's like treasure. Zen Tea Bowls!" she said.

"Well, I'll tell him. He's my roomie. I'm Robert. Robert Gray. But most people call me Sutra." I actually stood up now and held out my hand, which was awkward, I think.

"Cindy," she said, ignoring my hand. She seemed busy choosing a bowl. She picked one up and turned it over, looking at the bottom, and then set it back down, moving on to the next one. It was a very thorough inspection.

I went back to my spearmint tea and the *Register Guard*—something about a gigantic explosion in a country called the Ukraine—nuclear, I guess, a reactor melt-down—and Cindy went about the process of making herself a cup of hot water. I watched, somewhat surreptitiously, as she smoothly operated the stove to ignite a fire under the kettle—it required a match—and heat it up. It was like watching a ballerina—which, I suppose in actual fact she was, as a dance major—yes, it was like watching a ballerina do the Japanese tea ceremony. Her hands were memorable; not just in the way they moved but in their form. They were pale, like her entire body—I never knew Cindy to sun herself, and she remained untouched by the sun year-round—entirely vampiric—but this pale quality was more like ivory. Firm. When she held her fingers to her face and made a gesture, it was like an outtake from a kabuki play.

She sat down next to me and I could hear her breathe in the steam from her hot water. Her fingers gently touched the bowl like a sacred chalice. I swear, there was absolutely nothing in that bowl but hot water. No tea bag, no nothing. I know because I watched her pour it and saw the whole process. I had never seen anybody drink just hot water. Almost no one drinks out of a ceramic bowl, either. But if they did, one would imagine there would tea in it. Right? Isn't that so? It shook my whole philosophical outlook that this drinking of hot water was "a thing."

"Sutra," she said, apropos of nothing. "Is that a nickname?"

"It's a nickname."

"It's different."

"It started when I was in 11th grade," I said. "My school buddy and I were talking about something, and he said something and I answered by quoting from the Diamond Sutra. The Diamond Sutra is a Buddhist—"

"Yeah, I know what it is," she said.

"Oh. Well, anyway, ever since that time when he started calling me Sutra, it just sort of caught on, everybody started calling me that. Even teachers. At first it kind of pissed me off but then I started to like it. So I have kept it."

She didn't say anything and seemed absorbed in her hot water drinking. It seemed to be a very serious activity for her. As I have mentioned, there was a certain noticeable precision in the way her hands moved. I did not understand at the time that this was just how she was, it was her normal modus operandi. Surely it was an affectation? But suddenly I realized I was openly staring at her. I was agog. The paper lay now on the counter, the words on the broad sheet forming an indecipherable mess. She was not returning my gaze, just all self-absorbed. I said, "So what's with the hot water?"

"Hmm?"

"Uh...I guess I've never seen anyone drink hot water before."

"No?" She seemed puzzled.

"No."

"Interesting. Well, I do it all the time. I'm from Australia, originally, although I grew up mostly in the States. Ann Arbor. I think Australians do this. Actually, I'm pretty sure everyone does this, Sutra."

She seemed to be pulling my leg. Gently messing with me in her gentle ballerina way. She was dancing all over me. She had a kind of smile, a sleepy smile, as she spoke, and she still wasn't even looking at me. But...as it happens I was starting to be OK with all of it. I went back to my paper, or tried to, and she got up and began rummaging in the big fridge on the far side of the kitchen. "Damn, I'm starved."

"It's not yet time for breakfast." I meant the co-op breakfast. "Pretty soon."

"Yeah, there used to be some eggs...not on the counter?"

"Eggs," I said, stupidly. "I think those have moved into the fridge. God only knows why." I was no longer firing on all cylinders. It was suddenly like my mind was farting. But she took no notice.

"Ah...here we go..." She had moved over to the far cooler and, successful now, started the process of making herself an early breakfast. It had the general appearance of an omelette beginning to take shape, like a new-born being. I should explain that in the co-op we made all the food communally, including a breakfast, but at this hour—it was quite early, perhaps 6 a.m.—the cooks had not come down yet.

"So what's your major, Mr. Sutra?" she said, as she danced the cooking process, her fingers a blur. The scent of *Gallus domesticus* albumin tinged with yolk being rendered by heat, which I abstained from as a vegetarian, soon entered my nostrils.

"Creative Writing."

"Oh. Wow. That's pretty cool. So...you want to be a writer?"

"I am a writer."

"Really? Wow. What have you written?"

"Oh, just short stories, mainly. But I want to write a novel."

Yes, I was lying. In reality, at that moment I was just an English major. A brain farting English major. *Crap*, I thought, *I'm pathetic. I'm lying to this girl who is way over my pay grade in every particular. She's probably a fucking prima donna or famous somehow. And now I'm in for it.*

English majors were the kind of people that I always laughed at before the time I became an English major. I mean, Karen Tamlen was an English major. So, I didn't feel like telling girls or this new Cindy Sterling chick, this kitchen ballerina of the Zen hot water, that that's what I was.

I left, feeling rather irritable for some reason, not even saying good-bye or anything—another ridiculous social faux pas on my part, looking back on it—and went about my English major business.

But I kept thinking about Cindy Sterling all day.

***

I went up to my room, which as mentioned was on the second floor. This was a double quite close to the second floor front-stairs landing. Suddenly I realized I was measuring how far it was mentally to this Cindy's room. She was up a level and down at the end. It was like everything in my head was recalibrating.

Connor was just waking up. "Sutra, you pud," he groaned. "Dude! I was sleeping!"

"Good morning, Sunshine," I said. "Hard night?"

"No, just recovering...must be something I smoked..."

"What, with Foster?"

"How did you guess?"

I laughed and got ready to take a shower. "You groaned all night."

He groaned some more as I got ready for my shower. It was a shared co-ed bathroom, but with individual showers and stalls. I put on my bath robe and grabbed an almost clean towel out of my pile of rags. "Have you met this Cindy Sterling?" I asked.

"Uh...yeah. Like, at dinner? Where were you? Leo made the introductions. Dude! She's gonzo. I think she's a Dance major. Very introverted I would say. Flashing eyes. Skin like a China doll."

"Like Eva."

Connor considered. "Well, perhaps not exactly like her. I take it she's from the Midwest somewhere?"

"I don't know. She said something about Australia. But I was too mesmerized...it was like a hypnotic field.... She seems very Zen, though...." I laughed a little too loud. "She liked your work. Get this, she was drinking hot water..."

I told him the whole 'Hot Water, Zen Tea Bowl' story and as I did so, his eyes kind of brightened. "Ah. I see. Yes.... So does this mean your infatuation with little Karen Tamlen has run its course?"

"Oh my, what on earth are you talking about?"

"She's always standing so close to you. Telling you gossip and probably rubbing your dick."

"What, doesn't she do that to everyone? Of course she does."

"I was just wondering if she was now available. You know. So I could toast her waffle."

He was smiling and looking at me. He knew very well I thought Karen Tamlen was repulsive. I had said so repeatedly. In fact we both knew I protested too much. Yes, Karen was willing to stroke my dick and had indicated this repeatedly by both word and deed. Her turret-shaped head turned like a gun battery whenever I chanced to walk by. But I had not yet given in.

Even then, in my youthful ignorance, I understood Karen was the kind of girl you should never do, well— anything at all with. Certainly she was not the kind of girl you put your dick in; not if you don't want serious karmic consequences down the line. A moment of obscene pleasure delivered in marzipan staccato spurts, in exchange for decades of mind-numbing, soul-killing suffering.

This native soul intelligence would probably not have stopped me from falling down into the deep abyss of toaster waffledom eventually—after all, as Nietzsche said, to err is human; to toast a waffle is divine. But Cindy!

Perhaps my demeanour or my tone of voice, which was slightly elevated (as was my pulse) had given me away during the whole Zen Tea Bowl story.

He smiled again. "Yes. I see it all clearly."

"Oh, no," I said. "No, no, no. Hot Water Cindy? No way. I have to be free of desire! I'm on The Path for God's sake!"

He laughed. "Good one."

***

While we are on the general subject of the Campbell Club's kitchen and the first floor, or at least in the general vicinity, I need to tell another story or else we might neglect to introduce a side-character in our tale: Thomas Pincheon III.

Pincheon was a local boy from a well-established family who had applied the previous year to the co-op. At that time he clearly spelled out his situation. It was a first, and the requirement was discussed widely in the house; but most of that was before my time.

Yes, Pincheon was a quadriplegic and entirely wheelchair-bound; his room was intentionally on the first floor; indeed, the room had been specially outfitted by none other than Stan Harmon and Larry Caputo to work for someone in a wheelchair. There was even a special bathroom/shower setup right in the room. As far as his habit of leaving his own door continually open—this may have had some other trivial purpose, perhaps to let in fresh air; but I think the main purpose was to allow him to hear everything that went on in the kitchen—all the conversations there; perhaps even the smells and the feelings associated with those. I think even with his door closed he could hear most of what was going on, for the sound of the activity in the second and third floor halls above also travelled into the back hall, reverberating on the stairs; and echoed into his cavernous room like a great ear trumpet. There he sat, like a spider, listening.

Besides the room provisioning, there was the problem of access to the house. The covered front porch festooned with ratty couches stood a good four feet above the grass in the yard, and broad wooden steps led up to it. The great green wooden door, above which hung the proud Student Cooperative Association plaque, was equipped with a huge knocker, and was very secure, but was entirely inaccessible to a wheelchair. So, as part of the retrofit, it was agreed a ramp must be built.

The ramp turned out to be a significant project. Leo said that the co-op had never had a disabled person; that he was proud the SCA was able to offer this accommodation, but that much work would be required. And it was true, various people were involved. Johan Tunz was a junior working towards a Bachelor of Architecture, who put his hand up to design the ramp. It had to be strong enough to support a wheelchair (obviously) but also not create too much of a problem to those with working legs, or those carrying kegs, and so on. Finally there was the issue of the visual appearance. Johan promised he would design something elegant. His deep voice, amplified in a solid chest that was supported by washboard abs, gave everyone a feeling of security and mastery. And he came through with a fine design that Stan and Larry were hired to build out. That ramp still exists, along with the sunburst co-op logo that Johan helped make himself, which festoons the front of the house.[2] Everyone seemed pleased, and felt, just possibly, a sense of virtue, at correctly interpreting and meeting a crucial requirement of contemporary society, which is equity—fairness to the "differently-abled." But we did not say things like that in those days. This was all at least four years before passage of the Americans With Disabilities Act (1990).

However, when Pincheon arrived, he complained bitterly about the ramp, the room, and even the house itself. It was not immediately clear how things had failed so dismally, and Leo in particular was beside himself about it. Over time the core-problem, the underlying issue, emerged. It was Magda who realized what had gone wrong: "He's not making any friends," she told Leo. They had organized the physical structure; but it takes more than a house to make life liveable. Thomas would motor around in the dining room and bump over the living room carpet, and zoom in and out of the back hall, grumbling and sour-faced, like a gremlin on speed. No one talked to him, and he did not seem to allow anyone to do that anyway.

---

[2] It can be seen from the Street View in Google Maps.

It was Johan who befriended him, coming to his room for visits, sitting with him patiently in the dining room in the evenings. I think Magda had something to do with this. Thomas was an Oregon Ducks fan and regularly attended home games. This was something of an anomaly, the Campbell Club was not exactly sports-oriented. But Johan loved Big Ten Conference football, primarily as a way to gamble. It turned out this touched closely and serendipitously on one of Pincheon's passions: money. The two soon set up what over a period of months became a successful bookmaking operation that grew to the point frat boys were starting to hang out in the vicinity. I remember going down the back hall and being startled by "Frank" the frat boy, in full preppie attire, standing uncomfortably staring at the ceiling, as a line of representatives from all across fraternity row waited at Thomas's door to place their bets. Eventually Leo had to get involved after one particularly heated upset match, with Iowa losing to UCLA in the Rose Bowl. More than eight-thousand dollars changed hands before the game, with a lot of frat boy money disappearing into the ether after UCLA triumphed.

That night, things got a bit wild in Thomas Pincheon III's room, when he was thrown bodily out of his chair by an angry customer. Luckily Johan, who was in the kitchen, heard the disturbance and burst in.

"You hit the cripple, huh? Maybe you try hit me?" he said in his Lurch baritone.

The frat boy swung a sucker punch that landed on Johan's face. His head jerked back—but that was all. "Is it my turn now?" he said. Yes, Johan was enormous. Tall, with a torso of iron. He was like Ivan Drago in

Rocky IV. Well, perhaps not that big, but he was big; and seemed even larger and taller when standing near Thomas Pincheon III in his wheelchair, shrunken by his paralysis to the point he might have passed for a 60-year-old man.

So then Johan landed a hard right to the frat boy's solar plexus as he fended off a second punch. The frat boy went down. That one punch more or less ended the physical part of the conflict as the other two frat boys had no interest in taking on the washboard-ab giant who somehow had mastered the art of predicting Big Ten spreads. By now, Leo and a few others had arrived, including Stan and Larry. Stan had armed himself with a crowbar. They expelled the belligerent frat boy after lifting him up off the ground and wiping off some of the puke, and his friends went with him, cowed, their faces downcast, money gone, and then Leo finally put the kibosh on the whole gambling business. "You can run any business you like, guys, but not on Campbell Club property. I'm not even going to take this to the Board. I'm just saying, this is it."

Meanwhile, the frat boy who Johan had dropped like a rock went back to the Alpha Beta Gamma House and called the police to report Johan for assault. He also spilled the beans on the entire Big Ten Conference book-making operation. The cops showed up at the co-op later that night.

Things looked bleak, and Middleweight Johan was cuffed and taken outside to sit in the squad car, lights flashing, until they found out who Pincheon was. Turns out his father was a well-known fixture with the Eugene PD back in the day. The story of that worthy's son suffering a tragic accident—jumping headfirst into the brand-new concrete pool, when it had only received two feet of water, the hose still running—was widely known within the Eugene Police Department. Money had been raised through donations towards his support and eventually a college fund was set up, too. The boy broke his C5 vertebrae and despite rapid medical attention, lost the use of his legs. Considerable degradation of function in his arms meant he could barely move his left hand, and only two fingers and the thumb on the right. He could control an electric wheelchair with a joystick but not stand up or even control his own bladder. He was crippled for life.

Pincheon welcomed the two police officers who knocked on the open door to his room. He seemed to know both of them by their first names. The discussion quickly turned to his father, who they also both knew. When Thomas related how the frat boy had knocked him out of his chair and kicked him repeatedly while he lay on the ground, that he was in pain, and further that Johan, who had been in the kitchen minding his own business, had rushed in to his defence, the cops let Johan go, and more, actually thanked him for being a concerned citizen. There followed a quick discussion about the need to curtail any additional betting on football, to which Thomas assented. "It was fun at first, but it got out of hand. I messed up. I'm sorry about that. No more bets."

The very convivial discussion ended with the police officers asking if there was anything he needed, such as a trip to the ER for an X-Ray, to which Thomas replied in the negative. They left after making clear they would deal with the frat boys. "Don't worry, Thomas. They won't be bothering you anymore. Say hi to your dad for us." A raid later that night on the Alpha Beta Gamma House led to the arrest of several pledges on multiple charges including gambling, possession of marijuana, and underage possession of fourteen kegs of beer. I assume the cops later had a party of their own that night.

The outcome of the whole affair was actually to raise Pincheon's standing in the house, as the story was told and retold in different versions. Johan's in-house fame also went up several notches in this time period.

The secondary outcome was that Pincheon was now perceived as being good with money (he was a Business and Econ double-major anyway) and he was easily elected as the House Treasurer at the start of the following term. He did not grow many friends, but everyone now respected him as a fixture and understood something of his story, and it was a sort of ice-breaker. In some sense, he was finally integrated into the fabric of the co-op experience. Eventually a rumour circulated he had convinced Karen Tamlen to give him a hand job—with money changing hands also—and yes, quadriplegics can get erect, I have it on good authority—but I never believed the story. I think she would have done it for free.

However, this election to House Treasurer had the somewhat unpleasant effect of making Thomas the point of contact for all paying of fees, and also the person to negotiate a fee schedule with if someone could not make the nut. We ended up seeing a lot more of him than some of the house members wanted. Thomas was never very pleasant, even after becoming a hero of sorts, and the concept of a grace period on fees was unknown to him. More about this later.

***

Magda and Napoleon were to all intents and purposes a unit, a whole, a yin and yang. A marriage in all but name. And yet here was Raven, Magda's best friend, right there in the room with them. At night. Every night. I need to narrate how that exploded.

Raven Slecto was a big and somewhat ungainly girl. Not overweight, just a big person. What I mean is, for example, she tended to bump into things. Especially in the kitchen if she was in there it was good to stand clear. Slavic, blond (at least in theory), funny and kind in her own way; sort of a goof ball as far as I could tell. Not ugly, I would say, but not pretty, a girl who did not yet know love, and so did not see herself as an object of attention or worthy of attention; who never seemed to date, who did not mind her friend's romantic liaison, who in fact was genuinely happy for her friend's happiness.

But this day things had not gone well for Raven; there had been some difficulties in a class—something about a missed test—and some news from home that was also less than good. Raven was, perhaps, one of those people who seek to escape their troubles instead of facing them head on. At this moment she was trying to convince Magda to come with her to a club for a dose of much needed escape.

"It will be fun, Maggie!" she was saying. "Come on, let's try something *new* tonight. Let's get out of this stink hole." She niffed and involuntarily glanced in Napoleon's direction.

Magda saw this glance but ignored it. "Hmm...Well then, where do you want to go, my charmed one?"

"I have a place in mind. Can it be a surprise?"

"But I need to know what to wear."

Raven deflated a bit. "All right. Fine. The Riviera. I want to go to the Riviera."

Magda didn't say anything for a while. "Can we get in there?" she wondered.

"I think so," said Raven slowly. "I know one of the bartenders..."

"You do?"

"I do." Raven ginned mischievously. "You might know one of them too."

This was the first inkling that maybe Raven had a life outside of their little triangle—outside of Magda's extensive catalogue of social knowledge which included all things Raven and her entire school schedule, turn-ons and turn-offs, etc.

"Well...I have a test tomorrow, you know...."

But Magda agreed to go that night, even as Napoleon stood shaking his head. "The Riviera room? Are you crazy? Dat be a gay place."

Rastafarian is not without an element of conservatism, despite what anyone might think who just sees someone different than themselves in a funny cap, rainbow tie dye, and Napoleon hair.

Raven now tried to wheedle her way forward into this long held fantasy. "But Nappy, maybe Maggie and I can have a girl's night out? Just her and I?"

"Oh, I see...I see...yes. Maybe I be chillin' round the co-op tonight. Di girls need to bust out. And so you shall."

But an hour later Magda was insisting on including him. This set the tone for the evening: Raven clearly wanted time with her best friend, alone, without Napoleon's constant presence, without his influence, and Magda would have been happy to stay in with her man. She didn't understand the signals her friend was sending.

The Riviera Room was a bar down by Willamette and East 10th Streets, not so far from the bus station. It was actually pretty well known in certain circles. Like Cassidy's Tavern, it had a reputation and a very specific clientele. There was a bit of a 1940s nightclub feel but freaky and fun and disco. Some called it the 'Boom Boom Room.'

Napoleon sunk down in a booth of stained leather, his eyes slowly adjusting to the red glow. The sounds of 70s disco clogged his ears. Magda and Raven had gone up to see if they could buy a cocktail.

It became increasingly clear to Napoleon that Raven was a regular at the Riviera Room. More than one woman—and some of them were older women, not students—approached her, taking her in their arms, kissing, even. It slowly dawned on him what everyone except him already knew—that his girlfriend's best friend might just possibly be a lesbian. Then he saw Raven introducing Magda to some of these women— saw Magda not sure how to react, but swiftly adapting, smiling, trying to be her best social butterfly self.

Raven then had a teasing conversation with the bartender. He was a buff looking young man in his twenties in black tights and leather, very large and substantial. His shirtless muscled chest bulged above washboard abs.

Then, to Napoleon's horror, Raven pointed back at him and, seeing the Rastaman, the bartender smiled joyfully. He waved! Napoleon had no idea how to react; he raised his hand in a tentative gesture and made a peace sign.

Then the bartender went into action. Ice cubes popped in the air and liquid flowed freely high and low from various bottles; much shaking of canisters commenced. Finally, glasses were filled.

The girls returned successfully with cocktails.

"Something very familiar about dat bartender," said Napoleon.

Raven laughed. "Well, there should be! That's Johan! Johan Tunz! From the co-op."

Napoleon took a few seconds to process this news as Raven watched him react with amusement. "I-I don't understand. Johan? Our Johan? Who punched the frat boy? We were just talking about roots reggae."

But then the big man himself suddenly appeared. "How's my Blue Lagoon, Maggie?"

"It's good," she said. "Tastes like lemonade!"

Napoleon was beside himself. "Johan? Dat you?"

Johan sighed, and then briefly sat down in the booth, positioning himself so he could face Napoleon. He put his hands flat on the table. "So. I guess my secret is out."

"But Johan," said Napoleon. "You know I—I'm not sure what to say."

"It's OK. Yes, I am gay. You can say it."

"I can see that! But does everybody know?"

Johan smiled. "Yes, Nappy. Everybody knows. Only you didn't know. I guess because no one told you. And I have no idea why Raven brought you here." He looked at Raven now with a somewhat harder look. "Not the best plan, in my opinion. But now that you're here—"

At that moment an older man pranced happily over to the table. "Well, Johan, aren't you going to introduce me to this wonderful specimen of Jamaican manhood? Is he available tonight? Care to dance, young fella?"

"Bless!" cried Napoleon.

Johan was surprisingly harsh. "Lay off, Larry. He's from the co-op. He's with me and he's straight. They're just visiting. They won't be staying very long."

"Well, honeys, whether you're with Johan or not, it's still a two-drink minimum! Ta-Ta for now!"

Napoleon watched in horror as he flounced away, cackling.

"Sorry about that," said Johan. "Look, my friend, this is not how I would choose to come out to you. Let me get you a cherry cola. Or do you prefer a shot of good Jamaican rum? Maybe you need one?"

"Maybe. No—you are right, Johan. I and I. The Shirley Temple only."

"Coming right up."

"Are you OK, my love? Should we go?" said Magda.

Napoleon looked hurt. "I'm just out of my depth, Maggie. Like a fish out of the water. Someone please put me back in di goldfish bowl."

***

That night things just sort of blew up in room 24. I was down the hall, and I could hear the ruckus from there. Yelling, some screaming, stomping of feet, crying. But the weird thing was actually this: there was no soft music. It was The Day The Reggae Died. In the aftermath, Raven moved out of the co-op entirely.

This created an opening on the SCA Board, as you remember Raven was the Secretary. For a time, Rachael Day filled in at Leo's request. But it seemed her feelings towards Leo were beginning to sour.

Then something happened which definitely broke relations between Rachael and Leo. There was a weekend party at the house, a keg party, band, the whole deal, and I decided that I wanted to hitchhike to Florence and see the ocean.

I was making my escape out the big front door when Rachael accosted me on the porch.

"Bugging out?"

"Yeah. Sorry, not my cup of tea."

"I guess that makes sense," she said. "I heard you just like hot water!" She laughed then, a nice laugh at my expense, and soon went back to being a statue.

That trip is a digression to our current thread, so just to give the highlights, I hitchhiked out (had no trouble getting a ride) and spent a very cold night on the beach. I learned the interesting fact that wild strawberries grow on the beach; also that the ocean is very cold up in Oregon at this time of year. And then I tried to get a ride back, which took a day standing by the roadside.

When I finally got home to the Campbell Club, the party was over and the house was pretty smashed. I mean seriously broken. Lots of trash to pick up. Vomit, that sort of thing. Leo was running the vacuum, his face rather glum. I waved at him and went upstairs. The front room carpet looked even more disgusting than normal, and the whole house really needed a deep clean (which I'm afraid it never got). The only positive was that Leo had insisted on wrapping the Steinway in a protective cover of canvas, duct tape, and bubble wrap that had been recovered from dumpsters at the University loading docks. So at least Stein seemed to be intact and had not lost his Way.

The next day Rachael was out on the porch and I sat down next to her. She seemed distracted so I was very gentle. I told her the story of seeing the wild strawberries growing on the dunes out at Florence, and she brightened up a bit. "Those are *Fragaria chiloensis*, the Oregon strawberry. I've never seen one. How was it?"

"They're super small, the berries were about the size of a kernel of sweet corn. But tasty." I paused. "Are you all right, Rachael? You seem...just a little down."

She sighed. "Do you happen to remember, when we got the piano, there was a girl, a sorority sister."

"Babs, I think."

"Yes, Babs. You have a good memory. Well, Leo has been socializing with this Babs. For a while we were doing things with the three of us together. She seemed really nice but kind of fragile. It was all kept secret, skulking about."

I didn't say anything because I understood that Rachael needed me to be her friend in that moment and nothing more. I just signalled my understanding by nodding my head and leaned in a little.

"So, over the weekend, the party. Things got pretty out of control. Leo had set up a tent, the idea was the three of us would crash there after. There was a lot of beer involved...anyway, the three of us—"

I looked around to see if anyone else was in earshot. But things were quiet in that moment. She was almost crying. "We had a threesome, Sutra."

I considered a minute. "Well, that's beautiful, Rachael."

"No," she said. "No, it wasn't." Her eyes widened. "It was all wrong. It was gross. But I didn't realize that until about half-way through. I wanted to stop but I didn't. I made a mistake. A big one. Sutra, what do I do? I mean, when I make a mistake, a little one, I know how to handle that. But if I make a big one, this big, what should I do about that? How do I—How do I go on?"

I kind of froze, then, because I realized Rachael was at a turning point and I had to be very careful, very compassionate, and not my usual asshole self. I had to dig deep.

"When I was about 8 years old my mom remarried and my stepfather moved us to Florida. He worked for Lockheed as an engineer, for NASA, the space program. This was during the Apollo missions. Anyway, we lived in a subdivision that had these boat docks right next to the houses. There were canals cut, which lead from the marina right to the houses. So people could dock their boats. And me and the neighbourhood kids would play in and around those canals. So one day, I caught a giant horseshoe crab. You know what I mean? It's a very ancient looking creature."

"Yes, I know what that is," Rachael said.

"And I caught one and basically, I was torturing it. I don't remember what I was doing, something sadistic. And I will always remember, this woman came out of her house and started yelling at me. She was older, like a retiree, and she was angry. She yelled, "what are doing, leave that alone, that's a living thing!" And I suddenly felt something I never felt before."

"What did you feel?"

"Shame. That was the first time in my life I felt shame. I realized I was doing something wrong, terribly wrong, like a crime, I realized that hurting other beings was wrong. Not a sin, because sin is a very different idea. I did not feel shame because I was doing something forbidden; I felt shame because I was made aware, in the starkest terms, that what I was doing was hurting another being."

"So what happened?"

"To the horseshoe crab? Well, the lady made me throw it back in the water. But that was not end of it. Because I had woken up to the idea that hurting was wrong. Hurting anything. And so I had to then change my life."

"What did you do?"

"Well, eventually I became a vegetarian. Not for 'health reasons,' but for moral reasons. It's not the killing I object to, so much, as the fact that killing is hurting and harming another being. And that all goes back to that moment of shame, which I experienced when that old lady was yelling at me for enjoying torturing the giant horseshoe crab. I became a moral person."

Rachael thought about that. "I feel mainly disgust. And guilt."

"Yes," I said. "Guilt can be converted into the Positive Power. You don't have to tell anyone what happened, by the way. I don't think I've ever told anyone that story about the crab. In fact, I don't believe I even thought about it until just this moment. Spontaneous me, I guess. But now, thinking back, I can kind of see how things grew from there. These days, what I believe about animal rights and so on is far more radical than what other people believe. I don't think killing anything is moral, not even a bug. But obviously sometimes these things have to be done."

"So you're just saying I should try to be good? Try to be moral? That's not exactly what I need to hear. I'm not going on a moral crusade to stamp out, you know—"

"No, Rachael." I took her hand. "I'm saying Don't Skulk, as you put it. Honesty is always the best policy. Look at me, the hapless guy in a robe. It least I am out. Like gay people. My freak flag is flying. And I have the hidden satisfaction of thinking I am better than anyone else, because I don't eat meat or kill things."

She didn't say anything.

"You still seem kind of depressed," I said. "I take it my words of wisdom were entirely insufficient to guide your feet onto the Path of Truth."

"Yeah. No ideas here."

We laughed. Sometimes making a girl laugh feels pretty good.

"I do take your point," she said. "I got into a situation that was wrong for me. I was led into it by you know who. I trusted him. But now I understand. Now I know better. Never skulk!"

"I'm going to stop talking now," I said, "because if I keep talking, I'm going to mess this up. It's so perfect I need to write about it and put it in a book. All the perfect stuff."

"You do that and I'll shoot you. This business is gross." But she smiled then and did something I didn't expect. She leaned in and gave me a very nice kiss on the lips. I had not been kissed in a long time.

"What's that for?" I said.

"For the horseshoe crab. You stopped hurting it. Now go, please. I have to think."

I left her to do that. But what I was thinking, was maybe Leo was in for it.

Leo was toast.

***

What happened over the next few months was a classic psychological study in group dynamics; or, in my way of thinking, a vicissitude of karma, such that Rachael came to be aligned with Cindy Sterling and Eva Redbone into a house constellation, a power triangle. Not a power couple, which is more common, but rather a power trio: the ultimate rock band, I suppose. But here the power was all yin energy, Pussy Power (I think Eldridge Cleaver coined this term), not male bravado.

It actually started quite suddenly one day, almost as a spontaneous chemical reaction when the reagents are present in the correct amounts and have reached the correct temperature. Suddenly, the mixture began to fluoresce.

Socially, it was like a 'boys on the side' thing. The three girls were often seen together, occasionally sitting clustered at dinner, or in the living room in the evening, talking and chatting quietly, confined in their own mind zone, like mafioso capos plotting about their domain. Meanwhile the men in their lives were put on the side, not in a direct way; but just starved for time. Bled out for contact. Leo felt this the most, as his liaison with Rachael suffered a major breakdown when she failed to attend his big performance. He was playing a flute concerto by Bach, and Magda and Napoleon, Karen Tamlen, even Rob, were in attendance (I came late, but at least I showed up.) But not the Venus de Milo.

It turned out she had missed the gig to go on a bike ride with Cindy. Then later, when Leo wanted to work on his big poster for the music poster contest that was going on, she stood him up again to do something with Eva.

As things progressed, Eva became more aggressive and demanding towards anyone not in this charmed circle. She stopped even saying hello for a time and, as it was spring turning into summer, began wearing clogs.

I can understand how clogs are a kind of footwear a dancer would enjoy and appreciate. Not only because of the arch support, but also because they made a pleasant clop-clop sound and a clickety-clack that could be compounded into a cacophony. It was, in that sense, the ultimate dance shoe, even more than pointe shoes. There was also the fact that clogs had been used by ethnic dancers in various countries, not just the Dutch, which may have inspired Eva to buy some. I don't think she knew about the choreographic work of the Polish Jerzy Grotowski, which was mentioned in *My Dinner With Andre*, and involved clogs to represent the marching feet of concentration camp prisoners; but I knew about it. And I discussed it with Cindy, because by this stage I was deeply in love with Cindy and wanted to impress upon her how much I loved Dance; which was really only one of a hundred ways of saying that I loved her, and then Cindy told Eva—something, not sure how that information about Grotowski translated into Eva's Southern Belle mind—other than I got points for that, and then suddenly they were all wearing clogs and there was a tremendous racket all through the house on the wooden floors. And I tried to keep quiet about my role in that particular problem while people put their hands over their ears.

(There is a funny aside to this. After some of the initial hub bub wore down, Rob Meister was spotted wearing clogs that spring. I think in his case, it was through vanity; for Rob Meister was relatively short. Not of dwarf height to make fun of like Gimli in Tolkien's *Lord of the Rings*, but short. So I believe he came to clogs for one of their other properties, which was that they were lifts.)

***

With the approach of Spring Break, it seemed possible that Rachael had made her own break entirely from Leo. And when I asked him, he said "well, she was never really, officially my girlfriend."

I'm not sure what that meant exactly—some grand romantic concept in Leo's head no doubt—but Rachael left for Cancun without him. Leo moped around the house, which was mostly empty. Like me, he was far from home. The breaktime was good in that sense. I was thrilled to be able to sit in the dining room or on the front porch in relative peace.

Those days I tended to become more introspective (if that were possible). What I mean is, I began to dwell on the past. —Terrible idea, and also counterproductive. But it happened pretty often. I would sit quietly, my eyes closed, some people might call it meditation. I was just letting my mind calm down and becoming quiet. It's a wonderful, blissful thing if you can achieve it, because the only way to achieve it is by not achieving, by letting go and giving up achievement. I had that in spurts, just a taste of joy. But then, because of the way things had gone, and how I had been conned, I would start to think about my year at the Rajneeshpuram.

People sometimes ask me what it was like, if it was an orgy scene or a weird freaky scene. But it was nothing like that at all. We were building an intentional community and most of the time I was doing things like planting lettuce. Everything was very ordinary in that sense; but with a feeling of love in what we were doing. And in regard to Osho, or Rajneesh, the erstwhile guru, we hardly saw him. He would drive by in one of his Rolls Royce's, maybe wave his hand. That was about it. I never personally interacted with him at all. For me, the place was all about the people. By and large they were wonderful, and for one reason: it was a supreme good to be among people who all wanted to find something greater and better than the world we know. This world sucks.

So, it was all the more terrible when the experiment (as I thought of it) abruptly ended. Apparently, when you align yourself with a bad seed, then the fruit from the tree that grows from that seed is poisoned. Perhaps that was why all my efforts at getting back to normality had failed and every time someone learned I had been a "cultist" they tossed me under the bus or into the trash compactor. Imagine if C-3PO, finding that Luke was a cultist, had let the trash compactor crush him. That's how I felt sometimes. In those down-phase moments.

It never bothered me at the time that the outer world—the people of rural Oregon—basically, normal Americans leading normal American lives, watching television and voting for Ronald Reagan—hated us, literally hated our presence; because I knew they lived in *shoshaku jushaku*. Their condition was one of continuous error—choosing the wrong thing, like eating meat or indulging in sex and violence, over and over and over, until it became a lifetime of mistakes; and eventually their whole lives were, in the end, one continuous mistake. Death of the soul.

Thus, our very existence, our 'cult,' was to them something unacceptable, because we rejected their way of living and being and even openly criticized it. So the reason their rejection did not bother me was that I felt superior.

I imagine the American Indian felt much the same when confronted by the *Wasi'chu* on the prairie. There was probably nothing more pathetic to observe than a wagon train full of stupid white people, wandering lost in a land not their own, and trying to steal anything of value that they stumbled upon.

That is why, when all was revealed, and the inner core of the movement was demonstrated to have bad intentions, to be rotten, and Rajneesh himself to be a materialistic fraud, the pain was soul crushing. It was not being cheated that hurt but realizing that we were not better after all. We were all the same: the fools outside being kept in ignorance, divided, and used, by shady politicians and greedy business tycoons, or else, like us, being used by a different kind of leader, the "cult" leader. But cults are nothing more or less than rule by con-man. In theory, governments can be better. Businesses can have standards. Churches can be sincere and do good. People can be idealistic. But somehow all the politicians sounded to me a bit like Jim Jones. Or Rajneesh. The television preachers too. Their stained morality was as coarse as a dirty joke.

***

I realized during one of those meditation sessions of mine, that I needed to go and have a talk with our bookkeeper, Abigail West. So far I had not met her, although she was present at the all-house meeting and had given a financial summary. Probably when the co-op was quiet, like now, when most of the members were gone, was an excellent time for us to chat one-on-one.

That afternoon I took the short walk down the street to the Janet Smith. The fact is, I had rarely been inside. The SCA office, I knew, was on the second floor. I went up the stairs and peered down a hall. The door to the office was closed, so I knocked. "Come in," I heard. It was a small soft voice, like that of a 10-year-old girl.

I opened the door and there sat a very old woman with gray hair that was turning white at the roots, and blue eyes that twinkled from inside deep sockets. She looked a bit like Jane Goodall. She seemed surprised but not shocked, to see me.

"Hi," I said.

"You! Don't I know you from somewhere?"

"I think so. I'm Sutra. I lived at Rajneeshpuram for a year. But I'm not sure we ever spoke."

"I remember!" she said. "Yes. I remember your face. I was at the commune for two years, myself." She sighed. "It was wonderful while it lasted."

"Do you have time for a chat?" I said. "Maybe we could take a walk or something."

"I think that would be alright," she said. "I'm at a stopping point." We went downstairs and stepped outside, and she pulled the door closed. We stood on the porch of Janet Smith House for a moment looking out at Alder Street. She said, "We can walk down by the cemetery if you like. It's just a few blocks to the East."

"Sure. Yes, I know the cemetery." We crossed the street and began walking slowly in silence.

When we reached the cemetery, she paused. "I heard a story about a ghost in the Campbell Club, and was told that one of the students, apparently a Buddhist monk or lay person, helped to clear that up by finding and purifying the grave. Was that you?"

"I only helped by doing research at the library. It wasn't exactly an exercise of spiritual power. But we did help to get the grave cleaned up and tended, and it is now better maintained. I think Foster goes every week to speak to the dead girl. She was a student, you know, a sorority sister, but her father lost all his money during the Great Depression and committed suicide. The girl killed herself as well. Either that or she died from accidental poisoning. No one is entirely sure."

"How sad. Tell me your name again?"

"I'm Robert Gray. But most people call me Sutra."

"Sutra...yes. So glad to meet you. I don't see too many people from that time. It seems that we all scattered to the four winds."

"It's true. You know, I met a woman recently—she's the head of the Creative Writing Department...Mandy Reamer. Do you know her?"

"Oh my." Abigail put her hand to her mouth in surprise. "Did she mention me somehow?"

"It's kind of a long story, but basically, I was trying to get into the program, and she had read something I wrote about my life, and I mentioned, you know, Osho and what that all meant to me. And she hated it. And then I went to see what the deal was, and she just sort of went ballistic. I think she might have even denied me access to the program because of it. Not that it's anything strange to face prejudices."

"But how does that link up to me?"

"Well, she let on that a *dear friend* of hers was there, at Rajneeshpuram. It sounded like they were in a close relationship, you know? And she blamed the commune for that breakup. I think she hates Osho with a passion. Which is not strange. But she really tore me a new one, I can tell you. And the name of that dear friend was Abigail. So I just wondered."

"Oh Lord." Abigail stopped and sat down on a bench. "Sit down for a minute, would you? Yes, I see now." She didn't say anything for a while, and I just sat quietly. Finally she said, "Mandy and I were together for ten years. We were more than friends. We were lovers and partners. She had her school career, and I was a bookkeeper with my own business. We had some good times. But we drifted apart. She didn't have any interest in things spiritual, not really. Which is strange, because you would think someone who writes or is creative, would naturally have a connection to the higher worlds."

"Absolutely."

"But when I told her I wanted to go to see what was happening out in Logan County, that I had been thinking about it non-stop for a long time, she was dead set against it. She was just afraid, I think, and maybe a little bit jealous. A year went by, and then another, and finally I just said, 'look, I'm sorry—but I need to do this.'"

"I understand," I said.

"Of course, you might. Or it's possible that you don't, not really. You are so young after all. What was it like for you?"

"My interest in Osho? Much the same as yours, I would imagine. I actually knew someone from prep school who had met him over in India. He was totally convinced that this was the new Godman, but I wasn't so sure. And then he came to America. It seemed like a message, you know? I was always interested in Eastern things, even from a young age. I read the *Tao Te Ching* when I was ten."

Her eyes sparkled. "I'll bet you watched *Kung Fu!*"

I laughed. "Well of course I did. I had to get a special dispensation from my mother to do it, though, because it was on after my normal bedtime."

"That's very cute. Adorable." She didn't say anything for a minute. "Oh—wait. I see, you probably want me to say something to Mandy. Was that why you came over?"

"Absolutely not," I said. "I need to fight these battles on my own. I was just curious if you were the person she was talking about."

"I can talk to her. But I'm not sure if she will listen. Mandy changed while I was gone. She seemed to have hardened inside. It was as if, all those bad things they said in the papers, all the lascivious stories, she ate that up. She was radicalized, but not in a good way."

"That's kind of sad," I said.

"It is. You know, as it happens, I am going to have lunch with her tomorrow. So how's that for a cosmological coincidence? I haven't seen her in five years. And now today you appear out of nowhere and tell me about her when I have plans to see her. It must mean I am to talk to her about this. So you wrote something about Osho? I'd like to read that."

She wouldn't take no for an answer, and I begrudgingly had to accept the situation.

***

This was one of the periods when Connor and I really began to bond. Like me, Connor had read James Clavell's *Shōgun* at an early age. I don't know if this was a common thing at the time. It's a very long book.

"Did you cry when Mariko died?" he asked me.

"Nah," I said, lying. In reality I had cried like a baby. "But there are many other parts of the novel that I sometimes think of. The earthquake scene for example. And Yabu's seppuku."

"Mariko is what I remember most," he said.

So he had *Shōgun* close to heart, which meant something. But he had not read *Tai-pan*, *King Rat*, or *Noble House*. He was unfamiliar with the greats like Hemingway, who he had only perused. He did not know Steinbeck at all. In fact I was able to introduce him to *Cannery Row*, my favourite, which he loved. It seemed that he had read widely, but not with much depth. He liked Stephen King—several of the King novels were by his bedside—and he was just coming down off It. I had no interest in King, myself. "My world has enough anxiety in it as it is," I remember saying.

Nevertheless, we shared a lot in common. I took this remarkable fact completely for granted at the time, not understanding how rare it is to find a kindred soul.

Perhaps because of the new closeness with Connor I decided to sign up for Ceramics that Spring. It was just Ceramics 101; there was not a lot of pressure. And I had Connor, who was in the advanced class, as my inside connection. This got me acceptance and I eventually met the inner circle—the graduate students, who each had their own mini-studio spaces. Eventually Connor even secured a nook of his own, he was a rising star. It was in the studio that he would meet Janet, his first great love.

My decision to take ceramics was soon validated by the fact that Rachael Day was in attendance. I didn't know this until I walked in and saw her, radiant and flushed with the oxygenation of attempting to throw a ball of clay on the potter's wheel. I was impressed that she could do it. She looked up at me, kind of startled, and then suddenly the clay shot out of her grip and she lost control.

"God damn it, Sutra!"

"Uh-oh. Sorry," I said, and quickly moved on.

Her presence made it clear to me—like a message from the gods—that it was to be, that I was in the right place. Tools and techniques to be sure.

Even the Professor seemed glad to have Rachael in class. Bob James was his name. Connor rated him very highly. We didn't call him "Professor James" or anything. He was just Bob. This despite the fact that he was the department head, and had been there forever, was really the backbone of the Ceramics program and preferred to teach the beginners class just to be near to the creativity of the fresh students.

One day, Bob, who was very giving, heard Connor and I talking about Anagama, which is a traditional wood fired kiln design from Japan.

"Bizen is the most interesting Japanese pottery from my point of view," said Connor. "I'd sure like to see some of that."

The next day Bob came into the studio carrying a little wooden box. It had some Japanese Kanji on the side. He called us over. "Take a look at this, Connor."

It was a little Bizen-ware bowl. The color of the fired clay was tan and orange and you could see the effect of wood ash, which acts as a natural glaze, helping to vitrify the surface of the clay. The piece was rough and wild as Mother Nature herself. Bob had not only been to Bizen itself, in Okayama prefecture, but we learnt he had even participated in one of the now quite rare firings.

"Wow!" said Connor.

This bowl was entrusted to Connor, who felt the gravity of his responsibility, but being 19, did not quite know how to secure his possessions.

The next day Connor set out to the studio early, as was his habit. I came down later to find him in a panic.

Yes, the priceless Bizen bowl had been stolen.

"It's gone!" he kept saying. Connor was absolutely losing it and I didn't do much to help. I kept talking about how things in this world are transient and blah, blah.

"Shut up, Robbie!" Connor said. I could see he was serious because he used my real name.

Then it happened. Bob wandered into the studio. Connor had to tearfully explain about the theft. But Bob was sympathetic. "It's alright, Connor. Don't worry. It's just a material object."

But Connor was convinced he had failed. He was angry and broken for a long time and I tried to give him some space.

***

One day soon afterwards Bob was feeling especially generous. Maybe he had a sense of what was going on in Connor and wanted to help. He called us over. It was just me and Connor and Rachael. Bob said, "Let's play the Zen pebble game. You might like this one, Sutra."

"Zen pebble?" I said.

Bob produced a shallow wooden box that was filled with white sand, about an inch deep, almost like a game board. It was a little bit reminiscent of the sand in a rock garden. He opened a little cloth bag. "These are just random stones from the Willamette," he said. "Take a pebble from the bag."

"How do we play?" said Rachael.

"Connor, you start," he said. "Place a pebble on the sand so that it is Zen."

Connor was a bit puzzled. "How do I do that?"

But Bob didn't say anything. "Perhaps Sutra?"

"Sure," I said, smiling. I picked up a pebble from inside the bag and set it on the board.

"Let me go next," said Rachael. She took a pebble out of the bag and placed it.

Connor seemed to not yet understand the game, but he manfully tried. "Am I doing it? Is it working?"

"Zen is just an ordinary thing," I said. "The trick is not to think."

"But how can I not think?" said Connor.

We kept playing.

"When do you know who wins?" asked Rachael.

"You will know," said Bob.

"I think we're done for," I said. "It no longer looks Zen."

Bob smiled.

***

Connor seemed to be impressed that I was making it with Bob, who he idolized. I got points for that. But playing with clay felt therapeutic in and of itself, and I hung out in the studio for the remainder of that term. Ceramics seemed a lot more "real" than my literature class. I could care less about *The Castle of Otranto*. The only fly in the ointment was this couple, who seemed to be camping out in Ceramics, too. They made a lot of little sculptures that looked like an octopus monster— Cthulhu—so they were Lovecraft fans kind of like Connor—and laughed and bubbled away in vicious French while looking my direction, which I thought rude, although it was only another effect of Shock Buddhism, and so perhaps a reflection of myself. Connor seemed to be OK with them, but they kind of creeped me out. I didn't like them—the couple, I mean—and it turned out they didn't like me. It was Judith and Pierre. I'll have more to say about them later.

***

The Spring Break holiday was winding down and Connor came back from Evanston, and soon other co-opers were filling the dining hall once again. Rachael Day appeared the next morning looking tan and fit in shorts and a tank top, the sun shining on her smiling face, as she and a few other "Spring Breakers" piled out of a cab.

"Hello, Rachael, how was it?"

"Hey Sutra. It was great. So nice to get away for a while." She dropped her pack and plopped down next to me on the only ratty couch and just took in the air and the street for a while. It was a glorious day. Her body odour, which was far from unpleasant, washed over me.

"Kind of like home now, isn't it?" I said.

"It is."

There was a long pause and I didn't want to break the spell, but something in me was curious and a bit playful.

"So...the last time we were here, we spoke of other things. You and Leo...?"

She laughed. "What do you care?"

I smiled. "Oh, I care."

She put her hand on my knee. "That so?"

I put my hand on top of hers very gently. "Life is so fleeting. Fragile even. And I'm such a royal prick. I can never say what you mean to me."

She smiled then. "Sutra, when I was in Cancun, I met someone. He was so *hot*; I can't even begin to tell you. Really good looking."

"Muscles everywhere?"

"Oh yeah. And it was nice to be with a hot guy and have it all out in the open and do everything with no restrictions and know that I would never have to see him again. It was so freeing. I didn't even tell him my name. It was like a fantasy come true. I felt like I was in total control. That was the best part."

"That seems remarkable. Almost too good to be true."

"Oh, it was. It sure was." She got up and went inside, wistful.

And then two days later, the guy showed up in a rented car at the Campbell Club, having driven hundreds of miles to track her down, and she had to deal with him.

"Oh Sutra," she said later. "What have I done to deserve this? You men are all such bastards."

***

There is another story to tell about Rachael from this general period, when she was still learning that men are all bastards and life as we have constructed it is essentially a rat race of swine fighting for easy access to whatever loot they can most efficiently steal. It is from the time before she lost faith in me and I almost lost her forever. I tell it only because it relates to what comes later.

We were again down at the Ceramics studios. Bob had sent us on a mission to the Willamette. Of course it wasn't just me, the whole class was going, but I was tagging along with Rachael. Bob brought out an object, a walking stick of sorts, with a large decorated head on it, like something Gandalf or one of the lesser Istari might have constructed as a magic staff. He said, "This is a Pontifex. I want you to go down to the Willamette and make yourself one."

"But what is it?" asked one of the students.

"I'm not going to tell you any more than I have; other than you are not allowed to use any material or technique that involves modern technology. You must make your Pontifex using only what you can find by the river."

Now, I was perhaps a little ahead, in that I knew what "Pontifex" meant; it was Latin for "Pontiff." So I understood that it was the staff of a religious being, perhaps a holy man. But I did not immediately speak up about that. It's not really that often that knowing all the shit I know comes in handy; but suddenly my esoterica had an actionable value; perhaps even a good grade on an assignment.

The class walked in a loose assemblage towards the river. We walked down a bit from the footbridge heading west on the bike path. We crossed over the Mill Race, which was not much more than a ditch at that point, and then descended to the river bank.

"There's a lot of materials down here, basically everything you might need," said Bob, as he scanned the vicinity. "I'm going back up to the sheds, I'll come back in an hour and see what you've done."

I started working on the staff part of the thing first, while others, including Rachael, did their best, but wandered around like lost bees from a dead hive. Our efforts all seemed incredibly crude next to Bob's creation. But I was making progress and had somehow found a small natural deposit of clay in the riverbank, which made my task easier. My Pontifex was like a ragged Jesus crown of thorns on a pole. Quite hideous.

Rachael seemed frustrated. She had found a few fantastic feathers, perhaps from a bird of prey. But not much else had materialized from the Creative Realm. "Sutra," she said. What the hell is a Pontifex? I'm making zero progress."

"If I tell you, what do I get out of it?"

She looked at me and crossed her arms, her eyes narrowed. "You are playing a very dangerous game, my little friend."

"Oh?" I grinned wolfishly.

"I'll tell you what, if Bob likes my Pontifex, then after class we'll go skinny dipping in the river. We might even make it over to that island (she pointed across the water) it looks very private over there. Understand?"

Well, needless to say I was engaged to help, and rattled on about staffs and holy relics, and I shared the clay I had found and a few other things. Towards the end of class, Bob returned and asked us to stand up our Pontifexes for inspection by the river. It was like an impromptu art show. "These are fantastic," he said. "I especially like this one with the feathers. I think that's my favorite. Who made that one?"

Rachael put up her hand and smiled. I can tell you, friends, I was overjoyed. Like a pig in a puddle of mud.

***

School had not yet started, so some of the people in the house decided to organize an impromptu evening trip after dinner up to Spencer's Butte. It was a public landmark to the south that stood over 2000 feet above sea level. The co-op had a van—perhaps I have not explained—we used it to buy groceries and for the occasional house-sponsored, alcohol-free activity. There was no hot spring up there to lounge in after a long hike, and considerable discussion had floated the idea that Cougar might be a better destination, but in the end, we opted for Spencer's.

I had never been, but Leo said the view overlooked the city, and in March the snow could be expected to have all gone back where it came from; even as the pine forest would stand fresh with new life.

The trip was iconic in the sense of who was present in the van: Stan Harmon driving, Cindy, Rachael, and Eva, Leo, Johan, Magda and Napoleon, and a few more. Rob wanted to tag along, too. It was a good group, and Connor got to ride shotgun with Stan. Those two seemed to connect, perhaps due to their technical and process-oriented natures.

I found the climb in the gathering dusk exhilarating, and by the time it was fully dark, stars mingled on the horizon with the city lights in the Willamette valley behind us. I tried to stay near Cindy—the Trinity was walking together at a rapid pace—but soon fell behind and ended up back with Magda and Napoleon. They wanted to stop and have a smoke. "The view is pretty good from here already! Sit down, Sutra, join us!"

I felt like I should keep moving, though. So I kept climbing—the path was steep but doable—and I saw the main group up ahead already on the ridge. I finally made it, out of breath. The reward was a wonderful outlook and a bath of night air encircling me like a cold sauna.

Leo seemed intent on using the occasion to talk about the future—his, and ours. "This is my last year at Campbell Club, and I would like to propose that we do something that would be memorable. Something that we could commemorate later."

"Sounds more like a board meeting topic," said Cindy. "Don't you think?"

"Sure. You're right. But I'm just inspired by this view and all these good people. I just feel like this is a special crew."

Stan was certainly intrigued. "What sort of something are you contemplating, Leo?"

"I don't know yet. My first thought was about Earth Day. It's only a few weeks away. We could participate in Earth Day somehow."

"Earth Day! What a joke," said Rob.

Leo tried to point him in the right direction. "Try to keep it positive, eh Rob?"

"We could make a garden," I said. "Either do something with the Co-op's yard, or else maybe find another place to turn into a garden spot. Maybe a butterfly garden..."

There was general assent and head shaking towards this thought bubble. By this point Magda and Napoleon had reached the ridge and hobbled up. They looked pretty stoned. I was a little concerned about them maintaining stability while sitting on the edge—but they laughed and sat without too much problem.

"What are we talking about," said Magda, loudly.

"Doing somethin' big!" said Eva.

"Oh. Well, let's lead a protest! Some kind of protest march. Let's oppose Apartheid!"

Napoleon joined in. "Those bastards in South Africa are out of control! Have you heard *Biko* by Peter Gabriel?"

Leo agreed. "That's pretty good. We could organize some sort of protest march."

Rachael now piped up. "But maybe we should do something, you know, within our own house. There's lots of improvements. We could, for example, go Vegan."

"What's a vegan?" said Napoleon.

"A vegan is a kind of vegetarian, Nappy," I said. "They don't eat anything from animals."

"Nothing?"

"Sometimes they don't even eat honey, because they think it's stealing from the bees."

"Dat is nuts! On, sorry, Sutra, maybe dis is something you believe...?"

I laughed. "No, I don't have a problem with eating honey. And I think milk is OK. You just squeeze it out of a teat. Doesn't seem to harm the cow to do that. In fact, I understand it feels pretty good to be milked." Here Cindy laughed for some reason. "But at the commune we didn't drink milk because Osho thought it was baby food. And that's true enough, I guess."

"But you are a vegetarian?"

"Yes, of course," I said. "But that is for karmic reasons, for moral reasons. I try to avoid killing things."

"But we have to kill to live," said Stan.

"It's true," I said. "But a strawberry doesn't seem to mind being eaten, while an animal does. An animal runs away, if it can. In fact, you can make the argument that fruit is naturally food because it grows for no other purpose than to be eaten by some animal or insect. Isn't that so?"

Leo was sceptical. "I'm not sure how practical it is to try to convert the house to be Vegans. It's hard enough to convince people to not cook meat in the vegetarian-designated pans."

"And some of us actually think eating meat is perfectly natural and what humans evolved to do. That's why fire was invented, after all." Stan was known for loving a steak now and again, although he was by his own admission, entirely omnivorous.

Rob now stepped up with his own idea. "I think we should do an art piece. Something we could put in the yard."

"A sculpture?" said Rachael.

"Nah. A political piece."

"Maybe for the summer," said Leo, doubtfully.

"I have an idea," said Cindy. "What about if we started a new House?"

"A new co-op?"

"Sure. We could call it 'The Annex.' It can be an offshoot of the Campbell Club. We're too full as it is."

Leo's integrative mind, which was always putting disparate things together in weird but wonderful ways, like his peanut butter and pickles sandwiches, or French fries and ice-cream, seemed to light up at this idea. "Wow, that really is a *big* something."

***

So the trip was a success, in the sense that Leo got to jaw about what was on his mind, and everyone who went felt energized and refreshed. There's nothing like Idealism to brighten up a group of college co-eds. Even I, who at this time did not like to even identify as being human, due to a feeling of complete inferiority and failure, still found it refreshing to be among people so full of hope and ideas.

Something happened on the way back to the co-op that I thought was memorable. Cindy needed to pee, but instead of asking Leo to stop the car, she playfully dropped her shorts and positioned herself so she could pee out the back of the van. The window was the type that could be opened just a crack with a lever type assembly. I had never seen a woman pee standing up before; and in fact, I had no idea that it was anatomically possible. But she could do it. Moreover, it was almost like a dance. She didn't speak; she just went about it. I didn't know what to think about that; was it erotic? Perhaps in a way, but also it was just mind-boggling that someone would choose to do it and think it was funny to piss out the back of a moving van. "I'd hate to be behind us right now," I clowned. "Where's that yellow rain coming from?" Everyone laughed, including Cindy. Even Leo thought it was hilarious.

***

This was the beginning of a strange time in my life when my infatuation with Cindy began to outweigh all other considerations. It was not something that I planned. It just seemed to be fated that I was to suffer. We began to spend more time together, or perhaps more accurately, I sought her out. She would be in the kitchen or the living room or out on the porch, or even in her room, the *sanctum sanctorum*, which had a beautiful third-floor view of the surrounding neighbourhood, and I would find myself engaging her in conversation or more often just hanging out nearby, like a parasite attracted through smell to a host body.

I don't know what Cindy thought about that. I certainly was not capable of communicating anything intelligible about my own feelings or desires. But it turned out that without any explanation my intentions were entirely transparent to her. She was very experienced with the romantic and sexual life of human beings; much more so than I would have thought or guessed possible. As little Karen Tamlen had insinuated, she was "promiscuous." A word that means nothing, a label that we apply, which has very negative connotations, or else is used in a dry clinical context (where it again means essentially nothing). We have words like this because human experience is largely opaque and so varied that it has to be lumped together into an amorphous glop we call "sexuality."

But for Cindy Sterling, things were not at all conceptual. She did not want romance, or conventional conversation at all, or head-trips, or vacillation, or push-pull, or any of the nonsense that I understood about love (my education about it having been mostly drawn from television)—but rather silence. Silence and raw physicality: touch, gentle or rough, movement, flow. Scent. Skin, different kinds of skin and different apertures of the body, taken in their concrete form and functioning as they are expected to do, each function a minor miracle. But above all, everything in her world was a dance, choreographed to an inner soundtrack.

I soon realized I was overwhelmed; her soul had overpowered me. Just being near a person of that type was world-ending. It was like in *Steppenwolf*, when Harry finds out he cannot laugh, that he is too serious to be taken seriously, and must have his own self destroyed to find his true core. I am not a sensualist and have never been one; I understand the world through words, and to a lesser sense, though symbols and images, thoughts; but not in movement; and her kinetic sexual nature, which was silent and secretive but explosive, was far outside my experience.

For example, I was in the back hall of the kitchen one afternoon, helping Connor put up some of his ceramic tiles. He had made these cool little figures with extruded strings of clay, two dimensional, and they reminded me a bit of cave paintings. I noticed one or two of them had penises, which seemed significant. Sometimes art is neutered; but Connor was opening up. So, we were hanging these figures. The back hall was like a cave, I thought. Hanging them in an installation for the whole housing co-op to see was my idea. Connor had gone to the toilet or left for a few minutes. I was there alone.

I was up on a ladder, and had come down to get more figures, when Cindy quietly came into the hallway, looked at me, slowly climbed up on the ladder a few steps, and then turning and standing tall, unbuttoned her shirt. Slowly, almost as in a hypnotic trance, she exposed her naked breasts to me. She was smiling as she did this. I looked on in awe. Then as Connor rounded the hallway, she quickly and quietly buttoned her shirt, as if nothing had happened, and slowly and just as quietly came down the ladder as I stood there.

"Hey Cindy," Connor said in passing, not even looking at her face and not noticing anything going on. "Hey Connor," she said, still smiling at me. He then went back out into the main kitchen, and she said to me, laughing, "Wasn't that fun?"

A normal virile male, with normal levels of testosterone and all the regular cravings, would have been able to correctly process these overtly sexual games as being part of a mating ritual. He would have confronted her in some later part of the evening, in the quiet or the late part of the night, knocking and then being admitted, and coitus would surely have ensued soon after.

But I, who thought of myself more like a cumulus cloud than a man, did not know how to respond at all. I was like a small boy who thinks what the parents do and the noises they make in the night are absurd, ridiculous. And ignores them with a furious effort. But now I was forced to look.

***

At the risk of being accused of obsessing on a woman's breasts, I will say a bit more about Cindy's.

Yes, I know.

But perhaps you wonder, in the above, reading this account, did she lift her bra? Was she going around without a bra, perhaps due to some political views or feminism? I don't know the answer to that and obviously I didn't care. But Cindy was one of those lucky women who never needed a bra because she had the chest of a ten-year-old boy. There are women out there who have big nipples on a flat chest, that are always standing out at inopportune moments (as I have been reliably informed), but she didn't even have those.

What struck me later after this event in the hallway, was that it was probably the most erotic experience of my life—there are one or two others, but I won't share those, it wouldn't advance the story—but this "showing" this "big reveal" shook me to my core. The truth of it was, yes, this is going to sound very sexist, I had always thought of myself as an obsessive "tit" man. I thought breasts were blah, blah, blah—we can skip over that—but the sort of thing one learns from deep studies of Playboy magazine, furtive glances and late night sessions; and it seemed the breasts were the most interesting bits. But Cindy had nothing to write home about and was completely at odds, physically, with all of those surgically inflated ballons. She was so far removed from this obsession that she liked to tease me; so for example I said something about Alison, who is unfortunately not a part of the narrative, but was beautiful and kind and in my memories from the Campbell Club. I said something like, "Alison needs a bra or those are going to get saggy awfully fast," or some such stupidity, and Cindy said, "She has a fantastic rack, no doubt about that. Ten points at least. But I have no such concerns, thank God. So that's your problem, is it? You must not have been breast fed." This contrast extended further. For example, her haircut was short-cropped, almost boyish. She intentionally passed on growing out her hair. It's possible she even cut it herself, or had it styled in the most severe terms intentionally. Her hairstyle reminded me of those unfortunate French women who had liaisons with

German soldiers during World War II and ended up being punished by having the hair on their heads roughly shaved off; and yet in that condition were paradoxically erotically more interesting. Bald women. Cindy wasn't bald, but she wasn't exactly spending a lot of time or money on hair products.

Later, when looking at paintings by Rubens (who is well known for painting women who are "Rubenesque" i.e., fat)—I suddenly realized that Rubens did not obsessively paint every fold and curve of his model out of some need for painterly naturalism, or because it was required of him due to the style or mores of the time. He painted his model in that way because (as a historical matter of fact) his model was his lover and later his wife, Helena Fourment, who bore him five children, and his passion towards this woman knew no bounds. His obsessive rendering of her thigh cellulite in all its folds and delicate dimples was a testament to his devotion towards her, his love of her not in the abstract, but as flesh, as a living woman, as his whole world. He did this knowing other people would see it, and he seemingly made this the cornerstone of his entire *oeuvre*, to the extent that it became his trademark and "Rubenesque" a word that is now in the dictionary. It's what we remember him for in addition to his use of light and monumentality.

In much the same way, and perhaps for similar reasons, I later understood that the erotic element in what had happened that day with Cindy was not due to her body at all, but to her actions, her magic theater desire, which momentarily shined on me like a flashlight in the dark, pulling me inside-out. It was the erotism of the movement, the joy of show and reveal, the suddenness of the flash, which is one of the hallmarks of dance, that was on display.

The whole affair was a demonstration that my ideas about women and beauty were mostly made of cardboard cutouts and reconstituted pulp fiction handouts—my ideas up to then were the result of television and glossy magazines and the weird, sick taste of Hugh Hefner. But Cindy was real. And I was not able to grok. I had none of the tools required for that. Her body was not as I had imagined a lover's body would be; but I desperately wanted it. Every inch of it was booby-trapped. It was a mine field. Her thought processes were not like mine and her thoughts were completely hidden from me. One time when I was in her room I saw blood spots on her sheets on the unmade bed. "So that's—"

"Yes, Sutra. That's menstruation. I am a woman."

"But you leave it—"

"It's not just the Australian girls who do that, Sutra. Sometimes there's blood, it comes out of a woman's vagina at night. Does that embarrass you or frighten you?"

***

I think after a while the Trinity Friendship, as I called them (Rachael, Eva, and Cindy) must have discussed this—must have discussed me. I don't know that for a fact; but certainly I noted the three of them looking in my direction from time to time, eyeing me as they talked quietly amongst themselves in the dining room, or when lounging together arrayed on the porch, laughing, like a group of sheepherders considering who to cull. The trend of the conversation might have run along the following lines:

"*Do you think he's a virgin?*"

"*Well of course he's a virgin. Or the moral equivalent of one. Otherwise he would have come to me that night.*"

"*He's attractive, don't you think?*"

"*He has some good qualities.*"

"*I think I'm going to have to take him.*"

"*You're going to have him? Just like that? But he will be damaged.*"

"*I'll be gentle with him.*"

"*I'm rather doubtful that is possible for you.*"

"*[laughing] No, it will be fine.*"

And who would have said the last part? I was not sure for a while. This was all in my imagination and it could have been any of them. But I got some more looks and some purring sounds in the kitchen and I had a clue, perhaps an intuition, that something was up. It was the female sex drive, the mating ritual, which was so foreign to me, and at that time quite mysterious and strange to me also.

Then one night, Cindy was especially talkative—for her.

"Sutra, why don't we stay tonight down by the fireplace. We'll camp out. It's cooled down at night; I think we're having a cold spell. Let's make a fire tonight."

I was tasked with some of the preparations and got the thing going. At least I had learnt this small thing from my holy hobo Kerouacian days of absolute poverty "doing it rough"—I could make a fire. The sulphur of the wooden match fizzed and the flame quickly spread over the sticks I'd collected, supplemented with some detritus and shavings. The bigger pieces of wood were cut branches from the big leaf maples that lined Alder Street (no, Alder Street was not lined with Alder trees, as one might logically expect for a street lined with trees named 'Alder') that had fallen at some point and been collected for exactly this purpose of being burned on a cold night.

Meanwhile Cindy busied herself with moving a couch and a chair in front of the fire, not to sit in but to create a blind in which we could lay unseen by anyone coming in the front door. It was dark, and very late, perhaps 2 am, and so it was unlikely anyone would come through from the kitchen side; the only possible foot traffic would be from the front door, and that would probably route right up the front stairs towards the bedrooms and sleep, and not through the big living room.

Cindy then rolled out a sleeping bag—a single bag—and unzipped it; took off her clothes and beckoned to me as she got inside it. I was too stupid to undress, so as I got down on my knees, she undid my pants and pulled them down. I started to help out at that point and got the rest of my clothes off.... We were naked together....

***

A few days later Abigail West called me on the telephone. Perhaps I should explain a bit more about those phones (for the younger generation). The phones at the house were rotary, of course, but also black and older looking—very "Ma Bell" in their design and worn from use. They were like movie props for a film made in the 1950s, not the 1980s. There's one near the front door and then one each on the second and third floors. These two upstairs phones are in "phone booth" closets with doors. The phones are actually a long subject, with many stories to tell, with missed calls and cold calls, and stoned calls and happy good news calls, and all the other permutations of long-distance perception and time-dilation. But in general we had two camps of opinion: those who believed the phones were essential and that additional phone service was important (such as a phone-per-room) and those who believed the phones were a distraction, that ma Bell was evil, and we needed fewer of them. A few radicals even wanted them removed entirely; but Leo, being very sensible, insisted a level of basic services was essential in any civilized accommodation; and he was right. Yes, I was one of the radicals, but that was stupid of me. We have to learn in this world to choose our battles.

There was always a pad of paper by that downstairs phone, because the most logical thing to do when someone had an incoming call, was to take a message. Always a pad, but not always a writing device. The pens kept disappearing. We did try taping the pen down on a string. But that failed and then we lost the ball of string to poaching as well. Finally someone put a box of crayons down there by the phone, and the crayons seemed to stay around for much longer than the pens. The messages also became gradually artier, and certainly more colourful, until it seemed as if a new artistic standard had been imposed on us by a fanciful, if slightly mad, cooperative regime.

I suspect if someone really had something important to say, they would find other ways or other places to do that besides the house phone, as it was more like an emergency broadcast system than anything else. But the phone was the phone. Like everything in life, it had its minders and its keepers.

Karen Tamlen was one of those and often picked up the receiver (in the general case) and specifically (in this instance) and when she heard it was Abigail West asking for me, the little antennae that worked as her ears pricked up to attention. She said, "Oh hi, Abigail! Hold on" and called up the front stairs and then looked into the dining room. Luckily, I was within earshot in the kitchen and heard her. "It's Abigail West for you, Sutra," she said loudly. Probably half of the house could hear her.

"Thank-you, Karen," I said. I waved Karen off, as she did not seem to have disengaged and was loitering, hoping for more intel. I frowned at her. She went away a little deflated. "Hello?" I said.

"Hi Sutra! It's me, Abigail West."

"Hi Abigail. What's up?"

"I just wanted to let you know the outcome of my visit with Mandy, I mean Dr. Reamer."

"OK."

"I was wondering, could we talk about it tonight?"

"Sure, I guess."

"What I mean is, could you come over to my house for dinner."

"Um...OK."

"You're still a vegetarian?"

"Yeah, I am."

"That's good, because otherwise I don't know what I would feed you. Let me give you the address. It's a bit of a hike, you might need to take the bus."

She read off an address and I found a yellow crayon—Goldenrod, to be exact—and scribbled big letters and numbers down. "Sure," I said. "I'll see you then."

I took the scrap of paper and put it in my pocket and didn't really look at it until that evening. But I realized she was right, the address was on South C. Street in Springfield, which was quite close to the river but on the other side of Glenwood. I had to get moving. I asked Connor if I could borrow his bicycle. "Sure dude. Got a hot date?"

"What? No...I'm just going to have dinner with someone."

"But you never 'have dinner.' You never go out. To my knowledge you have no friends or social activity of any kind outside the house."

He was not wrong about this, but I didn't want to talk about it, so I just crossed my arms and looked at him like a transcendent and always wise Master Kan was being kept waiting.

"Fine," he said. "I'll expect a full report in the morning."

"I'll be back tonight."

"I have class at 9am so please keep that in mind."

"Don't worry. I have class, too."

***

I set out on his Raleigh ten speed and quickly realized sandals were the wrong shoes. But I was damned if I was going to turn around and go back for better shoes. Yes, I had put on my robe and beads, which I thought might please Abigail. But it was a terrible combination on a bike. I got honked at several times as I made my way down Franklin Boulevard, finally crossing the river on Main and then ducking off onto South Second Street.

Her place was very small, but it was an entire house, and not too far from the River, which was only a block or two away. The little garden in the front had a small stone buddha with a smiling face and a big tummy that I took as a good omen.

I knocked, and she came to the door and greeted me, smiling. "Come on in! It's so nice to have company."

Her small house was open and sunny. There was a strong smell of incense, and in fact there was a ceramic bowl filled with sand, sitting on an eight-petalled base, with incense stuck into the sand, just as we used to do it in the commune. Next to the incense was a small brass buddha, and behind it a flower arrangement, very delicate, with a pink Rhododendron in the center.

"What do you think of my place?" she said.

"Oh it's fantastic."

"Why don't you sit down?"

"Sure. But where should I sit?" This question was not so unreasonable, because her living room was as crowded as a forest full of plants. And as I soon learned every room of the house, even the bathroom and the bedroom, were filled with living things. It was like being inside a terrarium. Mostly plants, of course, but also a bird cage and bees and probably a lot of other critters. Yes, you heard right about the bees. She had built a beehive into her bedroom wall. The whole place, but especially her room, was filled with the smell of beeswax, and it mingled with the incense that burned perpetually on the little altar.

"Don't worry, you can move things. I want you to feel comfortable. Let me make some space over here—" and she moved some plants off the coffee table to make the sofa more approachable. There was just enough room for two, and she motioned for me to sit next to her. "I wanted to tell you all about my visit with Mandy."

"How is Mandy?"

"Oh, she's alright. She has had a hard time since we broke up."

"May I ask—"

"Of course." Abigail bet over and picked up a small box that was stashed behind a large potted begonia. "Ask away."

"Well, what I mean is, were you lovers?"

"Yes. I think I explained that to you last time. That's why she was so attached to me. And I think still is."

"Did she used to live here?"

"What a funny question. No, when we were together, we had a place closer to the University, over on Orchard Street."

"So these plants—"

"Yes, you're very perceptive. Some of these were hers, or gifts from her." Abigail had opened the box, and I could see a few small brownish, straw-colored lumps loose in the box and a larger lump wrapped in cellophane. "This is something special from Morocco. I've been there several times; I still have friends over there. Have you ever smoked hashish?"

"No, I don't think I have."

"It's really great. You know Lewis Carroll was a big advocate of hashish, right?"

"I'm sure."

"Sutra—may I call you Robert?"

"My mother is about the only person who does. But sure."

She laughed. "Well, I don't want you to think of me like *that*. But I just think Robert is a beautiful name. Robert Frost, Robert Redford."

"It's fine." I was wondering if I should "just say no," as the President's wife was so fond of repeating. As I saw she was gearing up for a smoke of some kind. And normally, that's what I would do. Of course as a teen I smoked a lot of weed, we all did. However I had tried to steer clear for spiritual reasons. I had ideas about purity, a Rocky Mountain High kind of idea. But for some reason, I didn't. Just say no, I mean.

Instead, I said something quite different. "I've never really been a smoker. I used to smoke Camel Straights when I lived in Idaho. I guess that doesn't count."

"So you're a virgin to marijuana?"

"Well, no. I've been in the room and surely have got a contact high."

I was lying, of course. At one time I was a pothead. I'd even smoked hash under the tutelage of my best friend Christian back at prep school, where we were considered total stoners. So, yeah, I was, as Jimi Hendrix had said, "experienced" with weed. Or so I imagined. But she seemed so innocent and old at the same time; so kind and gentle. I wanted her to feel I was the inexperienced one. I was trying to make her happy. And so I lied. But I also had an idea of superiority in the back of my egotistical brain. I didn't really understand that until later.

"This is going to be more than a contact high, Robert. Much more. Come sit a little closer to me."

She lit the bowl on a small brass-fitted pipe about the length of her middle finger, and took a draw from it, and then suppressed a cough and passed the pipe over to me. I took an experimental drag on it, not getting much throughput, and she said, "You have to draw the smoke in and hold it as long as you can. Here, let me put a match to it for you." This time I took a much bigger hit. She held the match to the pipe with a steady hand, and the hashish burst into flame, the small lump becoming a glowing coal. I held in the blue smoke as long as I could and then started coughing.

"Wow," I choked out. The shit was strong.

Abigail smiled. "It's pretty strong stuff. You OK?"

"Of course. But it's not doing much. Can I have more?"

"Let me get you set up. This whole lump will be for you. Don't worry, we'll get you high alright."

She put what I knew quite well was a significant amount into the bowl, a cube of resinous silly-putty about the size of a California raisin, and then helped me smoke all of it, encouraging me the whole time, like a mother hen helping her chick eat a fat earthworm. After a few drags the room began to spin. "Oh Lordy." I said. "We may have hit paydirt. But my mouth is getting dry."

"That's very normal," she said, as she loaded the bowl one more time. "Here, let me teach you something. Don't be worried. I'm going to take smoke into my lungs and then give you a kiss, just a friendly one, on the mouth, and breathe out, and you breathe in when I do that. Do you think you can manage it?"

"Uh, ok, let me try." And she took in a monster hit and gently kissed me in a way that was indeed new to me. I took the smoke in as best I could from her greedy lips as it pulsed out of her like electrified steam. We both ended up kissing a bit longer after each drag. Her tongue was so friendly....

I couldn't believe how stoned I was. Then, incredibly, we had two more rounds of this kiss-smoking with what I finally admitted to myself was the strongest hash in the world, or at least the strongest I'd ever been party to. I was higher than a kite in a Mary Poppins movie and now beginning to feel a bit anxious. *Idiot*, I said to myself. *Why did I lie? God, I'm so fucking stoned!*

"Uh, yeah. Wow. Well. Yeah." I was making sounds like that. "I think I must be stoned finally," I said. "You did it. So this is what it's like. I'm a little anxious for some reason though."

I was well underwater, drowning, but she seemed to want to take me all the way down to the bottom of the sea. All hands on deck, abandon ship.

"I'm here with you, my lovely boy," she said. "Don't worry. Is it good, Robert? Is it good?"

"Yeah, it's good. Uh...Can we do a bit more?" This was just total macho and downright stupid.

"We'll do another round of friendly kissing, don't you think?"

"Yeah, that's—that's really cool. I've never had that before."

We did yet another round, but this time there was a much longer, lingering tongue session after.

"I have a confession to make, Robert. Smoke kissing really turns me on."

"Yeah, I get it. I—it's just so intense."

"Do you think you can pass the smoke to me now?"

"I'll try," I said. "But, gosh, maybe I should just sit for a minute. My head is spinning."

"Let it take over. Just let go. Concentrate on me if you feel you're going the wrong way. I'll guide you."

I sniffed and looked over at her, expecting her to be about where I was. But I was wrong. She hardly even seemed high. Her eyes were clear. I got the sense she was photoelectric; her Chi was all around me flashing and tingling like a quantum field. "OK, Abigail, I guess I need to stop. You win. Let's get a drink. Hydration!"

She took hold of my hand then and closed her eyes for a minute. I felt the life energy pulsing through her body and into me as well. Her hand was throbbing and alive, a young girl's hand, not cold. And I suddenly thought I was a chimp. A dumb, stupid chimp, a hairy ape, or even an orc, sitting next to an elf queen. But I tried to stay cool and get on top of the high. She opened her eyes and then gave me another playful peck on the cheek and tugged at my chin. Just in a very slight reprove.

"Yes, I see," she said. "It's getting on top of you. You were not exactly truthful with me; perhaps I should have guessed. All men are the same, aren't they? But I love them. And I know just what you need. Let's see if we can make it to the kitchen. My dear boy. Yes, I know what will make you more comfortable."

Then she said three words: "*I have food.*"

"Food? Food?"

The thought of food hit me like a new idea she had just conceived of for the first time in the history of all the universe, and clearly must patent. A brilliant idea that would make a lot of money for us both, the white woman and her pet chimp. Or something.

"Oh my," I said. "I'm so starved. Food."

She made me sit at her dining table—really just a nook in the corner with a table that was also home to three or four potted plants—there was an Aloe vera, and a Peace lily, among others—and I sat and looked at them for a while and became a plant, trying to make oxygen, and then popped back into the present as she set a drink in front of me. "What's this?" I said. "It smells good."

"It's just juice. It's got some wheatgrass in it, and some carrot juice. And some apples."

I drank. My tongue exploded with an eruption of taste, like today they put on TV commercials for cheap fruit juice, but this was a real taste bud explosion. "Wow. That's just blowing my mind."

"Yeah, it's good."

We were sitting very close to each other, and I felt more relaxed than before. I wanted to be more honest, more respectful to her generosity. It was like peeling an onion, but I was the onion. It was coming off in layers, sloughing off like snake skin, but the onion wasn't getting any smaller.

The truth is that, in my mind, my lies began to sting. I could now see them visually, kinaesthetically. Each lie in my life was like a bee stinging my astral body, leaving a bleeding, black stinger protruding there. I had been so stupid to try and deceive her. She knew so much. I wondered idly if this was what love was like: being with someone who you never deceived.

I just sat there savouring the juice, juice that she had personally made somehow; it wasn't store-bought. Squeezed out of a carrot? I couldn't understand that concept. And it was so good. It was as if I had never tasted juice before. "This is like the first juice ever juiced!" I said. "God damn this is good. You know *Morning Has Broken* by Cat Stevens? This juice should be heavily mentioned in that song."

"It's definitely pretty good."

"Abigail—"

"Would you mind calling me Abbie?"

"You prefer Abbie?"

"I do. Between special friends."

"Sure. OK. Abbie. What a lovely name. Somehow it makes me think of mother of pearl." I had completely forgotten what I wanted to ask.

But I realized again that I was very hungry. I was about to speak but Abigail had already gotten up and was puttering in the kitchen. She returned after a time with two plates of steaming Basmati rice and a curry, a Tarkari, with a fragrant condiment of some kind in a little bowl, and then she put down some momos on the table. They steamed. It all smelled better than any food I had ever eaten. It was Nepali food, which in later days became my favourite Indian cuisine when I could find it. Nepali food and the true self of Abbie somehow merged in my mind through a process of neurons connecting and perhaps misconnecting and many years later, that was primarily how I linked to this very brief moment of time with her. Though the taste and smell of this meal.

"Oh my God," I said.

"Let me know what you think of my momos."

I started eating ravenously.

"Slow down, you'll eat too fast."

I tried to obey, but it was difficult. However, after a while it did make me a bit more conscious of my hostess. I looked over at her and saw that she was definitely watching me closely. "You're just watching me wolf this down?"

"Yes. I am taking pleasure in that."

"Hmm." I filled my fork again. After a while I looked at her and realized that she had changed. I actually stopped eating for a minute and looked at her face.

"What's happening?" She said.

"I don't know exactly. I was just realizing something. I don't think I have ever looked closely at your face. I've seen you, but I was not really *seeing* you. I think I was seeing only what I wanted to see, or possibly not seeing at all."

"Yes. That's right. Go ahead. Look at my face. Look into my eyes if you want to. Or if you think you are ready."

I didn't understand what she meant, exactly, but I reluctantly set down the fork and had another drink of juice and then I looked at her face and into her eyes quite steadily. I even put my elbows on the little table and leaned in towards her and looked really deep. She held my gaze, not flinching at all, totally open and kind, like a person who talks to chimps, and I don't know if she even blinked once.

"Tell me," she said.

"Well...originally I just saw an old person."

"Yes."

"How old are you?" I asked.

"Does it matter?"

"No. No, it doesn't matter. But for...shall we say, scientific purposes."

She laughed. "Well, if it's for science, I'm seventy-nine years old. I'll be eighty in May."

"Eighty!"

Her eyes became sad, so I said "No, don't shut down on me. Maybe I shouldn't have asked that. It doesn't matter. I see everyone as a soul. And in that sense, everyone is, like, 12 billion years old. You know? That's how old the universe is, right? At least according to the Big Bang theory."

"Big Bang, yes," she said.

"Our souls are not exactly new. We've been around a long, long time. So that basically means we're the same age."

She laughed then, almost joyfully, like a young girl at a birthday party. "Oh yes, Robert. That makes me so happy. You have made me suddenly very grateful to you. I want to shower you with my gratitude. Yes, we're exactly the same age!" She leaned in, then, and kissed me again. Yes, her tongue was on patrol, and it did all the right things, as if it had been sent on a recon mission but, being highly experienced, knew the terrain exactly already. It just went on and on, I don't know how long we kissed. Finally she pulled away.

"Robert, listen. I want something from you."

"You do?" I said innocently.

"I do. I—I also want to give to you. I want to give everything. Do you understand?"

"But Abigail—"

"Abbie, please."

"Abbie, I'm not sure I'm ready for this. I need to tell you about things."

"Don't worry," she said. "Let's eat some more and smoke some more hash if you want. And then when you're good and ready you can tell me everything, OK? I'm going to unplug the phone..."

***

That deep lingus felt like an irrevocable pact had been drawn up between our bodies; we were now connected on some lower level of flesh-honesty and physical commitment, like two people cold naked and alone on a deserted island, who must now fuck endlessly for the good of all humanity, or die. No choice about it at all. The species must continue; it was inevitable and necessary, like the musical coitus of angels that made the spheres revolve in heaven. That's how I conceptualized it. And that in turn seemed to allow for the barriers inside me to come down. Yes. We, Abbie and I, earth mother and her reluctant son, were soon going to join—full-fledged intercourse—wrapped together like serpents, and it was going to be everything I always wanted; what I had hoped for and fantasized about endlessly; better than any pulp fiction novel, better even than any torrid late-night movie on HBO. I had somehow hit the jackpot.

But perhaps in the back of my mind, there was Cindy, standing there with folded arms looking at me. Cindy and Rachael in garden gloves, and Eva in a leotard, all looking at me like the complete chud that I was.

"She might as well be your mother!"

"Idiot! What will the co-op think?"
"Sutra and the geriatric case. My God! Ridiculous!"

***

Those fears melted away when Abigail led me by the hand into her moist and humid herbarium-slash-living room and we stood together amongst the plants, illuminated by the pale light of a low wattage bulb. She held me to her so I could smell her skin, and whispered into my ear:

"We are exactly the same age."
I think she said this at least three times, like an incantation; or maybe my head was just reverberating.

I guess age really has no meaning to, in the quaint words of Robert Plant, "a woman who knows."

***

Probably what happened then was not in my power to avoid, because even though I had learned valuable life lessons, and gone a certain way down the Path, and knew intellectually a lot of the dangers and pitfalls, she was like the proverbial rock in the stream. I could not go around her. I had to hit into her and come in contact with her surface, all the edges of it, before I could continue further down the stream. She was more and more in front of me, more and more opening out to me and calling me to hit against her with full force. And there was nothing in the environment, in the general area of South Second Street, that would likely have any chance of interrupting. It would have taken an earthquake or some kind of an atomic blast to stop what was about to happen.

***

We were laying on the rug, I was looking at the ceiling, and she was reclining on one arm, her body warm, very patient, not servile, but not pushing, exactly as I had imagined a person of great experience would be like. An immortal. Mahadevi, who is all the goddesses. Abigail knew everything and was everything. She ran her free hand very gently over my chest and fiddled with my beads, rolling a bead between her fingers, like a child, waiting. Time had more or less stopped.

I said, "at the co-op, there's a girl."

"Ah. Yes?"

"There are actually three girls..."

"Women, you mean?"

"Well yes of course. But I guess in my mind, I am a boy, and they are girls. I'm sorry we don't have better words. But I feel that's how things are in my own mind."

"We'll work on that. Go on."

"And these three girls—there's Eva Redbone, she's a dancer. And there's Rachael Day. I think she's an Ecologist or studying some earth sciences. And then there's Cindy."

"Cindy Sterling?"

"Yes. Cindy Sterling." I paused for a moment, wondering what she had heard, and then rolled a little bit and looked into her face again. "I'm still tripping on your face."

"Yes?"

"It's like I see your younger self. I think of you like Jane Goodall. What a name, "Goodall." Remember I was telling you how I think your face changed. That's because, at first, I didn't even see you at all, you were a person off in your own zone, separate, and—"

"And old."

"Yes. Forgive me. You were just an old person. But after a while, after we smoked, and the kissing, then suddenly I had this image—it seemed so real—of what you must have looked like as a young woman. And that young person is still there, somehow. I see her."

"What you were describing first, the not looking, I think that is how everyone sees everyone. That is the general condition of being closed off. But then I awakened you."

"Yes. I suppose you did."

"But you were telling me about Cindy."

"Right. Cindy. When I think of her I shake inside. I think—I think to use your terminology, Cindy wanted to awaken me also. She, we set up the living room at the Campbell Club so it was private. It was late, no one was around. And we..."

"You had sex? Tell me everything."

"I tried to. I wanted to. But somehow, I couldn't do it. All of my attention was in the wrong places, I think. And of course, I had no idea how to do the things she wanted to do. The smells and sensations and all of it. She's—she's really very advanced."

"So you have never had sex?"

"Not really for real. Boobs in high school, you know. I've always been kind of afraid of girls. And some things happened at Rajneeshpuram, but I generally avoided that type of opportunity. I didn't want it, then. I was so serious about the Path. Anyway, things didn't go well with Cindy. I could see I was a failure. A loser. In the end, she just said, 'let's skip it.' And that was that."

"I see," she said. "When you think about Cindy, what are your feelings towards her? Do you love her?"

"Oh yes, I think I love her. I think about her all the time. Actually I think about all three of them."

"Do you masturbate thinking about them?"

"Well..."

"Right." She smiled. "Don't worry. You don't have to answer." She slowly sat up and began unbuttoning her top. "Robert, I am going to be your teacher."

"You are?"

"Yes. I want you to do an experiment. I want you to look at my body and see if you can see that young girl that you were talking about in my body and not just in my face. Can you try to do that?"

"OK."

"Take your clothes off, Robert."

We disrobed and she led me into the back garden. There was a tall fence, so it was private; but the property had a large yard anyway and not too many houses nearby. I could hear the road off in the distance if there was a car, but it was evening and there were stars. It's a very quiet part of town. My eyes slowly adjusted. She turned on a shower—a garden shower—and drew me into it. Our naked bodies reacted, perhaps contracted is a better word—to the cold water of the shower—it was probably just hose water connected to a shower head—and I cried out "Aaaargh! That's cold!"

She laughed and continued to shower anyway in the cold water, not minding, like a dolphin, washing herself with soap and then soaping me up, running the soap over me back and front. We both rinsed off and she towel dried me first, lovingly, and then herself. Then she led me by the hand back into the house and we went into her bedroom—it, too, was full of plants, many of them quite large.

"What's with the bees?" I said. "They're freaking me out."

Near her bed, right in the wall, there was a glass pane, and I could clearly see bees on the other side of the glass. It was as if a beehive had been bisected by a sheet of glass and then the whole thing built right in by a mad builder, a mad carpenter. "Johan would love this!" I said absently.

"Yes, those are my bees. I like having the hive near my bed. It makes a wonderful sound and smell, don't you think?"

"It's freaky. So who did all that work for you? And who put in that groovy skylight?"

"I did."

"You?"

She laughed. "I'm going to have to break you of that absurd male bias. Of course I did. I worked at Rajneeshpuram, remember? We built houses. I did electrical, plumbing. And I can cook and I can do so many other things. Like bookkeeping. I have a degree in that. Even beekeeping. But that's just a hobby."

"Whoa. You—you're incredible!"

"Oh my lovely boy, you make me so happy. What I'm going to do for you tonight, very few have known. But for now, let's take a second to sit next to the hive. We can watch it. This time of night the bees are resting. They don't work at night, they rest, much like people.

That will get you more accustomed to it. I'll even show you where the queen is."

We sat and lay and talked about the bees, and gently touched each other, but absolutely without hurry. I was mainly looking at her rather than the bees—she was nude, obviously—I'm not ashamed of the fact that I enjoyed looking at her female perfection. Physically, her body was obviously old, but she had retained a quality that does not have a name but is the product of doing Hatha Yoga for a long time. I'm not sure I can describe it, but "tone" comes close. Years of Hatha Yoga did something to her, such that her outer form was remarkably flexible and defined, but not to any excess, as Eva's body seemed to me excessively developed. Eva was muscular, excessively strong. Abbie was strong, even at 79, but not muscular. Her strength was entirely balanced and seemed to extend or be projected outward from some inner power. Even her body was proportioned perfectly. Most human beings are somewhat lopsided, as perhaps the right hand is stronger than the left, and so the whole body is asymmetrical. But Abigail's body was not like that. It was entirely symmetrical, sculpted from living flesh.

As a boy I used to watch a public television program called "Lilias Yoga and You," and Lilias the yoga instructor had this "tone," this quality of being fit and flexible and calm but simultaneously capable of graceful, energetic, dance-like movement. Abigail had this body type. I have to admit that Lilias, in her tight leotard and with her long hair braided and hanging down as she held an asana, had awakened sexual desire in me very young, even as Kung Fu had awakened the more spiritual side of my thought at the age when most children are learning to play Monopoly or Go Fish.

Abigail got up and said, "I'm going to put on some music, an Indian Raga. A night raga, if that is all right." She returned and said it was time for us to lay together. I almost felt like I was at school, but it was one of those occasional classes where I liked and admired the teacher.

"I'm going to teach you some tantra. It will take time, and you have try not to release too quickly. Let me decide when to do that. We'll smoke some more hash later and take breaks. It will be like a celebration of life. You do not need to feel any anxiety. There is nothing to prove. It's just you and me, and we are already fully committed to each other for this time. This is my gift to you for making me feel young. Anything you desire, anything you wish, we can probably do it. I am not quite as flexible as I once was, but I have not lost all my powers. And I know many secret things about a man's body and mind, things that you will learn about yourself and later reflect on."

"How will other women compare to this? Are you going to ruin me for life, Abbie?"

"Oh no, my dear boy. Everything you learn about yourself though tantra will be available for you, like new tools. In fact, in the future, you will find some women even attracted to you, women who, shall we say, sense that you have an understanding that other men they have so far been with, and have been disappointed by, lack. You will be able to please those women. Now lie back. That's right. We will begin."

***

It was two days before I left Abigail's house. We were naked most of the time, and I'm not going to narrate what we did or how I felt about it, or even what I learned, which as she suggested was quite a bit, mainly about my limitations because of all my stupid prejudices and culturally-ingrained bias towards women and their bodies and misunderstandings about sex generally.

But as I was leaving, Abigail finally told me what she had promised to tell me two days before, in our phone conversation (which seemed like a million years in the past). Dr. Mandy Reamer was willing to have me join the program.

"You just have to re-submit a new piece of work, preferably 'something more along the lines of what Karen Tamlen had submitted,' is what she said. Don't worry, Robert. I asked her to accept you on my behalf, as a special favour to me. She agreed."

"I'm grateful," I said. "Abbie, do you think you will get back together with Mandy?"

She looked at me and her eyes gave a knowing look. "My goodness you're fast. How did you know? I mean, about the possibility."

"It was just an intuition. And she really seemed, well, she seemed very attached to you."

"Oh she is. At my age it's good to have a companion."

"Abbie—"

"Robert, my dear boy, if you want to live here with me and my plants, if you want to be that person—"

I shook my head. "I'm sorry."

"Don't be. Thank-you for the last few days. I hope I didn't impact your schooling too much."

And then it hit me—Connor! "Oh my," I said. "I do need to get back to the co-op."

"Good-bye, my dear lovely boy."

I rode back barely under my own power to the co-op—not sure exactly how I made it—it seemed to be night, but I had no idea really of the time—and crawled up to our room.

I lay there on my bed, finally in the familiar comfort of my own room. Connor slept soundly over by the north-facing window. And then suddenly I realized—*idiot!*—that I had been unfaithful to Cindy. 'Oh no!' I thought. I almost cried out. I was convinced she would be lost to me, that I would become a laughingstock, and the Trinity Friendship would one and all reject me. 'Tomorrow is really going to suck,' I said to myself. I slept fitfully.

In the morning Connor woke up and immediately said, "Dude!" which woke me.

"Connor...Ugh...I am so out of it."

"Dude!" he said again. "My bike?"

"Yeah, sorry about that. But when I tell you the story, you'll see the justness of my cause and ultimately forgive me my impudence."

"That must be some story. Listen man, a lot of people thought you were dead."

"Me?"

"Yes, you. You dropped off the face of the earth. And remember you had committed to bringing back the bike, and, probably, by the way, going to class."

"Yeah," I said, hesitantly. "Yeah, I think I blew off a few classes. What day is it?"

"Dude! He doesn't even know what day of the week it is. Do you know which planet you're on?"

"Third rock from the Sun?"

"Yes, that's close. Or possibly hell for you. Yeah, it's all out in the open my man. Oh boy."

I looked at him in shock. "What?"

"You can mostly blame Karen Tamlen."

"Oh my god." I was mortified. My time with Abigail had been completely confidential, private, totally secretive, and while we were together, it felt like we were the only two people on earth. We were Adam and Eve, fornicating under the influence of the apple hashish; or perhaps, we were mother and son, Eve and Cain, pounding away in incestual privacy. But sure enough, somehow everyone in the entire co-op, in fact, all across the SCA, because the news spread to the Janet Smith house, I found out later—yes, everyone knew. Everyone somehow had got a 411.

"Sutra lost his virginity to—get this—the SCA bookkeeper!"

"Sutra and that old broad? That's bonkers! Hilarious."

Leo said his head was spinning over it.

Even Thomas Pincheon III looked at me funny, and in his begrudging sort of way, smiled, as he whizzed past in his electric wheelchair moving through the dining room at his normal breakneck speed. And Johan! Johan slapped me on the back. "Sutra! You're a real man now. What would Buddha think?"

But it was Cindy who had the most interesting reaction. Cindy Sterling, who I was convinced was lost to me, was all attention and kindness that morning in the kitchen. "Sutra...well, well, well, I guess I didn't have quite what you needed. But I'm glad you were resourceful enough to figure something out. Right as rain, are we?"

I sighed. "Cindy, I'm sorry."

"Sorry? For what? I'm very impressed with you. Half the girls in the house are now fantasizing about you."

"What?"

"Of course. Any man who can do hard yakka like that—a grown woman for god's sake—post-menopausal—is worthy of all our trust."

"But you don't understand!"

"Don't I?" She laughed. "Oh I think I do. I'm just not your type."

***

It took time for me to get back to reality—the reality of school and classes—after that experience. The time available in the term had suddenly contracted like an accordion and everything I was supposed to do was late or behind. It was unnerving. The turtle had gone into his shell. But I felt I had made a commitment to school, even to classes that I thought were ridiculous, and so I had to knuckle down.

It was hard to do that for a variety of reasons, but one thing that started to get under my skin was Eva's constant banging up and down on the stairs. She would charge up the front stairwell in her clogs moving in the direction of her room, which was at the top of the third floor and just to the left of the landing.

Now, it happened that Terry and Mike were in a double just across the hall from Eva. Certainly they got the brunt of the noise. It did not take long for Terry to start to see the situation as a thing to deal with. And Mike concurred.

Terry began to court Eva. He did this in a very gentlemanly traditional fashion. There were things like flowers, chocolate, he may have bought her a dress. I was not aware of all the details. But over a period of a few weeks, he put forward his masculinity, which was certainly robust, and she responded in kind in feminine energies. Being a Southern Belle (of sorts) her instinct was to take all the attention from the male of the species in stride—but this was Terry Bradman. He was an impressive specimen, as I have said; and she also knew the story, that he had turned down a football scholarship. In her mind this was the same as having played football. Bradman had shown interest in one of the girls at the Janet Smith House: Martina was her name. She was a sophomore, a Latina, very dark skinned, and certainly not the kind of girl he could ever take back to white-bread Green Bay. But they had chemistry. It seems that he told Martina that he needed to take care of some things with Eva and that, in his words, "Not to worry, I'll be back. You're my girl." But this was only revealed later. Meanwhile, the night came when Terry and Eva went out for a special dinner, and some music was involved—I think maybe he paid a mariachi band to play something just for her, maybe "*El Son de la Negra*, or *Volver, Volver*. They drank margaritas. Tequila is a funny thing. At any rate, the night progressed, and a good time was had by all and they headed back to the co-op. Terry had to listen to her *clop, clop, clop* up the stairs, but they made it up to the third floor landing, and she invited him into her room. One thing led to another, and his pants fell to the floor due to the force of gravity, along with her party dress. Or so I imagine. The clogs were pushed into the corner.

I wasn't there, but what I understand to have happened was that upon their return, Mike Dix, anticipating, had slipped into Eva's closet. He was armed with a polaroid camera—a popular choice in the 1980s.

Terry then proceeded to make love to Eva, who was spread out on the bed. He had not yet penetrated her— he did not want to be potentially accused of rape—but had mounted and spread her legs wide, her arms wrapped around him in an embrace, his glorious Achilles thighs lifted off the bed, when Dix burst out of the closet. *Flash!* Went one flash bulb, with her vagina spread open. *Flash!* Went another bulb, as Terry, laughing, held her open and she writhed on the bed. They got off one more picture of her in the nude, wailing, trying to find a covering, and another of her pulling a blanket over herself, her face a mask of discomfort. "Give me those!" she yelled. "Give me those pictures, you bastard!"

Terry stood up and pointed his finger at her. He spoke calmly and chose his words carefully.

"Now listen to me, Eva! Listen very closely. You stomp those clogs again on the stairs, or anywhere in this house and I hear you clomping around, even for one minute, and I'm going to have Mike take those polaroids down to Kinkos and have a hundred—"

"—Five hundred!" laughed Dix.

"Five hundred flyers made up with your face, and all the rest of you, spread out like a tuna fish sandwich. Then we'll post them all over school."

"You bastard! You bastard!" she kept saying in her Southern drawl. Which I think proved definitively, that it was not an affectation. She really was a true southern belle. Perhaps even a sort of Blanche DuBois. She was crying now.

Dix laughed and pretended to lick one of the rapidly developing polaroids and waved it in her face as he went out. Terry and Mike then high-fived out in the hallway saying something about 'mission accomplished.'

That was the story I heard. Eva never clomped on the stairs again; and I do believe the reports that she threw away her clogs the very next day. Certainly I never saw her wearing them after that.

This period in the house melodrama was probably the height of the Trinity Friendship's power and dominance, and so what passed between Terry and Eva was largely written off as a comeuppance and compensation for the emotional and hormonal reign of the Friendship. Not that anyone had a problem with the three lovely young women running the roost. In fact, it was perfectly natural from the point of view of human social and cultural evolution for women to lead; and my only comment about it was that it was high time for women to come into their own, especially in a 501(c)(3) such as this one; but all things rise in great circles of up and down motion and all beings are on the *Bhavacakra*, the great Wheel of Life, with *Samsara* (ignorance) at the centre, holding the wheel upright like an axle. And there is no escape from this wheel other than understanding the causes of suffering.

***

However, Eva did get her revenge. After that night she spread the rumour that Bradman had a micropenis ("It has a head, but no shaft!") She worked so hard spreading this particular salacious detail about his anatomy that eventually word got around. Things came to a head (so to speak) when during one particularly rough game of Ultimate, the opposing team kept muttering "micro-dick, micro-dick" to Bradman, driving him fairly mad. Any man will tell you that there is no practical counter-riposte to this sort of attack. Bradman knew he could not walk about pulling out his dick to every man, woman, and child in Lane County, shouting, "See! See! See!" Eventually he surrendered and went and begged Eva for forgiveness. And Mike reluctantly handed over his prized polaroids. But the clogs did not return. - DRS

***

And so I must narrate something else that happened in this period which initiated a chain of events that will be important later to the story. This was the much discussed "dick rubbing" incident.

In truth, this is the most outlandish event I have to recount about the Trinity Friendship. I was not there—what I know is merely second or third hand—and it could be completely made up—but the story is so gonzo that it must contain elements of the truth.

It must be understood, first, that horse-tonic strength pot was involved, which can make things that normally do not happen become actualized on this physical plane (as I had recently experienced). None of the participants except Napoleon were in a position to understand what extremely strong marijuana is really like. Nowadays this might sound strange, but back then, there were plenty of people who thought like Nancy Reagan.

Napoleon himself would have developed a very high tolerance and so was less impacted. Magda could have warned them; but she was busy elsewhere. And Raven, who minored in joint rolling, was nowhere to be found. The putty-like nut-brown hashish that Abigail treated me to was intoxicating and mind expanding; even hallucinatory; but Napoleon was in contact with sources of ganga within his own scene, which was a music scene, but also an actual religion, of worship through pot, and those sources were comparable, if not stronger, to what I had been dosed with on South C Street.

Cindy was the most experienced with pot, mainly just with the terminology and the general practices of getting stoned, but through vicarious observation, and not necessarily direct inhalation; and then Rachael, who had experimented a little with Leo up in his room when they were all alone and still an item. It was a sneaky business, like in *Animal House* when the Professor locks the kids in the bathroom and they sit in the tub. And then finally Eva, who at this point in time had never smoked pot before in her life. It was locoweed, as far as she knew. She kept giggling hysterically at the prospect of trying "the bad-bad."

So Napoleon had sourced something strong on advice from Cindy that Eva wanted to have an experience. Not just a puff, but a real "up and out, Willy Wonka" kind of thing. Eva was so flirtatious that she constantly tested Napoleon by touching him in a way that today we would call inappropriate. I suppose that she meant the attention in a good way, but it was poison, he reacted innocently to it and with naive pleasure where a more experienced soldier in the battle of love would have avoided Eva like the plague. In a word, she was a tease. She did it to everyone. There was no way that horse was going to drink; but Napoleon kept bringing her water through his kindness and his genuine human charity. I suppose this type of interaction is unknown in the South, where all the women are still chattel and must fight in the only way they know how.

The bud he showed them was purple, sticky, and sweetly pungent; even words like crusty were employed. The girls had never seen anything like it and Rachael, the ecologist, was fascinated with it just as a plant and wanted to have the baggie passed around for everyone to inspect. Eva realized suddenly (perhaps somewhat stupidly) that it was a flower, and Cindy explained it was a female flower; that there were both male and female flowers but the female flower was much stronger than the male. This seems to have activated Eva's interest and certainly, she felt herself becoming moist inside. She was aroused and said she felt like dancing, and actually stood up and did move her hips, her head bobbing back and forth like a deva in an illustration from the Kama Sutra.

***

There is something of the East hidden in marijuana flowers, a mysterious quality that speaks of their origin. Indeed, many ordinary things in life are like this; but we have lost the ability to see the mysterious in the common thing due to familiarity. The plant originated in exotic and esoteric India or perhaps deep in South East Asia, where it still grows wild today. If you compare the apple, which grows best in the temperate zone and likes a hard frost, with the mango, which is tropical in origin and wildly succulent, where the apple is merely sweet, and sometimes even sour, then you have a sense of the true nature of the Cannabis Sativa: tropical, exotic, sensual, plant, with a life and a history and a reality of a hundred generations of human experience all hidden in obscurity; and probably it's God's gift as a medicine that can bring on sleep; but it is also a plant watched over by a powerful deity. And that deity is a goddess; that deity is female.

***

It seems that Cindy had discussed the idea with Eva the night before; planted the seed, so to speak, of a Jah experience for her slightly younger and less experienced dance contemporary that would not just be chemical, but also sexual. "Napoleon will help us. It would be good for you...free your mind. And we need to thank him. Thank him in a special way. Maggie has been holding out on him. I'm sure he needs release by now."

"Napoleon, he's so Rasta," Eva said. "He's cute. We must do something for him, of course."

She had worn a rasta cap that day, and played with it like a fashion model, just to tease him.

In one version of the story, the Trinity Friends went to Napoleon's room when Magda and Raven were away at the Riviera. There, a joint was rolled and passed and Eva taught how to inhale. In other stories, things are more explicit; but I will not tell those.

They sat on the floor, Indian style, and the combined pheromone emission of the three girls was released into the tightly enclosed space of the room, where it mixed with incense and sweat and the smell of dirty clothes. Initially Rachael was inclined to merely observe, but she soon became relaxed, enjoying this opportunity to be near to Napoleon with his girlfriend absent. "I have so many questions, tell me about your dreads."

And then Eva, "We're so interested in Jah!"

And there would have been music, softly playing music, not Bob Marley but something much more roots, more esoteric, which only Napoleon would have known about, thick with drum beats on 1 and 3, so that the bass can breathe. And they would have discussed music, concerts, and then Jamaica, the island nation, which is an entire world away in both life and fantasy.

***

The joint is now moving in a clockwise direction, and Napoleon carefully guides Eva, at one point even comes into her personal space to help relight the joint, and runs a hand innocently across her back, as he gently encourages her to breathe in. The conversation eventually—perhaps several more joints were involved? I don't know. I suspect they are all now higher than kites—but eventually the conversation goes in the direction of a comparison—a contest, the three girls. Cindy pipes up now.

"We girls are becoming beautiful young women, so soft, so smooth. Don't you see that, Napoleon? Don't you see us? What we have become?"

Which does he prefer? Which is the best? Eva insists that she has softer skin than the others, speaks of lotion, of showers. Rachael laughs at this and runs her hands over her own naked thighs below her khaki shorts. Rachael's legs are unshaven, and the hair, Napoleon notices, is the colour of straw against amber, on unblemished tan skin.

Now Cindy, the most experienced of the three in all things erotic, and the most sexually competitive, observes intently, as they all have a final round of this insanely strong bud and the deity finally awakens.

Rachael coughs and sputters, laughs, unconsciously runs her hands over her breasts, exhilarated, and cries out in ecstasy: "Oh my God, I am so stoned!" she says. "Oh, my God!"

Eva then begins laughing hysterically and even maniacally, looking around her, as her personality changes under the influence, her inhibitions coming down, one by one. She sees Rachael touching herself to the beat. Eva's own body then responds, rocks back and forth to the soft hypnotic Jamaican pulse, her hand out in front of her, palm up, vibing to the music, in and out, in and out.

And all as Cindy looks on, her small grin playfully expanding into a smile under bloodshot eyes. And then she says, finally, almost like a magic spell, "Mirror, mirror, on the wall, who has the softest skin of all?"

***

Her initial idea, which did remain unspoken, merely a fantasy, but which she told me about later in confidence, was that they would all have sex with Napoleon, one after another, and that the girls would judge each other's performance (in this I thought I could see Cindy's rapacious nature)—but it seems this was far too ambitious.

"Yes, it was impossible. We were just too high."

Instead, Cindy proposes that he, Napoleon, should rub the head of his penis against each of their faces to determine which girl has the softest skin. "I want you to test us. The skin on our faces, on our cheeks, is a good place to test."

Napoleon, for his part, is sitting stoned and silent while much of the preceding conversation has evolved. Outwardly content, he was far from that inside. His thoughts were actually elsewhere. He has been worried about his relationship with Magda for a while now; she seems to always be slipping out to find Raven and her new 'dyke' friends. He doesn't trust Raven. And he has no understanding of lesbianism or why the two would keep going to the Riviera. It's just beyond him.

And then he begins to realize the influence of the Trinity has been at work on his mind. He had no intention to get the girls so high as to encourage them to do something irresponsible. Nor is he infatuated or really, even all that interested in the Trinity, despite their good looks. From his point of view, he has a mission: to spread Love. Love, he believes, is the greatest force in the universe, even though this world is filled with evil. Love is the answer, the Power, and the true wisdom. He is deeply devoted to Jah, first and foremost—almost in the way an Evangelical is deeply but abstractly devoted to Jesus, if Jesus were black and loved to smoke Ganja—and he feels his sacred duty, his command, above all else, is to spread the love of Jah through the miracle sacrament of cannabis. 'That is what Rastafari was all about,' he says to himself.

Besides, he would never dream of betraying Magda. He has even planned to propose marriage to her as soon as they both graduate; the last thing he wants to do is alienate her or drive her deeper into the fever dream of the dyke butch assembly at the gay bar.

But the three had prevailed on him, first to indoctrinate them into the ways of the 'reefer madness' (as Eva called it), and then in going along with this business of dick rubbing. "I still don't know how dat all came about. It was never my idea, da for sure."

And so we visualize Cindy, nefarious in her glory and unyielding strength—much stronger than Napoleon was able to handle—trying to convince him to do this thing, this contest, as what is best for all of them. It is the *Judgement of Paris* by Rubens, all light and monumentality, but with cannabis: she is able to prevail upon him to decide which of the three is 'softest.' But what is to be his reward? "The one who is softest will thank you in a special way." But even as he is doing it, he thinks this absurd. He does not want it. He does not even become erect, although quite naturally there is some tumescence due to the mechanical action of rubbing.

In the version I am telling, Magda now bursts into the room and witnesses her boyfriend, her lover, with whom she never does anything except missionary position intercourse, because in Rastafari, both oral and anal sex are generally forbidden—she sees him standing, his pants down, penis pressed against Cindy Sterling's face, the three girls all gathered around him and looking up at him, 'like a coven of young witches celebrating a black sabbath.' She then cries out, "Nooo! What are you doing!" and runs away in tears, hysterical. In other versions of this story, the whole affair takes place elsewhere, perhaps on the roof under the night sky, filled with stars, or in the living room next to the fireplace in the early hours of morning; in those versions Magda does not directly witness what happens, but only learns the truth later through a tearful confession from Napoleon.

Meanwhile the night proved to be the end of Napoleon's relationship with Magda. After that night, Magda would not speak to him. Her dull cried-out eyes seemed to fill with tears for days. Her anger and frustration also blasted the Trinity, especially Cindy. "What were they doing IN MY ROOM?" That friendship was now in ruins.

After a week of scenes and melodrama of a high order, that most people avoided by being elsewhere (but Karen Tamlen closely observed and recorded verbatim) Magda moved out of the co-op. She went to live with Raven. It seems they carried on for a time in some lesbian-inspired farce. It was the beginning of a bad period for Magda, who lost weight and began wearing sunglasses to mask her crying, and a nightmare of recrimination and guilt for Napoleon, who sulked and moped, sad and sorrowful, leaving plates of uneaten food on the dining room tables. His stereo turntable, normally spinning in joyful celebration, remained silent and still. Two-thirds of his records had gone with Magda. He could not face looking at that void in his collection.

But Raven was fine. Raven was happy. When I saw her a few weeks later on the street she didn't say hello, but she smiled and waved as we passed each other. The sun seemed to be shining just for her.

Part Three. In Which the Annex is Born. And the Co-op is Overrun by Orcs.

"The butterfly's wings get filthy as it is chased by a village child."
—*Kobayashi Issa (1763–1828)*

Summer was coming on and I planned to stay at the co-op. Most people left and enjoyed a summer at home or abroad, or wherever they could go to have a change of pace. Only a few of us, like Connor and myself, chose to hang out in Eugene. For myself, there really wasn't anywhere else to go.

Connor had announced his intentions to stay because the studio would be quiet, he said, and he 'felt he could get a lot done.' I sensed there was another reason, which turned out to be one of the grad students—Janet was her name. She was a bit older and blond and reminded me of an elf princess; I fancied she might be a character from a Tolkien fantasy come to life (maybe Galadriel). Connor was smitten with her, but when I mentioned the Tolkien idea, he took it badly. "Don't say that! I hate Tolkien," which I thought was a bad omen about him generally. The *Lord of the Rings* was a favourite of mine and Connor would probably have been able to guess as much. I have never really been friends with anyone who did not like Tolkien. Then I made the situation worse by singing some lines each morning from the *Rocky Horror Picture Show*: "Dammit, Janet, I LOOOVE YOOUUU!" as he was going off to the studio. Yes, she had not a small physical resemblance to Susan Sarandon, including ample bosom and hips on an adult chassis. Connor said she was 32. She had apparently even had a child. There was a twelve year difference in age. But jokes about dating older women were definitely not OK. I did not understand until later when we were no longer friends, that he was sensitive about such things; that his romantic love was his Achilles Heel. His sarcasm and biting wit did not extend back upon himself to his own feelings; he took love remarkably seriously.

Janet was an interesting person. She was what they called a "hand-builder:" she didn't throw on a wheel like Connor, but rather rolled out sheets of clay to make tiles or hand-built pots made from coils pinched together, or in her case, furniture. Yes, her project was building an entire set of furniture from slabs. It sounded quixotic; and it was. But beyond that, she had life experience and apparently had lived in the woods alone for a time and had made interesting friends. It was through Janet that Connor and I got hooked up with Deon the Survivalist.

That summer turned out to be what Connor and I called *The Summer of Love*. At first, Connor didn't like it (it was my idea to call it that) but after Janet heard me saying it, she adopted it as well, and Connor reluctantly got on board with the concept.

You see, it wasn't just Connor who was having a good run with girls. *Cindy* had decided to stay in Eugene. Hot Water Cindy of the Clogging School of Dance Academy was hanging out, occasionally to be seen at Sy's Pizza or manning the counter at the bulk food store on East 24th. She was in town to help actualize her idea about the Annex—the co-op extension—that got floated in that mad brain-storming session at Spencer's Butte. It was a big project, and I didn't know what was going on except for reports occasionally from expat Leo, who would drop by the CC house to hang.

So Cindy was suddenly no longer at Campbell Club, much to Karen Tamlen's dismay. She had now moved into this beautiful shared house out in Whiteaker that they said felt a lot like a Japanese Ryokan: it had a garden that was at least verifiably Japanese inspired, I would say, and the house was made of dark wood with trim that reminded one of bamboo, and it had a large covered porch made of old-growth sawn planks. That platform looked out onto the back, secluded garden.

When it rained, it was blissful out there, a place to soak up the negative ions while sitting nude holding someone's wang; or else standing on two toes drinking boiled plain water from a temmoku mug. It also had a wrap-around porch out front, my favourite kind of porch design. Yes, Johan had been out to see the Annex and he came back and gave it a big thumbs up. That happened weeks before I even got out there.

When the sun shone down, warm and vibrant, the smell of the pine and other garden plants in the neighbourhood combined in the glowing air to create a natural intoxication that would have satisfied even John Denver. That is what Cindy said, more or less. "Even John Denver would approve this shit," to be more exact.

Or maybe it was just Cindy. Her body in motion, the graceful mudras made by her hands, as sunbeams erupted through heady cumulus clouds. I could see and imagine it all without actually having the need to go there. But eventually things came my way, like a paraplegic finally getting an erection. The ties of fortune and the inevitable binding nature of karma came to fruition and my suffering had to commence in earnest.

"Sutra, I think you'd really love my new place. It feels so *Eastern*." Yes, Cindy one day said this to me. I was having an actual conversation with her, not just a passing 'Hello.'

"That sounds cool," I said.

"So...why don't you come out sometime? Maybe this afternoon? Not too many people will be there, but you can still see the place."

"Uh...sure. OK."

So I had to go back and ask Connor again to borrow his bicycle, for another long ride about a girl, which sounded suspicious even to me.

"Ah...Cindy Sterling out at the Annex. Hm. Well, well, well," he said.

"Yes. Yes. Yes. Sounds suspicious when you put it that way."

He was tight lipped.

"But can I borrow your Raleigh?"

He sighed but said yes. "You might just consider buying a biiiike...!" he said, echoing down the hall, as I hurriedly rushed out of the room.

***

The address was in the Whiteaker neighbourhood, as I mentioned, and seemed to be in a very wholesome setting. Eugene had some really nice old neighbourhoods in those days and the Whiteaker had an art vibe and a feeling of counterculture which was to follow it forward in time. But at this moment "The Whit" was not a place of political bumper stickers or late night "Anarchy in the UK" style shenanigans. It was peaceful and arty and Zen.

The address looked quite close to the Owen Rose Garden. I got there, winded, and stood for a while in front, thinking how Cindy was inside. A quick fantasy hit me hard unbidden, about all of it, but I realized, no, that would not under any circumstances govern my visit. I was the world's biggest fuck-up glutton for punishment and wanted none of it right now. Wait, Satan.

Architecturally, the house stood out in my mind as being exceptional, and Johan had patiently explained certain things to me and even named the period of the style, praised the Victorian, almost castle-like design, and so on, but I immediately forgot what he told me because in my mind it was only about Cindy. I wondered how they had managed to rent such a nice old place and what the rent was. Out front, there were already some raised beds where most likely it had only been lawn before, with strawberries planted in rows covered in fresh straw for mulch. There was Buddha on a tree stump, smiling at me with an immutable smile, and I could hear a wind chime. The vibe was certainly good. Very good.

I put Connor's bike out of sight at the side of the house (he had no lock) and then walked around again to the front and knocked on the big, gracefully appointed front door. Eventually Cindy herself opened it. She smiled at me. "Hi Sutra. You made it!"

She seemed genuinely happy to see me. "Cindy. So this is the Annex. Incredible."

"Yes, we've been working on this for a while. Leo has been involved in a big way."

"Is he going to ditch Campbell Club to live out here?"

"I don't think so. He's almost done you know, with school. So he'll be moving on. But some others may jump ship. Johan was gushing."

She led me in silently and we stood in the living room of the comfortable old house. "Wow," I said, this place is great!"

"Come and see the back."

"I want to see the kitchen first," I said.

"Oh, yes, the kitchen is very nice. You would like it."

We went in and looked at the kitchen. For a private house, it was fantastic, basically a big farm kitchen in layout with drawers and cabinets galore, a big stove, and a sizable utility table off to the side, good for sitting or preparing.

"Would you like some hot water?" she said.

We laughed. I was pleased she remembered our first meeting. It was a sort of a confirmation that somewhere inside her, and therefore near her heart, I had a small nook of my own. I was not just a passing, transitory moment which is then forgotten and becomes oblivion. (As of course, is the cosmic truth).

She stood a little bit closer to me, I noticed. I was looking at the kitchen, admiring everything, and then she beckoned silently with her hand, which then took mine, and we went to the back hallway, and through a passage to the door which led out to the back yard. The door was painted yellow, and there was a hand-written sign that said something about taking off one's shoes, or clothes, or something like that. We stepped through the yellow back door, which swung closed due to a spring latch, and it snapped closed sharply, and I suddenly felt time dilate. The broad covered porch wrapped around here, too, with the sawn planks of old growth trees eyeing us through knot holes. The backyard, which seemed to extend out a ways, was shaded by fir trees and had ferns and ornamentals, topiary style, beside a bubbling water feature. I could see the whole yard was loosely cordoned off with a lattice style fence. And on the side to the right was a wooden structure that looked an awful lot like an old water tank.

"Wow," I said. "You have a hot tub."

"I know, it's really quite a place."

We stood silent for a while just holding hands. I didn't want to break the spell. But she spoke, and that was OK because it was still a part of the spell. "Sutra...everyone's away. I've got the house all to myself. Until tomorrow."

I sighed. She looked at me, a knowing look, and I understood what she wanted.

"I can get the hot tub going. Don't you think it would be lovely in the afternoon, to have a bath and a soak back here? Look over there, there's a garden shower." And she was right, I realized there was a little concrete pad wrapped with natural stones, possibly collected from the Willamette River bank, and a shower head on a metal rod that ran down into the ground. It was a bit more sophisticated than the setup at Abigail's with actual plumbing. More refined. Almost decadent.

"Cindy, I—"

"Let's not talk," she said. "Let's just be in the moment."

I came over to her, and put out my hand again, which she took, and I tried to dance. She smiled and laughed and swung around in a pirouette. I pulled her towards me and held her for a moment uncertainly and just looked at her chin. I could see her ears and neck very close to me. She had no jewelry. I realized she never wore anything of that sort; her fingers were bare and unadorned as well. I don't think her ears were even pierced. Cindy was what you might call a completely natural woman. I don't think they make them like that now. These days they all seem to have ink and septum piercings. But Cindy was a temple. A temple with Buddha eyes, like on a Tibetan Stupa. An ivory Venus of Brassempouy.

Finally I stopped musing and nodded. "OK," I said. "I guess hot tub it is."

She went off, satisfied. Her face often reminded me of those I have seen in pictures of the Kabuki theatre: she moved like a dancer because, well, of course, she *was* a dancer. But there was more to it, and her eyes, as I recall, were never like those of a normal human being going through a normal tedious earthly existence; they were continually rolling up; which suggested an ecstatic state, like a saint high on God, which was part embarrassment (the embarrassment of being seen), the intake of breath, and part exhibition (the pleasure of being seen), which comes on an exhale. I realized that I didn't really know much about Cindy. 'Tonight,' I told myself, 'I will try to find out a bit more. There must be more...'

"We should invite Connor and his new girlfriend over," Cindy said. We were in the hot tub, quite relaxed, and I was looking up at the pine tree, which was giving us a certain amount of privacy, as the branches seemed to enclose the whole area of the tub (the tree was huge). There was the lattice fence, as well, but it was day, in the shade, and the lattice was not exactly a privacy fence, and we were both nude. I felt a wave of anxiety about this beforehand, as I was taking off my pants, but when the moment came to be nude together, it all seemed so perfectly natural. She was so comfortable in her nudity that it created a surrounding quantum electrodynamic field. It was like being children together playing in a kiddie pool. I was sure Cindy would want to have sex somehow, that sex was her goal and this whole situation had been carefully choreographed for that purpose; obviously. What else? She wanted me to provide for her, what I had provided to Abigail West. They may have even discussed what happened between Abigail and I, woman to woman. It would have only been natural, and once I had had this thought, I almost convinced myself that it was true.

But I was completely wrong, at least about that bit. "Cindy, have you spoken to Abigail West? I mean, about me? About what passed between us?"

"Oh heavens no. I would never think to do that."

"Really?"

"It bothers me that you would think that" she said, splashing the water, almost in anger.

"Cindy, when I was with Abigail, she and I had extended sexual intercourse."

"Oh?" She smiled. "How was it?"

But as I started to speak, she covered my lips with her finger. "Don't analyse." She paused and then said again, "How was it?"

"Mind-blowing."

She laughed. "Really? Did she know some special techniques or something?"

"Have you heard of tantra?"

"Oh my lord. I was only making fun of you. You mean, she really *did* know things?"

I thought about it for a while and relaxed back into the water. "Yep."

"Well, can you show me?"

I laughed. "I don't know. That's a tall order."

"Why?"

"Because I was not in love with Abbie. Abigail. We were not in love. It was about, I suppose, gratitude. She was at Rajneeshpuram. I reminded her of the times and the feelings that we all had, that some of us had, about that place, and about each other as sannyasins. But we weren't—you know—I didn't *love* her."

"Oh my."

"Yeah."

"The Big L? With me? You mean to say you are in love with me?"

"Yeah. Fraid so."

"Well that's terrible, Sutra. You have no right to Love me. You don't even know me. WE have hardly ever had a proper conversation!"

"I know."

"Holy crap." She paused. "But wait a minute, why does that mean you can't, you know, why can't you teach me what she did? If you 'love' me, as you say, then shouldn't it be easy? Natural?"

"I'm not sure. I don't think I should say this. But the fact is, I desperately want to be with you, to make this more than it is. And I want that so badly, that of course it can't possibly work. Nothing is ever going to happen. I mean look at me, we're naked and I'm not even erect."

She laughed. "Well, that can easily be organized."

"No," I said. "You don't understand. I'm going to completely muck this up. It will be a catastrophe. Just like, you know, when we were in the living room at the co-op."

She considered that for a while. "But, what about Be Here Now? Wait a minute—how did it work with Abigail? Is it that she was old? I mean Sutra, she is not just old, she's like, ancient. Are you—are you some kind of weirdo?"

"No, no, no. Not at all. Oh God! I knew this wouldn't work."

"Calm down. Explain how it worked with her. Was it technical? Did she do oral? Did you go into her from the rear? What was the kink?"

"Well, I guess we smoked a lot of hash."

"Oh. I've not done that before."

"And then I started to hallucinate that she was younger. I was completely tripping out. You know, I didn't think marijuana was hallucinatory. But this was. She looks physically, you know, kind of like Jane Goodall. You have seen her, right? She's blond and thin, and has a kind, sort of a gentle, face. She's a lovely woman. And somehow, the hashish caused her to look like a young person again—I could actually *see* her soul, the soul of that young girl, in that older body. That young person wanted to be with me—she was apparently grateful, or at least, she was very pleased to be wanted. I think that was it."

"Yes. Maybe she hadn't been wanted in a really long time."

"But then there was also the tantra. You see, she understood inner energies, energies that flow in the body. She could feel them, in me and in her. And we were having intercourse—full penetration—like a oneness—I don't think I should say—"

"Go on! Now you have to." Cindy was deeply fascinated with what I was telling her. Probably in a past life she was a practitioner. But I could not tell her that.

"Spit it out, Sutra. I have to know."

"We did some postures, yoga postures, and she kept me erect for so long using just her vagina, her thighs. She had control over the muscles in her vagina. She told me we could do any sexual thing that I wanted, that I was completely free of constraints, and she knew every part of the male body, how to stimulate and control it. It just went on and on and on. I mean I was at her house for two days, and we were naked most of the time. And then there were other sorts of postures, other positions, meditations, chanting, for different times of the sexual act, times of rest, times of arousal. And we just kept smoking more and more hashish."

"And you came from all this?"

"Well yeah. Not always. That's kind of the point, to not come."

"But how many times? Over the two days?"

"Oh, I don't know, maybe ten or twelve."

"Ten or twelve times?"

"Or maybe more."

"Wow." Cindy looked stunned. "I'm so envious."

"Well, maybe you should hook up with her."

"Damn. Maybe I should. Sutra. Look, I realize now that this may have been a mistake. I can't love you the way you want. Could we just be friends?"

I sighed. "Sure." I felt like a complete failure. My whole fantasy just slipped out the window, then. It was like she pulled the plug on the hot tub, with the water just swirling out the bottom, and me with it.

Then she said, "We can be friends. But we can also have sex, too."

"What?"

"But it's just for today. Like a today-only special kind of deal. And I want you to try to do some of the things—you show me what she did, direct me, and I'll try to do it. You'd be surprised how much control I have over my body. It's called Isolation. It's not a ballet technique. And ballet is mostly what I study now, it has everything you need to be a dancer. I am a modern dancer—you know that much at least, right?"

I didn't, but I lied and said, "Sure."

"—But in other kinds of dance, not in ballet but in many ethnic kinds of dance, there is a focus on just isolating one body part, like the neck or the belly."

"Right."

"Well, I can do some of that." And then she did a head wobble, the way an Indian dancer does, which was completely like an alien thing to do.

"So you're asking me to be friends, friends who also have sex once in a while? I don't see how that can work."

"No. No. Not at all. It can't work, you are right. What I am asking you to do, is to be my friend. *Be my friend.*

Right now, here. In this moment. There is no other moment. There is only *this*. And come up to my bedroom with me, right now, naked. I don't suppose you would be comfortable doing it here in the hot tub."

I sighed. "Probably not."

"We could lay in the garden, in the dirt. Like animals. Haven't you ever fucked in the forest? It's really fun. To be naked in the dirt and writhe around. Like children. We could smear mud and leaves all over ourselves as we fuck."

I shook my head. "No."

"Well then, you see? We have to go upstairs. It's the only logical thing to do."

And that is what we did.

***

Afterwards—it was towards evening by then, and I was getting hungry, but Cindy seemed to be resting— just softly sleeping—and I lay in her bed next to her and thought about what had happened. I suddenly realized that Cindy could never be what I wanted her to be; it was totally impossible. And the heavy weight that seemed to be lodged in my heart, like an iron anchor sunk to the bottom of the sea—that feeling was in me and nowhere else. She had none of that. It was like I was playing one-handed solitaire.

Cindy, I realized with astonishment, was far more Zen than I was. Hot Water Cindy was like an itinerant saint, going from one bed to another. She was a guru, teaching the transitory nature of reality and the ultimate absurdity of the flesh, except that she didn't know it, and because she didn't know it, her teachings were fresher and stronger than any guru's teachings I had encountered.

But I also knew, as a tremor of horror washed over me, as if I were being forced to watch an alien eat a cockroach or endure a slasher film—that Cindy would tomorrow, or the next day, or perhaps the day after that, go and do everything we had just done with someone else. This realization hurt, and probably not since I came to terms with Osho being a fraud and a conman, did I have this intensity of pain. But I understood it with a sense of clarity. It felt like an icepick *Satori*.

I didn't realize enlightenment was, or could be, a state of pain, that it could be *painful* to have clarity. I always imagined higher understanding must be some form of pleasure. That is, I thought truth and pleasure must be aligned. But there it was. And as it would turn out, even many years later this 'anchor in my heart' would not go away; and even though I eventually married and divorced and remarried and had a family and children and friends and a career, and a whole life—and I would have many relationships and be successful in love—that anchor would never be drawn up. It would always be embedded inside me.

***

So the Annex, which was a mere idea Cindy had floated casually back on our trip to Spencer's Butte, was now fully actualized. I was impressed by that feat. It was an artist's gift to actualize things. Secretly, those things aligned with higher powers. That much I knew. As a writer wannabe, I had so far actualized almost nothing of value. I was a fake, a fraud. But now I had seen the thing happen. A Green Revolution? Co-op values? Perhaps a start. Leo certainly had something to do with it, although this house was not actually a part of SCA and was merely a rental. But it was an actual shared house, with co-op values and ideals to whatever extent that was possible.

One other idea that got actualized was the one from Rob—the concept of an art piece. And this project actually got us some notoriety. Rob initially wanted other people from the house to get involved, but because it was his idea, and because he had a very clear notion of what he wanted to do—which no one else could really grok—he set about doing the piece himself. Only trouble was, Rob had ideas, he was an ideas man, but he was not an artist—he did not have the technical knowledge, the craft part of being an artist. In fact, his first efforts were so discouraging that for a time he shelved the idea.

But come summertime he met a guy named Pierre, who was from France, who claimed to have read *The Communist Manifesto*, and had spent time in the Ceramics studio (so Connor knew him, I realized it was the same guy) and now said he was part of a revolutionary collective of students. "We are postmodern Surrealists," he said.

Pierre and Rob sat brainstorming on the front porch for a long time—probably a few days, just talking about philosophy and politics and Europe and America. And soon Pierre's paramour, Judith, who was apparently Canadian, and possibly half-orc, joined them. Judith didn't say that much, mostly just agreeing with Pierre. But they seemed very close.

It turned out Judith and Pierre were formerly U of O students, but Pierre told Connor he had overstayed his visa, and neither of them were taking classes presently. But it was summer, and they were looking for a project. Also a place to hang out. After considerable discussion and basically dominating the front porch for three days, which none of us really appreciated, the three of them began Rob's "Big Ronnie." It was to be a monumental art piece that "targeted" Ronald Reagan (as Rob put it). They initially approached the house, such as it was—there were about ten of us at Campbell Club for the summer—for money. Rob made the request, his sullen new friends quietly kibitzing from the rear of the meeting, as the house discussed it. According to Rob, the work would be about three stories high and thirty feet long.

"So what is it exactly?" I asked.

"It will be something like a billboard. It's a play on advertising."

"And it will be a picture of Ronald Reagan?"

"Exactly. A giant blowup of Reagan. This is the picture we'll use—" and he held up a fairly nondescript image of Ronald Reagan, long before he became President, wearing a cowboy hat.

"So you're going to blow that up to the size of a billboard."

"Yes."

"And then—put this billboard in front of the Campbell Club?"

"Yay, the monk gets it!" cried Pierre, and his glee club of one, Judith, began laughing.

"This is a house meeting, guys," I said.

"But we're going to help Rob implement his design. We'll need to participate."

"I notice you've joined Rob for dinner the last three days," said Connor, who I think was also on to them. "And I've seen you in the kitchen a lot." But Connor's take was a little different than mine. "If that's what you plan to do, then you need to start participating by doing chores."

"Naturally, we all must work, the art is the life," said Pierre in his Parisian accent.

But as time passed, I was not aware of them doing any *actual* work. It eventuated that 'doing art'—and their particular take on art, their 'mission,' the work they were doing with Rob and the cause of surrealism—was in their minds, all the contribution they needed to make. "Don't you think art is important?"

"Sure. Very," I said. "But this is a student co-op. You're not students, at least according to what Rob said."

"We *were* students. Besides, it's the summertime and school's not in session. What does it matter?" said Pierre.

To that I had no answer. And because room number 14, the triple on the second floor, was now vacant (Magda and Raven both having moved out, and then Napoleon, finally, at the summer break) Judith and Pierre moved in there. "It's just for the summer," said Rob. "I need them in the house; we're doing this huge project. They're my crew. Besides, they fit right in."

I didn't see it that way, and I had a bad feeling about it, like Aragorn thinking that Hobbiton was not safe, but I was busy with my own things.

Due to Janet's influence Connor was bit by bit coming out of his shell and now wanted to be more social. At first, he was all about the love interest and was nowhere to be seen—they'd go to her place and he'd ghost everybody else. But as time passed, she wanted to be more social, and they would come to the co-op and hang out. Yes, truly, it was The Summer of Love. For Connor it was an explosion of feelings and experiences. They took a trip to Portland one weekend, apparently with the goal to "climb Mount Hood," and the next week, it was off to Florence, the quaint little beach town, and Janet wanted me to come with them. I didn't know at the time, but Connor didn't really want my presence. He was completely wrapped up in what apparently was the first serious love of his life. However, his lady was insistent, and so that was how it had to be. It was her car, anyway.

We set out in her beater Ford Pinto on a fine morning that quickly became overcast. The road out is numbered 126, the Florence-Eugene Highway, and it winds along the Siuslaw river eventually meeting Pacific Coast 101 at Florence. It's a fine stretch of road. In the rain, things became a bit sketchy, and we had to pull off once in a while due to the heavy downpour.

When we got to Florence, though, the sky cleared up and blue and gray clouds sought their escape on the horizon. The ocean was turbulent and dramatic. I didn't even want to get out of the car, but Janet was all gung-ho and happy, and Connor got happy when we started looking at driftwood. The variegated shapes and forms seemed to spark Connor's imagination, and he got high on it. Suddenly he was gathering pieces and building spontaneous sculptures. Janet got into it in her own way. I preferred to watch and was asked to judge and assess.

As evening came on, we sought out a diner and sat drinking coffee and talking and laughing, sharing a single slice of pie, or opening packets of crackers. Nobody had any money, but the waitress didn't seem too fussed. Eventually we needed to move on.

Sleeping on the beach was pretty challenging. We had sleeping bags, and Connor brought a borrowed tent (it was Leo's) which he gamely set up as best he could in a sand dune, but the wind came up and blew the sand like bird shot. The tent quickly came undone, ropes loose, sides wildly flapping and then collapsing on top of us, and we ended up huddled in the dark in the car at some stage, freezing cold. Nevertheless, I had gone through much worse at an earlier stage of my life, to me a night outside was nothing. I rather enjoyed it because I was with other people. And I appreciated Janet's resilience. She knew how to laugh in adversity, which is a great gift, and seemed to be teaching Connor useful things about life. I was pleased. And she never complained even once. It was Connor who was obsessively concerned, mainly about her, fearing the trip had become a disaster in her eyes; when really, it was only a disaster in his.

We decided to return to Eugene the next morning, as conditions had defeated us. The witchy weather seemed to disappear almost as soon as our resolve to leave became fixed; but we left anyway.

When we returned Rob and his crew had begun construction of their monstrosity. It was basically a billboard but set up in the front lawn of the co-op, more or less obscuring the house. The original design had concrete footings that really did seem rather permanent, and of course, the Big Ronnie also obscured all the light on that side of the house so nothing could be seen through many of the windows except the back of the billboard. "But it's summer, don't be a spoilsport." I tried to focus on my own problems. I was supposed to be writing.

***

The summer was rapidly ending when Connor and I decided to take up Deon the Survivalist's offer of a training course. Deon was a friend of Janet's and when Connor heard his girlfriend had been through his course, he wanted immediately to do it. I was less excited, but I said, "sure, why not."

Deon was a very quiet man, older, and his clothes and general demeanour had hobo written all over them. I understood about such people, that they could be dangerous and violent in certain situations, not because they were evil but because they had nothing to lose. I was pretty sure Deon had also been in prison, based on his tattoos, which were of the hand-pricked variety.

These red flags turned out to be of no consequence. Deon was kind and gentle. He might have been what we today call autistic; but there was no word for it then that we knew. He had difficulty looking into another person's eyes, and he liked to keep the emotional temperature at a bare minimum. His was almost a technical nature, even a military nature, like a Spartan war pig raised in the pack, to live, to fight, to survive;

but he had no detectable formal education. This was not an unpleasant aspect of the man, rather the reverse.

He wanted fifty dollars each for his survival training class, but when we explained we were recommended by Janet, and that we were poor students, he lowered the cost to twenty dollars. He rarely spoke except in some operational way, such as to point out a plant or signs of an animal, or how to make a fire without attracting attention, or to demonstrate how to tie a knot. He was very proficient with rope, canvas, and other traditional survival materials; but he also knew everything, it seemed, about the plant and animal materials available for free in the vast reaches of the natural environment. Lastly, he understood how to treat the urban landscape as an environment in which certain necessaries could be found and scavenged. This included, but was far from limited to, dumpsters and trash bins. Places to sleep, sources of water, even potential food sources—all for the taking in a situation of need. Deon carried only a very small pen knife on his person, rather than a bowie knife or something more substantial; this was to avoid problems with law enforcement, he said.

There's a footbridge that crosses the Willamette out past Franklin Boulevard, past the Urban Farm and the art studios, and from that bridge one can see an island in the middle of the river. Deon operated in the area past the bridge, which to us was nameless parkland, and was forested and home to the Alton-Baker community gardens and had paths and walking trails. If one kept walking, eventually there was the Athletics Department and the football stadium. But prior to that was a sort of natural wonderland for recreation and exercise. It was a magical land of nature and wildness or a wasteland ready to be "developed," depending on your politics or your imagination.

The bridge has a name, and the island also probably has a name of some kind. But as Alan Watts said, when you don't give something a name, you can begin to actually see it. And that is true enough both with that part of Eugene, and also with Deon himself. As to the island, I used to call it *the Island in the Stream*, after the Hemingway novel. And that was where the training started.

"How are we supposed to get down there?" asked Connor.

Deon smiled. "That's your first challenge. I'll set up a base camp on the far end of the island. See you there on Saturday at about 5 am."

***

So we got out of bed at a ridiculous hour and walked in the direction of Franklin Boulevard. It only took a few minutes to get to the footbridge; but now—the island.

"I guess we gotta swim."

But it turned out the water was not that deep, perhaps waist-high at some points, but not more. We scrambled down the side of the bank and then tentatively made our way out into the riverbed. The water was fast-moving but the main thing was the cold. The water was freezing.

We arrived, soaked and shivering, and dragged ourselves up onto the bank. "Didn't it occur to you boys to take off your clothes before you went in the water?"

Deon chuckled. "I thought you'd be OK on this challenge. But now you're all wet. Well, take off some of it, and hang it so the wind and sun can dry it. Come down to the far end of the island, where it's harder to see you. Stealth is part of this course. Stealth is actually a huge part of Survival."

The day was full of interesting ideas, and I was not sorry about taking the time to learn from this man, who had clearly understood much and discovered much about life in deep solitude. We learnt how to make a shelter, and the little island actually seemed much more welcoming once I understood how to conceivably live there; I became excited about this and for a few minutes even visualized how wonderful life would be. No more school; free, naked, unfettered, living on what nature provided. But Deon reminded me of the obvious. "Sure, Sutra. But what do you do when the river level rises? Floods, my boy. Floods."

Deon taught us next how to make and use a bow drill to create enough friction to start a fire. But then he taught us more creative ways to invite the god of fire. A magnifying glass or even the broken bottom of a clear glass bottle might suffice. We moved on then to animal (and human) tracking—useful, Deon said, primarily in regard to self-defence, to understand who (or what) was in the area. Then trapping and fishing, which Deon said was quite feasible. "The Willamette has trout: steelhead, rainbow, and cutthroat, but also Coho Salmon, Chinook, and many others like Kokanee and Bass. Most any fish you can catch, you can probably eat it."

"What about regulations, licenses?"

"Yep, in theory you need a license. But that's for a fishing rod. We're not going to use one. As far as size, basically anything small, you have let it go. If the fish is big, adult, then likely that's just fine. Even with The Man."

Deon showed us the principle of a fish trap: basically making a structure using rocks, where the fish could enter but then easily be caught as they had no escape.

We then moved on to foraging and general ecology. I thought of Rachael a lot during that lesson, and of that miracle day when we were together at the Urban Farm. Deon said something that stuck with me, a thing that might interest her. "There are about six butterflies in the area that are blue; but there is one—people say it is now extinct. It was last officially sighted during the Great Depression era."

"But is it really extinct?" I said.

Deon had a twinkle in his eye. "Oh, I don't think so." But he would say no more other than the name and the general details. "Fender's Blue, it was called. Like many butterflies here, it needs the wildflowers for food. We've cut those down and cleared them out through mowing to point only a few places where there are gardens of wildflowers that can support them."

It began to get on into the afternoon, and after a very odd lunch of berries, bugs (yes, one or two, on which I gagged), and fish, Deon said he had a special treat for us. "You're really going to like this," he said. We walked back into the more heavily wooded area after taking an almost imperceptible path (the cut to which thanks to Deon's teaching, we could now perceive). And then we saw it: a tree house.

But this was no ordinary tree house. "The Sheriff's Office every now and then comes out and destroys my treehouses; I've built seven of them over the years. But so far this one has withstood the full brunt of law enforcement."

Connor and I looked at each other in shock. I could understand why the cops had not torn it down: the thing was ridiculously high up in a huge tree, and the miniscule platform, if there even was one, must have been at least sixty feet off the ground.

"You boys are going to love this! The view is great."

"But Deon, that's nuts!" I cried.

"Oh, well, your friend Janet liked it."

Connor was stunned. "Janet climbed up there?"

"She sure did."

"Well, then I have to go. Sutra, I'm sure you're too fragile for this. Stay on the ground, my dude."

"What? I'm not fragile. Just terrified. The thing is 200 feet in the air!"

Deon laughed. "Oh by no means. I reckon it's more like 50 feet. Of course, if you fall it will still likely kill you. I don't have insurance. So, if you're scared of heights, I wouldn't attempt it."

Connor was already up on the first stage of the ladder, having steeled himself with the thought of Janet, her eyes, her face, and what she would say—or what he imagined she would say—if he could not also do this climb. Perhaps it was male pride. But I think it more likely to have been a desire to prove himself to her. I realized how much he must love Janet, to put away all fear, even this most obvious and rational fear. Also, he would probably prefer death to failure. Not exactly a good guy to follow up a tree.

The tree-house ladder was constructed of sawn two-by fours, apparently nailed into place. The design was quite clever, it leveraged the fact that the tree actually had twin trunks, which diverged higher up, but at the base it made something of a natural ladder frame when the cross-pieces were added.

"But Deon, is it safe?"

"Well, nothing in life is really, 'safe,' if you know what I mean. Walking around on Franklin, if you don't pay attention, you'll be dead in about 5 seconds if you wander out in the road. This is much the same. But yes, it is fairly safe. I've been sleeping up there in the good weather. It's a great way to avoid the usual hassles from the cops, I can tell you."

I couldn't believe the audacity of the man.

Connor meanwhile seemed to be making progress. He already had reached a midpoint; but his progress had slowed. He was moving more cautiously with each rung, looking around him, as if his sanity was slowly returning.

I started climbing, too, but I had not gone far before Connor called down. "Sutra, what are you doing, dude."

"I'm coming up!"

"Stay on the ground, dude! One of us has to go back and tell the tales of brave Ulysses."

"I'm doing it!"

"You're crazy, man!"

Meanwhile he had almost reached the top. He stopped talking for a while. I proceeded slowly, one rung at a time, and had got about half-way up, when he pronounced his ascendency.

"I'm there, Sutra!"

"You're a godman, Connor!"

He stood on what he described later as a small platform, which was hardly more than a large plank. There was no guard rail.

Connor rose up to his full height and yelled into the universe, doing his best Muhammad Ali: "I—am—the—greatest! Float like a butterfly, sting like a bee!" Off in the distance, birds were disturbed by the racket and took flight. The world was suddenly silent for Connor, honouring him, and the sun broke out from behind a cloud as if the gods were applauding, and all I could hear was his breathing. Then we could both hear Deon far below. "It's getting late, guys."

"I'm not going any further," I said, groaning.

Presently, Connor responded. "Yours was a futile effort, Sutra."

"A lot of life is like that," I yelled back.

"I gotta figure out how to get down myself." He was talking now more to himself than me. But he started slowly to navigate his way down. "I don't even know how I got up here."

"Adrenaline," said Deon. "And pure nerve. No one in their right mind has ever made it up there without it."

***

The feud between the "Rob Squad"[3] and Thomas Pincheon III began in earnest a few days before the start of the Fall term. As I have described, the Big

---

[3] Or the orcs as others said. I preferred to call them the *Deplorables* (due to the deplorable state of their hygiene).

Ronnie was positioned on the Campbell Club property in such a way that it took up most of the front yard. This made the front porch into a cave of darkness and the windows on the front side of the house became blocked. Even the second story was impacted, and some rooms (all right, Connor's and my room was one) were blocked. Minimal to no sunlight could get in. That was all bad enough, but for reasons that seemed inexplicable, the work had been built in such a way that it blocked the wheelchair ramp.

Thomas Pincheon III had spent the summer at his parent's house, which was out in North Springfield. So he didn't have occasion to drive down Alder Street. Yes, Thomas had his own specially fitted van and a driver's license. I was surprised by this. One day I was out and about and I saw Thomas in his van. He honked and pulled over, rolled down the window, and said "Sutra. Beautiful day! You need a lift to the co-op?"

"Sure."

"Well get in. Come around to the passenger side."

I opened the passenger door and got in.

"Put your seatbelt on," said Thomas.

"Uh, sure."

From my passenger side viewpoint I could see his setup. The van had a lift arrangement so that he could get in and out from the rear door; in the front, the driver's side seat had been removed. The steering wheel had special push-pull hand controls.

"This is quite a rig, Thomas," I said.

"Yes. I love my van." He stepped on the gas, then, (somehow) and the van began to accelerate.

"I have to admit," I said, "I didn't know quadriplegics could drive. I mean, it just shows my ignorance."

"Well, don't feel too bad. Most people don't know these things. Disabled people won the right to drive in the United States all the way back in the 1930s. But the big change was after the war."

"World War II?"

"Exactly. A lot of soldiers came home without limbs or paralysed. Ford and GM both started making modifications to their vehicles about that time."

Meanwhile I noticed that Thomas was pushing the van hard. He roared down the road like a kamikaze.

"Whoa Thomas!"

He just laughed. Speed was clearly his adrenaline. And we were back to the co-op faster than I thought possible.

***

But that summer, just a few days before Fall, Thomas arrived at the Campbell Club for the new term. He parked as usual in the back, and descended from his van using the lift, then motored round in his electric wheelchair to the front of the house—and found the Big Ronnie in the yard. He stopped, almost stunned. "What the hell is this?"

"That's the Big Ronnie," said Pierre, with an amused grin.

"Who the hell are you?" said Thomas.

Pierre ignored him and continued painting. He was working from a ladder on the top right section of the billboard, up by the hand, which seemed to be either waving or pointing.

Thomas turned away in frustration and motored down the sidewalk towards the ramp—and his chair came to an abrupt halt. Yes, the Big Ronnie had been constructed in such a way that the ramp was blocked.

"I can't get in!" shouted Thomas.

"Oh well," laughed Pierre.

"What are you doing! You idiot! I live here!"

"No need to be abusive."

"*L'infirme semble être contrarié*," laughed Judith, who came around the corner.

"*Ce n'est pas notre problème*," said Pierre.

"Fix this!" shouted Thomas.

"You will have to talk to Rob. It is his design," said Pierre.

"We're just workers in the cause," said Judith.

"Cause? *What* cause?" shouted Thomas. He was nearly in tears now.

"*La grande cause de l'art*," laughed Pierre.

"Art and Revolution!" said Judith.

They paid no more attention to him. It seemed to give them a kind of sadistic pleasure that Thomas was angry. He went back to his van, slowly used the lift to get inside, closed the door, and then cried.

***

Fortunately, Johan had come back to the United States from his trip overseas. Thomas left and drove his van to a place where he could use the telephone and called the one person who perhaps in all of the world, he felt he could count on. Johan.

The next day, Johan arrived. He had not planned to come back for a few more days. But this situation was intolerable. You will remember it was Johan who had designed the ramp in the first place.

Now, standing and looking at the billboard, he was shocked. "Unacceptable," he pronounced. "Where is Rob? They've poured concrete footings in the front yard! And the lovely hydrangea are all destroyed!"

It seemed that both Rob and his 'workers' were out and about. So Johan did what any builder would do: started making alterations. He first gathered some materials and tools from the basement and then cut a large void into the Big Ronnie's left breast, going all the way up about as high and wide as the left-side breast coat pocket. His saw stabbed into and through Ronnie's carefully painted surface. Johan then cleanly trimmed the void with two-by-fours and created bracing to hold things in place.

Meanwhile Judith and Pierre returned and saw Johan at work. They stopped and gawked in anguish.

"Imbécile!" said Pierre. "You cannot do that!"

It was Judith's and Pierre's turn to be ignored, as Johan worked on what we started calling the "Brandenburg Gate." A structure of considerable quality. Everything Johan touched was like that. I was proud to stand with him toe to toe and admire his craftsmanship.

"You are destroying a great work of art beyond your comprehension to understand," yelled Judith. "We are in the papers! Don't you read? There are two articles in the *Register Guard*! We even made it into the *Oregonian*!"

Johan just sneered at her. In response, Pierre rushed up, shaking his arms violently, a faint or bluff, I suppose. Johan's significant physical appearance—he was a head and shoulders taller than the small Frenchman—caused Pierre to come to halt at a safe distance of about three yards away. The little man pointed and gesticulated wildly as he spoke an English slur. "Asshole!"

Johan then crossed his arms. He gave Pierre his best, most stern 'look' and spoke very quietly. "Don't even consider touching this bypass I have cut through your ridiculous Postmodern nonsense. Yes, I know all about it. You cannot fool me. I know you are scoundrels. Eurotrash," he said, chuckling in his brass baritone voice.

"You—you—Nazi!" But Pierre shut down as Johan marched in his direction, hammer in hand. The pair fled.

***

So Thomas was able at last to enter the co-op. He zoomed up the ramp at high speed to general cheers from a number of the members who had taken an interest in the affair. As I have said, Thomas never was popular, and his handicap was something that certain people felt uncomfortable with at times, but this incident made him into an underdog and highlighted the absurdity of the Deplorables. His gratitude to his friend Johan was such that he later organized a $1,000 betting pool on the first Big Ten conference game that season and worked as a bookie once more "for old-time's sake" so that his friend could get some action on the game. It was a "one-off" and Leo said he quite understood the gesture.

Meanwhile the general attitude towards the Big Ronnie was mixed. Everyone liked the general idea of an art project, and we had done things like hang posters in protest of Apartheid, and things like that (so we were not apolitical) but no one could really explain what the Big Ronnie *meant*, and Rob was intentionally coy. He insisted everyone had to assign a meaning, that he could not do that for the viewer. And he was gratified and validated by the attention the Big Ronnie generated. Sometimes it got an egg or a rock from a passing car; sometimes a cheer would go up from a passing ROTC cadet or Young Republican in a Chrysler. It was a strange and thoroughly polarizing *objet d'art*, considering Rob's claims of ambiguity and the necessity of interpretation. The more violence and chaos it seemed to generate, the happier he seemed to be.

***

One afternoon I watched Rob give an interview about the Big Ronnie to a visiting newspaperman, who brought a photographer. Words like 'postmodern" and "revolutionary" could be heard emanating from Rob's grinning mouth. Apparently they were from the *LA Times*. Rob introduced himself as the "leader of the co-op house," which of course was untrue.

The Deplorables were also massing their forces—orcs and dark goblins—their rag-tag friends—in the so-called "Student Art Collective." Suddenly various unrecognized non-members wandered the halls making comments about this or that, trying locked doors, and eating what foods they could find in the kitchen refrigerators. It seemed things were getting out of hand.

"It's like Hobbiton under Saruman around here," I said to Rachael.

"It's a disaster," she said. "There are fleas in the couches on the front porch. And I think someone pissed in my room." She left, disgusted, to try and find some bleach and cleanser.

***

The Fall term saw a lot of change. Cindy had decided to stay at the Annex. So I saw her less. And that fucker Jay was there. I had got the 411 on him but I won't waste your time. Leo was back but only for the term; it was to be his last at the Campbell Club. I was thrilled for his presence, not least because things seemed to be breaking down and falling apart, but he was also my friend. It was a simple thing; but friendship, I came to understand, means everything as regards happiness.

The elections for SCA Board were upon us, and I was looking forward to seeing Abigail. She seemed to be moving a bit more slowly; to be a bit more frail than I remembered. But when I greeted her coming into the Campbell Club front hallway, her eyes lit up as they always did. I called them "Jane Goodall" eyes. They lighted on everything and understood everything without having to be involved or interfere. I noticed other people looking at us but I didn't care. I gave her a hug and she reciprocated warmly with a motherly kiss on the mouth and asked me motherly questions to which I gave properly dismissive son answers.

And Leo was there and said warm things to her as well. Leo was the person who had hired her originally, back when she was shunned (as we all were) from other opportunities.

Abigail gave a good review of the finances and it seemed that things were going well. We had money in the bank. I saw Rob and the Deplorables listening carefully to this part.

I half-hoped that Leo might not be serious about leaving, that he would stay on; but when it came time for the meeting to start, he officiated but didn't stand for any positions. He was breaking the ties. So who stood, you might ask?

I was surprised and impressed when Rachael put her hand up to be SCA President. She was a junior this year and was blossoming out into a woman (to a greater extent) if that was even conceivable. The truth is that we don't have very good words for the changes a woman experiences in this time of life, the period from about age 12 to 25. So much happens inside a woman: the first experience of love, the pain and embarrassment of menarche, the search for identity in a world dominated by men, even the simple problem of what to wear, pants or a skirt, seems to have broader implications. We have no words for those many stages. We say "girls" (and I have done this many times even in this book out of habit) but that word no longer works. And "young women" sounds patronizing. I perceived then, and still believe now, that we have made things much too difficult for women and that has prevented them from becoming what they can and should be—the dominant social and political force on the planet.

I then had one of those realizations which come once in a lifetime. I thought that perhaps women were a different species of life and needed to be studied as such: this insight might have led eventually to a new matriarchy based on their superiority as a species. Men were like Neanderthals, lumbering warlike idiots; women were the true Homo Sapiens, the wise. But this brilliant idea I chalked up to my usual absurdity and I forgot all about it instantly.

As far as I could tell, Rachael seemed to have navigated those landmines put in her way and found a safe path through many, if not all of them. She was strong, yet supple; fresh, yet gathering in experience; keen to understand, but not overbearing or obnoxiously reactive, as scientists often are (because Science is very much a dogma, just like any other religion); beautiful—as you know I have compared her to a Greek statue—and that beauty would ripen, the way a green fruit ripens and becomes sweeter and sweeter until it cannot wait, and at the peak of ripeness must be eaten.

That's how I thought of her for a long time. But now, she was entering public life; I was suddenly proud of her for entirely different reasons and had to come to terms with my earlier shallowness and rank misogyny. Yes, the truth was, Rachael was the perfect woman. But when I said this to Cindy, she laughed, and said, "Well, of course, she's blond and has big boobs. All men think like that."

Her opponents for the position were the perennial candidate Stuart Longfellow, who was going into his last year at Janet Smith (he was tying off a PhD in some complex subject.)

And then there was Rob.

Leo had the candidates come forward and I couldn't help asking. "Hey Leo, maybe I speak for a few of us, but you are not in the running?"

"No, Sutra," he said. "It's my last term and I want my free time. I'm coasting, you might say. Possibly even free-loading. Time for others to step up."

Rachael then gave a wonderful speech about how her experiences over the last year had changed her and given her insight into how special the co-op was. Her plans for the year included revamping the house kitchens, replacing all the cutting boards, buying a new dishwasher at the Campbell Club, implementing a recycling program, and in short, improving sanitation and overall "green" profile of the houses. "We're going to move towards a green future. It's the Green Revolution. Just our small part."

Stuart gave an interesting plug for more graduate students, citing the need for high value members who cared about the house and the co-op values that the SCA represented. He avoided looking in the general direction of the Deplorables (at this point Judith and Pierre, and Trip and his girlfriend Sue Ellen, none of whom were enrolled in classes that term) and got general applause from both houses. Everyone knew there was an underlying issue and Stuart's way of bringing it out into the open without directly challenging what was going forward was appreciated.

Finally it was Rob's turn. "As everyone knows, it's a big year going forward. It's my last year, too, I expect to complete my master's thesis. And then it's on to bigger and better things. But meanwhile, I'd like to help make the co-op a success this year. It really is a special place."

"What's with the Big Ronnie?" came from somewhere in the back. Calls of "Tear down the wall!" came from my general direction.

Ok, yes, that was me. I was the one who shouted, "Tear down the wall!"

Leo stepped in at this point. "We will take a few minutes after the election to discuss the, eh, 'art project' that some of the members have put up. But meanwhile, we need to complete the business of electing the new Board."

"While Leo was speaking, and in fact all through the speeches of the candidates, the Deplorables were chatting amongst themselves, seemingly incapable of granting respect to the speakers by listening or staying quiet. I don't know exactly why these people had got so far under my skin, but it probably had something to do with the fact I understood their type: they were con-artists, one step up from the street. I had learnt from Rajneeshpuram if not before, all the tactics people can use to subvert and destroy civil society; how to flout the rules in order to bend and break them; how to ignore in order to fend off, and now these things were being acted out in front of me. But the other trend of mind inside me was to see everyone as soul, to understand these fools as minds clouded and deluded, who potentially could be helped or saved. Of course, that was probably wishful thinking in their case.

"Point of order?" I said to Leo.

"Yes, Sutra?"

"Apologies, but this is an SCA joint-house meeting. Some people are present who are not members. They have not paid any fees for this year, for example. I think they should wait outside."

"Is this true, Thomas?" he said.

"Yes, I've complained about it. They won't come and talk to me about a payment plan. I've approached those two" —here he pointed at Judith and Pierre— "but they just ignore me. In fact, they say rude things. They say I stink."

"All right. Please can we just complete the elections before we get into this business."

The votes were cast and counted. Leo stood up and reported the results. "It seems that Rob has won! Congratulations Rob!"

"Wait a minute," cried Stuart. "I'm pretty sure those folks voted. Are they members, or not?"

There were a number of people who had observed the Deplorables voting, and they now voiced their concern in support of Stuart.

"All right," said Leo. "I guess we need to have this out. The vote is nullified. We'll discuss membership and then we'll try again."

"But Rob was elected!" cried Judith. "What gives you the authority to toss out the result?"

"Well, I'm running the election, as stated in the By Laws. It's part of my job."

"I'm not sure that's fair," said Pierre. "Seems questionable. You are not abiding by the will of the houses."

The room was rapidly becoming chaotic and the meeting seemed to break down. Which, of course, is exactly what these people always want: they're chaos agents. Leo did the smart thing, though, and suggested we take a 15-minute break. "But before that, I think it is fair that we vote on the central question, which is if Judith Stimmer, Pierre Benz, Kip Turner, and Sue Ellen Rogers are allowed to participate. You four cannot vote in this round. Also, please go outside for the time being."

"That's not fair, either," said Judith.

"It's necessary for you to leave the meeting in order to make sure you don't vote." Leo said this kindly, but with firmness. "Clearly you participated in something just now that some members don't think was appropriate. The least you can do, if you are interested in living here going forward, is to respect the wishes of those who are currently legitimate members."

The logic of that was undeniable, and so with that the four, now thoroughly disgruntled, continued to grumble as they made their way out the front door. They stood around on the porch, looking in or pretending not to.

After they had gone out, Leo closed the door, which had been propped open up until then for purposes of air flow. "All right. Let's discuss the question. Five minutes. Who would like to speak first? Rob? Maybe you should represent your crew."

Rob was quick to disavow the Deplorables by throwing them under the bus. "They did a great job on the Big Ronnie. But if the House doesn't want them here, well, we should vote on that and they can be on their way. This is supposed to be a housing co-op. Obviously they want to live here. I suspect this is a challenge to the powers that be, because they are working class people. They feel—"

"Working class? But they do no actual work!" Someone shouted.

Yes, unfortunately that rude someone was me again.

"Don't interrupt, please," said Leo. "Rob has the floor."

"As I was saying, before I was so rudely interrupted, these are working class folks and their understanding is not necessarily the same as yours, like me they are interested in socialism, but that shouldn't matter. My view is that if they live here, they are de facto members, fees or not. And should be able to vote."

"Thank-you Rob. OK, who would like to speak next?"

I said nothing, but Foster and Rachael and a few others pointed at me.

"Fine." I stood up. "I think the facts are pretty simple and Rob has not gone over those. He is intentionally deceptive to gain a political advantage. You know, at Rajneeshpuram, Sheela eventually brought in busloads of homeless people from all over, to swell our numbers and win in the local election. That was morally wrong and probably illegal. Now I see the same thing starting to happen here. Anyway, these are the facts: this summer, Rob brought in some friends—"

"Workers!" shouted Rob.

"—workers for his art project. Most of the members weren't here, so there was not much control over what was happening, and he didn't ask anyone if that was kosher. He just did it. But it was summer. That's a pretty relaxed time. Now, Fall has come, and people who are not members have not left, as they probably should have, and are basically free-loaders. I don't think many of you have experience with that scenario. The co-op works because we're all students, and also because we all have some shared ideals. These guys don't share those ideals. They're con-artists. I know their type. But look, basically, if someone is not a student, and if they don't share the ideals of the SCA, then they should be asked to leave."

"Rob, any rebuttal?" said Leo.

"I think the problem is with the definition of Student. Judith and Pierre are students, or were. They're just not enrolled at the moment. Same with Kip. I don't know for Sue Ellen."

I wanted to respond, but Leo waved me down.

"All right, time's up," he said. "I think it's obvious that the definition of a 'Student' is someone who is enrolled at the University. It's defined in the By Laws. So there is nothing to decide on that point. However, by show of hands, who agrees with this definition?"

I was surprised to see the number of people who seemed to disagree. I noticed that most of them seemed to be new this term, and probably did not understand how the co-op worked as well as they could have. This was part of the blow-back from losing Magda Slater as Membership Coordinator. After her departure, this function had gone to Karen Tamlen, who was very excited to take on the job, but seemed too busy to actually do much. She probably just approved anyone, good fit or no.

"All right," said Leo. "It's agreed by a majority that 'Student' means 'enrolled.' So that should be considered settled. Now let's tackle the question if people should be allowed to live in the co-op if they are non-students. I think the way that *could* work is if they are not considered members—don't vote—but still reside here, perhaps on a temporary basis, that is a reasonable thing. That's actually what seems to have happened over the summer. I'm not supporting or defending the idea, I'm just saying, we could go that direction. So the question is this: 'Should we consider applications from people as residents, grant them, say, residency visas, to live in the houses even if they are not students? Show of hands, please?"

This was voted in the affirmative. I voted against it; and so, I noticed, did Rachael. But we seemed to be in the minority.

"All right then. So the proposed process is for the four outside to apply with the SCA Membership Coordinator in the new category of 'residents,' and also I imagine they should pay their fees right away if they are delinquent. The normal rules should be in effect. I mean, people who live here have to do chores and follow the house rules which are agreed to. Fees are part of that. I hope everyone agrees with me on this?" Leo was looking at me, here, and I nodded. There was general assent to what he had said. "So let's take a half-hour break and have something to drink. I'm parched."

I watched as Rob went out to explain the decision to the Deplorables. I could see him talking though the front windows, see their unhappy reactions, and then Judith noticed me and gave me the evil eye. I admit, I smiled as I walked towards the kitchen.

We reconvened and Leo ran through the election, as everyone was getting tired of the process and dinner was waiting. "All right, let's vote on the SCA President."

This time, Rachael Day won. I was so happy that Rob had been defeated. I saw how much this meant to her, too, as she was being congratulated. Her face was shining. Even Rob congratulated her.

But my exhilaration was short-lived when Rob ran for Membership Coordinator and won. Karen Tamlen had done a lackluster job, but she was at least predictable; with Rob there was no telling what would happen to the house population. The faces of the Deplorables, who sat in on the meeting, told the story.

The other positions were filled with Eva as SCA secretary, Thomas Pincheon III as the SCA treasurer, and the house representatives for Campbell Club were Terry and Foster.

***

Two weeks later, I got a visit during dinner from Thomas Pincheon III. He motored up to me at his normal high speed, almost but never quite ramming the table with his electric wheelchair, and came to an abrupt, almost bouncing, stop.

"Thomas?" I said.

"Sutra. How are you."

"I'm good, very good. What can I do you for?"

"It's about you know who."

"The Deplorables?"

He smiled a devilish smile. "So is that what you call them?"

"Uh-huh."

"Well, the Deplorables—none of them have paid their fees yet."

"That seems bad." I knew that the deadline for everyone had passed the week before. "I can't say I'm surprised. They don't have jobs. Probably they're destitute. But they know a good fat cow to milk when they see one."

"I don't know what to do," said Thomas simply. "They're noncompliant. They're troublemakers. They don't belong here."

"I agree."

"Can't you talk to Leo or Rachael? You're thick as thieves with the two of them."

"Sure. I will."

But I didn't honor that request. I was too busy with my own problems. That was probably a mistake.

***

Judith and Pierre made their play at the next Campbell Club House Meeting. They wanted to trade 'painting skills and services' for rent. "We'll create a large mural in the second-floor hallway in lieu of the fees for this term."

"And what will this mural look like?" Asked Foster. He was still across the hall and would have to look at it.

"We work in a style inspired by Salvador Dalí. We're surrealists working in the Postmodern age. So it will be dreamlike but reject capitalism; de métacritique. Our images come from the subconscious. You can't tell what will emerge. It is in the act of painting that these things come out."

"So you have no idea," said Foster.

"I can see you don't appreciate art," said Judith.

"I also have concerns," said Thomas Pincheon III. "These people have never paid a penny in fees, ever. They've lived here, eaten in the kitchen, and hung out for at least four months, and never paid any fees. That's not a viable situation. Also, they don't seem to bathe very often—I think they have lice."

"That's a lie!" shouted Pierre.

"This cripple cannot judge us," cried Judith. "He has no right to talk about smell. He doesn't exactly smell that great, as far as I know. Pew!"

Thomas was enraged. I had never seen him so angry, and he began to become physically agitated, but Leo stopped him.

"Everyone, this is not productive, so let's move on to the vote. All in favor of allowing Judith and Pierre to make their painting in lieu of their fees for this term?"

I was surprised when a fair number of hands went up, but it was not enough to pass the motion. I'm afraid I cried out openly with pleasure at the thought these two would be expelled from the house. But then Rob sabotaged the entire vote by claiming as SCA Membership Coordinator, he had final authority about who could stay in the house. He quoted By Laws to support his position.

"So it seems we have to put up with these two con-artists," I said, "and I use that term literally. Or is it three con-artists?" I wasn't very nice, obviously. But I was angry at what I saw as the destruction of the community that was the co-op, the soul of the Campbell Club was at stake. It was all going to hell.

We then moved on to discuss the "Big Ronnie" which Leo explained had been determined by the city council to have violated several zoning laws and must be removed immediately from its permanent fixtures. "I'm not going to call a vote on this, because we got notification from the city about it. So party time is over for the Big Ronnie, folks."

"We can keep it up as a political protest! The First Amendment guarantees freedom of speech!" shouted Pierre (who I knew was a French national on an expired visa and thus had few, if any, of those rights). But Rob was no fool, and he understood, if nothing else, that the Big Ronnie needed to come down, if only to keep him personally out of trouble. "What we'll do is make it portable."

"Yes!" cried Judith. "It's going *Portable*! Voilà! We can put it up outside the University Administration building!"

"Art show!" cried Pierre. "Rolling art show and protest!"

"You can do what you want, Rob, but it has to come down this weekend. The alternative is I will forward the bill for the fine they imposed to you. Abigail says they've fined us $2,000."

It seemed that we would be stuck with these two chaos agents for the term at CC. A number of the co-opers looked depressed. Rachael sunk her head into her hands.

***

I know it was unkind to scheme ways to get the Deplorables out of the house, but sometimes I'm like that. Maybe I do have a little bit of Osho in me, God help me.

I had never been in Thomas Pincheon III's room before as a visitor; but always before as a payer of fees. I'd bring cash, the little money I had stashed away from various enterprises, and he would write out a receipt, and that would be that. But today I had something else on my mind. The door was perennially open—I've talked about his penchant for vicarious observation and eavesdropping. I knocked on the open door anyway and peeked in.

"Thomas?" I said.

"Sutra! This is unexpected. But not unwelcome! Come in, come in!"

We exchanged pleasantries, and Johan was there. "I'll leave you two to talk," he said.

"Wait, Johan. Maybe this would interest you. And we might need your help."

Johan seemed pleased. "Of course. Anything."

"Thomas, uh, do you mind if I close your door? This is somewhat confidential."

"Go ahead, Sutra. This is starting to sound interesting."

I went to the door and gently closed it.

"All right. Here's what I've been thinking. And Johan, your input here is very welcome. I think we have a problem. Perhaps you both know what I'm talking about."

"The Deplorables," said Thomas with a smirk.

"Deplorables?" rumbled Johan in his thick Bavarian accent.

"Yes. That's the term Sutra coined for these shiftless con-artists, these street people who have invaded our home."

"So here's what I know. Connor encountered these folks early on down at the Ceramics shack. And in conversation he said that Pierre admitted his student visa has expired. He's not an American. He's a French national. I think Judith is Canadian, I don't know her visa status. However—"

Thomas's grim mind immediately reacted to this news. "Ah-hah!"

"Now, Johan," I said, "forgive me, but are we going to lose all respect in your eyes, if we use the powers that be to shut them down?"

"It's certainly not very cool, Sutra. If I didn't know better, I'd say this was a trick worthy of the Rajneeshi."

"Ugh!" I cried. "That hits hard, brother."

"But we must do something, Johan," said Thomas. "I can see it coming. They will eventually destroy the co-op."

"That seems unlikely to me. More likely they will just light out some night and disappear. But I admit sometimes something must be done. They are harmless parasites in my mind. But not very convivial."

"And they called you a faggot, Johan!" said Thomas. "I was present when the incident happened!"

"Well, that does not bother me."

"Now I have a question, Thomas. I know you have some connections to the local Eugene Police. But how does one go about involving the Feds? Isn't deportation a federal issue?"

"Yes," he said. "Of course it is. It would help if they could be picked up on some charge. Then the PD could hand them over—in custody—to the Feds."

"Hmm." The wheels inside Johan's head were spinning. "Yes. Perhaps I have an idea about that. Leave it with me."

***

I didn't hear too much more about it until the sirens were outside the co-op a few days later. It was early evening. I went down to have a look in the living room. Both Judith and Pierre were down there shouting and gesticulating. The cops, having pushed them back, were talking to Johan. It was clear they remembered him. At that moment Thomas Pincheon III rolled up.

"So what's this about stolen money?" asked the cop.
Thomas spoke up. "During the summer I noticed things
starting to go missing here and there from my room. It's
true, I've always kept the door open. And those two
were here all summer. Anyway, Johan suggested we try
a little trap for them. He's a builder, he knows about
paints and things. So we put some green dye powder
mixed with a little baking soda on three hundred-
dollar bills. I put those in my wallet and then put the
wallet into a laundry basket. You could barely see, but
the edge of the money was visible, and the wallet was
on top. Then I had Johan put the laundry basket
outside my room."

"We knew the routines of those two; they usually go
up the backstairs for whatever reason. We knew they'd
walk by."

"So you're saying you set a trap for them?" said the
cop.

"Not for them, but for whomever has been stealing.
We guessed it was them. Looks like we were right."

Both Judith and Pierre's hands were stained bright
neon green. The color seemed to have transferred onto
Pierre's shirt as well as his trousers, while Judith's
white top was also stained green.

The cop seemed intrigued. "Where'd you get the dye
from?"

"We know grad students in the Chem department."
"Smart. Yeah, kids seem to be making all kinds of
things today."

The cop called his Sergeant, who came out and
greeted Thomas and Johan warmly, and they had to tell
the whole story again. Then the Sergeant got Judith
and Pierre's side of things.

Pierre spoke up first. "Those two have it out for us. We didn't do anything wrong."

"I saw the laundry basket and was just taking it down to the laundry room for the cripple. But he must have had something in there that got all over us." Judith said.

"But Thomas says he put dye only on his money—which was in his wallet. By the way, do you happen to know where his missing money is?"

"We know nothing about that. You cannot search in our room either. We won't permit it."

"I see. So that's what you're going with here? Tell you what, you tell me where the money is, and I'll talk to Thomas about dropping the changes. No harm no foul. The other option—since you're literally caught green-handed—is for me to get a warrant and come back in three hours. You sit here until then. And then we toss your room. I've got a feeling we might find other things besides the money in there."

Judith and Pierre looked at each other. "If we give him back the money, will he drop the charges? You're sure?"

"No, I said I will ask him to drop the charges—no harm, no foul. And I am a man of word, I will ask."

"Fine," said Pierre. "Let me go up to our room and I will get it."

"I can't do that, but if you tell this officer here where it is, he will go and look."

The officer soon returned with the cash.

"All right," said the Sergeant. "I'll talk to Thomas now about this."

"What do you say, Thomas? We've recovered the cash. These two may have learned a valuable lesson. You also have the right to press charges. What do you want to do?"

"I don't want to press charges, but I do want them to have some punishment. I also think if they were booked you might find they have priors or have done other crimes you might want to charge them with."

"That's what would happen if you pressed charges. Of course, if tomorrow you changed your mind, and let the charges drop, that would be your affair."

Thomas Pincheon III smiled. "Let's do that."

"Charge them?"

"Yes."

"Will do." The Sergeant motioned to the officer, and he cuffed Pierre. Judith started shouting. "You said the charges would be dropped! You lied!"

"No, I did not say that."

"Bastards! *Espèce de salaud ! Je vais t'attraper !*"

"What did she say?" inquired the Sergeant.

"Nothing good, I think," said Thomas.

***

"Let's hope someone checks up on their visas," I said to Thomas after the police had left and things quieted down.

"Oh don't worry, I already spoke with my father. He's going to make a call to the Chief of Police. I have a feeling our Deplorables will be looking forward to a trip home to wherever very soon."

One positive that came out of the situation was that, after the arrest, the cops went through their room and a certain box containing a Bizen masterpiece was found amongst other items.

"Holy shit!" I said. But Connor was glowing. This thing with the Bizen bowl had been like an albatross around his neck for months. He took the box immediately down to the studio and because Bob wasn't there, waited all night until morning, just so he could return it. But Bob told him to keep it.

"What? But this is yours."

"No Connor," Bob said. "It's yours."

***

This was not the end of the story for the Deplorables, and I've left out gruesome details like Judith's messy attempt at a chemical abortion in the shared bathroom. Their kind eventually killed the Campbell Club in the decades to follow; today it is a shadow of its former glory, filled with hungry ghosts. If you try to visit you will discover that for yourself. Our idealism could not triumph. But that's a story for another day.

Part Four. In Which I Get a Message From God. And Also, We Take Ecstasy.

*"The butterfly and Chuang-tzu are both
dream-essence."*
— *Matsuo Bashō (1644–1694)*

"Sutra? Look at you. What have you done to yourself?"

It was Carrie Anne Kyber, and we were in the Campbell Club living room. I have not mentioned Carrie Anne before in this story except in passing. The main reason is, as I explained, Campbell Club had a capacity of 38, and I'm a pretty good storyteller but even I can't tell the tale of every single person who lived in the Campbell Club during this period; it would have become rapidly confusing, but more to the point, some of it would be less interesting. Not everyone has an interesting life. (Yes, I'm sure that's not fair. But sorry, it's true).

At any rate, Carrie Anne was the girl—the woman— the athlete—who you may remember Rachael mentioned early on as someone who could "probably bench press more than you can." Which was undoubtedly true. Carrie Anne was in training for the Olympics, she was another Alaskan, like Leo. I found her to be a little rough around the edges, but pleasant. Her sport was cross-country skiing or maybe even downhill slalom, and I often saw her walking or running, cowboy hat on her head, Lycra suit on her lean, immensely toned body, with ski poles (perhaps these are called trekking poles?) in her hands.

The only story that I knew about her, which I can tell, came from her own explanation of how she got the money to go to school and train for the Olympics. "I'm not much of a talker. And you see how I dress. I'm a Levi's and hiking boots kind of girl. But I really wanted to try out for the Olympics. And so I made a slide show, a little PowerPoint *pre-sen-tation*, and I sent invitations to all the community leaders, and Elders, you know, the people who live in my town, of Anchorage, that's up in Alaska. And I put on a dress, a real fine, pretty dress, and pantyhose and high-heeled shoes. I had to go and buy those things; I had never worn those before. And I had all those folks come to an auditorium. It was my school auditorium, the principal let me use it. And I stood up there on the stage, under the lights, in my high heels and my little fine dress, wearing pantyhose, and told them all about how I wanted to go to the winter Olympics."

"But to do it, you needed money," I said.

"That's right. That was the nub. I needed money. And I explained what I needed, I asked them to support me. 'I am a local girl, from your own community. I'm not from out of state, I was born right here. I can do this— I can win this competition or at least bring home a medal. I'm not going to lie,' I said. 'It's hard to win gold in this sport. But I can bring home a medal. I'll be damned if I won't do that. I'll bring that home to you. I've thought about nothing else since I started skiing at the age of four. This is my life's dream.' And they listened. I didn't know what they were thinking. The lights were down; I could not really see the faces. Was

I having an impact? Was it working? I prayed then that it might work. I did, it's true. I prayed to Jesus, silently, when I was done talking. And afterwards I stood at the back to see people out. And what do you know? Several of them pulled out their check books. Right there, right in front of me, in that auditorium, and they wrote checks. Substantial checks. And over the next week, more checks came in the mail, and letters from people wishing me well and including some smaller amount. But fifty dollars or one-hundred dollars—that was real money to me. And I cashed those; I got the money in my account right now. That's how I got to come to school here. Because I have a scholarship for the tuition, see. But I needed money for coaching and equipment, and for travel. There's a lot involved with trying out for the Olympics."

So that was the story that Carrie Ann told me, and pretty much all I knew about her, other than the reason she had come to the Campbell Club. "It's cheap," she said. "Dirt cheap. Vegetarian food? Well, it's food, ain't it?"

And I liked that attitude. I liked her, even though she was completely the opposite of my "type." And so, when I went into the house, higher than a kite on Ecstasy, she happened to be there in the living room. It was just a coincidence. But I said hello, and that I had taken Ecstasy, and was really high.

Her reaction was swift. She first took me by the shoulders and turned me a little to face her. Then she took my face in her hands, and pulled me in closer, so that my face was directly in front of her face. We're about the same height—she's pretty tall—and so we were eye to eye. "Sutra," she said. Look at you! What have you done to yourself?"

"I got some of this new drug."

"Listen. This is not for you. I have watched you these last few terms, I have always looked up to you. But this is not right. God is Love. Don't you know that?"

"I—I think so," I said.

"Well, He is. He is the great ocean of Love, which encompasses all of existence. And if you come closer to Him, then He comes closer to you."

I looked into her eyes. She was not angry, but just seemed sad, like Jesus speaking to the scribes. And also very energetic. The goddess of energy and activity: surely that was Carrie Anne. Out in all weather, apparently unaffected by heat and cold, a Kwai Chang Caine of the track. I had not known this goddess. In fact motivation was not exactly one of my better attributes.

***

OK, in order to tell this part of the story properly I need to go back a few days, possibly even a few weeks.

Connor had started it. I've described how Terry and Mike dosed. We all knew about that. When Connor met Janet, one of the things that eventually came up in conversation between them was her interest in MDMA. She had heard about it and Connor, being very interested in pleasing her, started to investigate whether someone could get their hands on it.

It was me. Unfortunately, it was I who suggested that Mike Dix probably could get it; and I even asked Mike about it on Connor's behalf. According to Mike, it was easy to score. "Not a problem, at least not to get it. We know a cook."

"A cook?"

"Yes. He cooks in his kitchen. He's a good guy, used to be a grad student. But why stay in school when you can make a lot more money using knowledge you already have? Do you know what it's made out of?"

"No, actually. I don't know anything about it."

"It's kind of cool. The precursor is the thing that makes root beer."

"Root beer? You're putting me on."

"No, man."

"Root beer. Sounds harmless. Well then, can you get us some? It's not for me, it's for Connor."

"Connor? The guy who made all the cool ceramic mugs?"

"Yeah."

"That's OK. He's cool. But we don't just sell 'E' to anybody. There's a test."

"Really?" I was surprised.

Dix laughed. "Bradman's rules. You have to play 'Truth' with us. Then we can decide about you, if selling you what is now a Schedule 1 substance is worth the risk."

"I see." I was worried now, because I assumed, from what little I knew about Terry, that the test was some form of physical endurance or other type of painful initiation requiring strength or agility; and I would obviously fail.

"So you want to do this?"

"Yeah," I said. "When can we do it?"

"How about this weekend."

On Saturday night I knocked on their door, but I was too early. I could hear a strange electronic drum-machine heavy groove totally outside my experience; it was seeping out from under the door. A voice, probably Terry's, said "come back later, man."

***

Sutra's recollection from all these years later, was that the music he heard was by the Microwave Prince (Le Petit Prince, the great Steffen Müller-Gärtner, the godfather of Trance). But my research shows that is impossible; the Microwave Prince was still a full eight years away. Such are the vagaries of memory. But we can be sure it was a primal techno beat that echoed what was to come in the future. - DRS

***

I had nervous dinner and then saw Terry and Mike come down the front stairs. Terry came over then. "Hey man," he said. "We're going out for a bite, but when we come back then we can play 'Truth.' We need a private place for that. Have you ever been on the roof?"

The fact is I had not. When they got back we went quietly up to the third floor. No one was about at that moment. The way up to the roof is by a vertical wooden ladder that is bolted to the wall. I'd seen it many times; it was near Cindy's single, actually. So I knew it. But I had never been up it. You had to climb about twelve feet up, and then go out through an access panel hatch at the top, which was locked. But Dix had the key.

"So tell me, Mike," I said conversationally, "how'd you get that key?"

"From Stan," said Dix. "It's kind of like a legacy. Stan got the key from Foster's brother, who graduated four years ago. And when Stan moved out, he gave it to Terry."

This made sense, because I remembered that in the summer term, when Stan had been working on a few things for the house, he had taken a room as part of the compensation for his labor, and sometimes slept under the stars with his cool girlfriend Mira on a futon. I'd seen them on the front porch one or twice. But I also remembered seeing them dragging the futon up the stairs in the direction of the third-floor landing. But I didn't know anything about the key.

Dix went first and did the honors, and I clamored up onto the roof, then, and was stunned at the view. It was fantastic! The sun was beginning to set. Terry came up last, and then we all took a minute. "Damn!" I said. "This is magic."

"Yeah," said Terry. "That's why we keep it locked. Come and sit down over here, Sutra."

There were some milk crates on the far side. The roof was just an ordinary tar-papered flat roof, with here and there a vent, with sides that were knee-high and tar-papered as well. But it had been partly covered in a sort of lattice deck—I sensed Stan's handiwork—and this meant less damage on the tar paper. There were no rails.

It was Dylan's Eugene Skyline all the live-long day.

"What was that music I heard at your door, Terry?"

"Oh that? That's Techno. They play it at Raves. All-night dance parties. You're not quite ready for any of that yet, Sutra."

"No, I suppose not," I said.

So we sat on the crates. I said, "Terry, Mike told me there is some kind of test. But I'm not exactly in the best physical shape. In fact I'm a total gimp."

They laughed. "It's not that kind of test," he said. "And it's not really a test, it's just a game."

"'Truth.' Yes, I heard. What is that?"

"What is 'Truth?' Well, it's just Truth or Dare but there's no dare."

"So you're saying, you ask questions and I tell the truth?"

"Sure. But first we take E."

"Ah." I realized now that I was in a little over my head. I was thinking it was Connor who was going to be the 'guinea pig' as it were, with this new mystery substance. But now, it was me. I was the guinea pig.

"Don't worry, Sutra. As far as we can tell it's relatively safe."

"Is it like acid?"

Terry and Mike looked at each other. "No, I wouldn't say so. You've dropped acid, have you?"

I wanted to say, "of course," but I was trying to stick very strongly to the truth. So I said, "No, I just hear things. You know how it is." Which I'm sure came out about as pretentious as it sounded. But they didn't care. Mike was getting out a film canister from his pocket, and I noticed Terry had come prepared with some Gatorade. We took the pills—they were small gelatine caps with a white powder inside. The Gatorade tasted as bad as I remembered. Dix laughed. "So you're not a big Gatorade fan?"

I then told the story of the first tasting, where one of the football players tries Gatorade and spits it out, and then tells the inventor 'this stuff tastes like piss,' and they laughed. And Terry said, "is that a true story?"

"It is," I said. "It happened in 1965. It's on film, actually, they were recording the first tasting."

"I think I knew about that. But how," said Terry, "did the guy know what piss tasted like? That's what I really want to know." We all laughed.

We chatted for a while and Terry asked me some questions about Rajneeshpuram. I didn't mind. He actually asked interesting questions, the important stuff like where we peed and if we slept in some sort of communal bunkhouse, or had our own rooms, and not about sex parties or something absurd. And I explained that things were pretty good until the busses of street people were brought in from all over the country, and the street people were exactly what you would expect and did all the wrong things, which destroyed the community. But before that it was just very loving, kind sannyasins trying to build an intentional community.

"Do you regret going there?"

I was going to answer, but I stopped. "I think something's happening."

"Yeah, you should start to rush pretty soon. Just stay calm. If your jaw gets tight, massage it a little bit and have more of that stuff that tastes like piss."

I nodded. "So...anyway, to answer your question, no, I don't regret it. I always wanted to be a monk. From the time I was little. You see, I watched *Kung Fu*."

Both Mike and Terry immediately grinned. "Ah," said Terry. "Now we're starting to get somewhere. *Kung Fu*, that was the best thing on television. I don't even understand how it got made."

"Pure magic!" said Mike.

"Right," I agreed. "Yeah, I have no idea. But that basic idea of just wandering around and doing interventions and being a monk. That was so cool. Suddenly I knew what I wanted to be. But of course, I was 9."

Now Dix, who was clearly starting to come on, chimed in. "That was such a great program, man! But think about it, what if Master Po had never been killed? Caine's life would have been completely different."

"And boring as hell," said Terry.

"Exactly. It was only because Master Po died, that anything interesting happened to him."

"That's true," I said.

"So are you into Karate or martial arts, then?" said Mike.

"No," I said, "sadly no. I was coming to it from the perspective of the Eastern religions—from Zen."

"So you like Zen, huh?"

"Yeah. I like Zen."

"Are you feeling it now, Sutra?" said Mike.

"Yeah."

Terry suggested we stand up a bit and stretch. "I'm kind of scared of falling off this roof," I said.

"Then don't fall off," said Terry.

"Right." I looked at them and realized that they were pretty good guys. "You know, Terry, the truth is I have not paid much attention to you guys. But I now see that I was missing something."

"That's good, bro," said Terry. "But mainly it's just the E talking. Do you feel up to playing Truth?"

"Yeah man, I'm into it," I said. "It's not like I've been untruthful to you, actually, as we've sat up here."

"That's good. So, tell me. Did anything ever happen in your life that you were embarrassed about?"

"Yeah, man. Lots of things."

"What do you think was the most embarrassing thing? Don't lie, because we'll know."

"The most embarrassing? I guess there's a lot of embarrassing family stuff, but that wasn't me directly."

"Sure, that's pretty normal, most people have stuff like that."

"But you mean, me personally."

"Yeah."

"So how does this work, do I get to ask you questions too, or just me gets to bare his soul?"

They laughed. Terry said, "You can ask. But you have to answer a Truth question first. This is on your dime. You want something from us. So you must demonstrate your character. Truth."

He said this expansive sentence like a demi-god speaking to mere mortals. The task before me, then, was to rise to the occasion, like an oath-taker before a sacred altar.

I sighed and thought about it. Suddenly I knew exactly what I had to talk about. And it was a doozy.

"OK," I said. "Well, young Robert Gray—I'm going to tell the story in the third person, is that all right?"

"Sure man, that's very cool. Very creative, don't you think, Dix?"

"Absolutely."

I was not convinced Connor was worthy of this humiliation. However when I thought about Connor I remembered suddenly that I loved him. It was like a truth to itself. "I have to tell you first, that I love Connor. He's my brother in arms. I mean he's very different from me, but he's got a good soul. It's just underneath all these layers of mind and cynicism and sarcasm. And he's drowning in that. He's drowning in mind and matter. I really wish I could help him. I wanted to get that out of the way. To make it clear what this is about. It's him that wants the pills."

They nodded. "Go on," said Terry.

"So little Robert Gray, he used to rummage through his mother's things. His mother is divorced, and there's no father in the house at the time. And he finds something in her drawer."

"Yes?"

"It's a feather duster. Soft and frilly on the front end, with a round and knoblike handle."

"Ah." Terry was smiling. "I think I know where this is going."

"You could put it that way. And so little Robert takes the feather duster and goes into the bathroom, where he's supposed to be taking a shower, and he turns on the shower and then instead of going in, he uses the feather duster on himself. You know, on his little penis. And then, when he starts to feel really good, something different, a feeling like he has not had before, something big starts happening, and it just feels so incredibly good that he can hardly stand up, when he decides to put the knob end into his rear. I think he finds some lotion to help with that. He's just got the feather duster handle lodged in, far up his rectum, when suddenly the door bursts open. It's his mother. She doesn't even knock. I should explain, this is her ensuite. So it's not that strange, probably she wanted a hair-band, something from the drawer under the bathroom sink. And she sees what he's doing. But *he* doesn't see her. He's too busy with all these new feelings and sensations with a feather duster stuck up his ass. But then suddenly he sees her, not directly, but he sees her angry face in the mirror."

'What are you doing!' she says. 'That's my feather duster! Why is it stuck up your bottom?"

And then little Robert says, he tries to lie his way out of it, see—he says he wants to use the duster on the cabinet in there. Or something. But she knows he's lying. His story is completely absurd.'

"This is good!" said Terry. "Oh man! So what happened next?"

"Well, little Robert dislodged the feather duster from his rear and let it drop to the floor, like a sad, dead bird, and stood small and naked in front of his mother. She pointed at the offending dead thing on the floor. "Give me that!" she demanded. He slowly bent over and picked it up and then handed it over. She left, closing the door, to wash it off or disinfect it, or something.

Then little Robert did what he was supposed to be doing, he took a sad shower, tried to wash his little bottom, which now felt strange, dried off and got dressed, and went out the bathroom to find his mother sitting on her bed, crying. And then when she looked at him, he just kind of knew. She had seen him do something terribly sinful. In her mind, obviously, this was a bad-bad. Way beyond the pale."

"And so what did she do then?"

"His mother? She didn't do anything. She just looked hurt and angry. And then over the next few hours, she would castigate him, complaining that he was so much like his father, who she had recently divorced. A sicko. Someone broken inside. And Little Robert Gray knew she had now changed her feelings towards him. Inside her a window pane had shattered. She never looked at him in quite the same way after that."

"Was she aroused; you think?"

"Impossible. She was just so deeply disappointed. Disappointed, I think, that men are the way they are, that even her little boy was suddenly like that, was growing up, was one of them."

"So what did little Robert do then?"

"Well we—he and his mother—had a few difficult days after that. He started spending a lot more time outside to avoid her, when formerly he was always inside and hanging out with her and watching the TV. But eventually we all move on, I think. Everything does. So, anyway, that was the most embarrassing thing to ever happen to me. I hope you enjoyed my reenactment. Maybe we can get it onto PBS."

Terry and Mike clapped.

"So, you got anymore?" said Mike.

"What, anymore of the most embarrassing things? God I hope not."

"Were you, like, abused and stuff? Because I was."

"No, nothing like that...." I was feeling the full effects of the drug by that point. "God this stuff really rushes. I don't know if I can talk. My jaw is tensing up."

"Yeah, it can hit hard. Just rub your jaw for a bit. Do you want to stop?"

"No, I can hang in there I guess. You guys are really all right. I didn't realize it till now."

Bradman wanted to discuss something and made a point to be casual about it. "Have a drink of this Gatorade. By the way, are you and Cindy together?"

"No," I said, "not at the moment. Why do you ask?"

"I just wondered if you knew."

"Knew what?"

They looked at each other. "I guess the question is, what *do* you know?"

"Gosh, guys. This is not very fair. I love Cindy. I love her. That's, you know, that's probably all I'm going to say about her. If that's a problem for you, well, you can both fuck off."

"Whoa, slow down. It's fine. I see how it is. So, you LOVE her. That's big."

"Yeah. Kinda feels big."

"And she knows this?"

"Yes. She knows."

"Did you maybe want to know any stories?" said Terry. "I mean, about her past. I'm not going to be mean. Just things that we were aware of. Stuff gets around. If not, that's OK."

"I have a feeling what you're going to say is there's a lot of guys at Campbell Club who have 'known' her, but in the biblical sense."

They both laughed. "Yeah. That's about right."

"But I don't care about that." I said. "I mean, I'm lying in the sense that I do care, but I had an experience—an awakening—about that. And I realized that I don't care in some cosmological sense. In the big picture, she can love me back or not, but that doesn't change anything from my point of view."

"Hey, that's cool." Terry seemed satisfied. "That's very admirable. I'm impressed, actually. Well, if you want the 411 later, I don't mind giving you the details. But I see that you are really serious about her. Or at least, you think you are."

I didn't say anything, and so we moved on to other things. I asked Mike about his bad experience, because it seemed he wanted to share. It was the usual stuff. Apparently nine out of ten American families are perforated by incest, child abuse, or drunken shitfuckery. The more 'religious' the household, the more toxic it turns out to be when the covers are pulled back.

"Well, this is the Kali Yuga after all," I said, by way of explanation. And Terry told some stories about Outward Bound, how it had changed him forever for the good due to the extremity of it. He said he was never afraid of anything after that experience, not even death. He also talked about his father. I had imagined him as a typical American Dad—that is, an abusive asshole, and Terry pretty much confirmed what I imagined. Then Terry said they needed to leave. Achilles had plans. "Party crashing. Yeah, there's some frat boys we want to fuck up tonight." And so we said our goodbyes.

***

A few days later Mike dropped by our room. I was out, but Connor was able to buy a couple of doses. "Sutra checked out. So normally, just go through him," is what Dix told him. When I came back that evening, I was a little disappointed that he had bought just two doses—one for him and one for Janet.

"It happens to every dude eventually, my dude. Paul has to give up his unconscious homosexual attachment to John, due to Yoko coming onto the scene. Don't worry, you'll get over me."

"That's all right. Well, have fun. You can tell me all about it." I didn't tell him that I had already had the experience, though, or what it took to get where he now was.

"Janet says it's supposed to be really intense."

"I'm sure it is. Bring water. And stay hydrated!"

"Yes, Dad," he said.

Connor shuffled off to his girlfriend's place for the weekend armed with the pills in a little black plastic film container and came back on Sunday morning with a story about a mind altering, soul-changing experience.

"Connor!"

"Dude! It was nuts. I don't think I can even put it into words. I'm still trying to get a handle on what happened—I feel different. Changed."

"Was it good?"

"Yeah. Yeah. It was good." He sat down on the bed. "But, first I thought we had got ripped off. It's in capsule form, see, a white looking powder. We both took the capsule at the same time. After about half an hour, it seemed like nothing had happened. But then Janet started to get happy. She was smiling and talking about how good things were between us, how she was so happy I came along. She took her top off. She has such an amazing rack. Anyway, I was really bummed out because nothing seemed to be happening for me. I didn't even think what was going on with her was Ecstasy. But then I started to feel it. It was like a rush. A really hard rush. My mind was going a mile a minute, or maybe time slowed down. My jaw started to clench hard. I was beginning to freak out. But then a wave of what I can only describe as complete peace came down over me like a lid. I felt like Janet and I were in a spaceship or something, traveling together through time and space. And she stood up and wanted me to stand with her, and we did some yoga stuff—she loves to do yoga, I thought that was all bullshit but she asked me to do it with her, stretching, and then, suddenly, I was like 'this is amazing!' and she asked me to do this yoga pose where we were leaning together, I can't describe it. It was a trust thing. And suddenly I trusted her completely, and I told her that, and she said the same to me. And we hugged and held each other and had this moment and we went for a walk and looked at nature. Everything was—it was like turning holy. And we were not wearing clothes, it was out past the foot bridge, you know where I mean. Adam and Eve. I think we looked at flowers and trees and bugs, and I looked at her, of course, because she is a real looker, for about an hour. And then suddenly I wanted to go to the Ceramics Shed. God I was desperate to be creative. And she felt it too, and we both went. Man was it a gas."

"Did you try to have sex? Out in the woods? I've heard that can be fun."

Connor looked at me strangely. "Dude! No way man. Outside? No way." Connor laughed. "I think that would have been impossible anyway. I can't imagine getting an erection under the influence of that stuff. But the fact is I didn't even want to. I was so into Janet at that point. It's Love, man! It's like the love drug. But you come down hard."

I digested this information over the next few days, and I watched Connor closely. He definitely wasn't making this up, something had happened to him, something big. And as the days went by he seemed subtly changed.

For example, one morning he went into the dining room, looked at all the tables, and then started systematically folding them up. (They were metal folding tables with Formica tops, if that helps here). He folded up all the tables in the dining room except one and then went up and got this incredible ceramic pitcher that he had made, it was a full-sized pitcher, like something from an Italian painting, and then gathered flowers and put those into the pitcher and placed it on the lone table. And then he sat at the table and read a book.

These aesthetic moments were a function of the drug. However, I knew that creativity is from the god, and enthusiasm, taken literally, means 'en theos,' that is, "in the god." It was Bob who had told us about this way back in the Pontifex-making class, where we learnt about creativity by doing rather than talking about it.

So Connor was in the god in that moment, and doing it, living the Creative; and if that was all that the drug did, then maybe that was all right. Maybe what we had done was useful, in some small way, and not a gigantic mistake. But I don't think Bob would have approved of us taking Ecstasy.

Anyway, I was not deeply concerned about Connor's transformation or that his behaviour was out there; we were all a little out there by now, the collective consciousness was engaged. Leo had been seen taking E; and so had Stan Harmon according to little Karen Tamlen. Rachael was entirely against it; but Eva, still fresh from her first experience with the Reefer

Madness, now wanted to jump to something stronger. (I thought that unwise, and I said so.)

The only problem, what worried me, was that he, Connor, wanted more. He wanted to do it again as soon as possible—for me to get him more pills. I didn't think that was a great plan, and I said that. "Less is more. Try to absorb what you have been given," and noises like that, which he took as ridiculous drivel. He left $40 dollars on my desk with a note that said "more."

***

A few weeks of weirdness passed by and a thought—it was more of a fantasy—kept recurring in my mind. I am ashamed, actually, to admit what that fantasy entailed.

It occurred to me, one day as I was watching Connor, who was now quite emotional and not his usual acerbic self, that if only I could get Cindy to take this love drug, perhaps if we could do it together, then she might come to love me the way that I wanted her to. *It may change her*, I thought, *in a way that I could benefit from.*

However, I understood myself well enough to know that this idea was both selfish and borderline criminal: using a drug to alter someone else's feelings for gain was an immoral, probably even evil, thing to do. How in God's name could I even think like that? Was I so craven and disgusting? Yes, it seemed that was true.

Thus, it was a real conundrum when Cindy came to me and asked about Ecstasy. Apparently others were starting to take notice of 'the Experience,' as it was being called over there. It was happening at the Annex; but she didn't feel comfortable asking for drugs there;

for some reason she thought I was the right person to ask. "But why me?" I had said. "Because I trust you," came the response. I was gob-smacked, my mouth hanging open. It was like that scene in *Animal House* where Pinto's 13-year-old date passes out, and the angel and devil stand on his shoulders; he has to decide between fucking and sucking the girl, on the one hand, and being a good person, on the other—taking her home, keeping her safe.

Except in my case, this was not a 13-year-old girl and not someone I met casually in a grocery store. This was (in my own private, completely twisted fantasy) my absolute soulmate, the regular object of distraction as I sat in class day-in and day-out listening to nonsense and absorbing useless factoids about Homer or Guy Maupassant. Only Cindy made sense; only Cindy mattered.

Of course, this tissue of nonsense and fantasy had nothing to do with the real person who was Cindy Sterling, which I also knew. I was not stupid. I understood what had happened that day at the Annex when we were in the hot tub, and the things which happened later, were exactly as she had advertised. Her Zazen moment with me had passed. Now was a new moment, a new guy. I knew the truth, the whole truth, and nothing but the truth. But such are the obscene joys of *Maya*, and the darkness of *Saṃsāra*, that illusion almost dominated and blinded me. I almost succumbed. It was only with great effort that, at last, I could do the needful. *I will tell her*, I said to myself. *I'll tell her everything. And she'll never speak to me again.*

"Cindy, we have to talk. You have to understand something."

"Yes, Sutra?"

"The truth is that I had thought to dose you with this stuff to make you love me. I know. I am ashamed of it. I don't think I can possibly help you with this, when I had—have—those kinds of thoughts in my head. I am a bad person. I am no friend of yours. For that I am deeply sorry. I think you should discontinue our friendship."

Cindy gave me a rather hard stare and sat thinking.

"Good Lord." She sat for a while longer. "You know, Sutra, I was wondering if I could be allowed to call you Robert. What do you think? Since we're getting to be so very friendly and all."

"Yes," I said, "You may call me Robert. That is the name my mother and father gave me. It is actually the name of my father's best friend."

"Well then, Robert, you said that you loved me. And I 'love' you too (here she used air quotes). But you have to get past that. I'm with someone right now."

"You mean, that you have a regular boyfriend?"

Cindy looked at me and I could see she wanted to laugh but held that back, like a teacher speaking to a five-year-old in a way a child can understand. "Something like that. The point is, I can't be what you want. That is impossible. It will always be like that. I can never, ever be what you want." She actually filliped me on the forehead then, with her middle finger, quite hard, to punctuate the fact that she was serious.

"Ouch! Yes I know that. You don't have to take out my third eye."

"So this news you were scheming—"

"No, no!" I said, already denying everything. "It was just a fantasy. A bad idea. Are fantasies illegal now?"

"No," she said. "OK, I get that. Fantasy is fantasy. But if it was just a fantasy, why can't you help me?"

"Fine. Tell me what you want from me."

"I want you to be my friend."

"Yes, so you have said. OK, friend. What do you need?"

"Well, can you hook up Jay and I with this stuff?"

"This Jay—that's the guy you're with now?"

"Yes."

"What's he like?"

"Are you sure you want to go there, Robert?"

"Of course, it's fine," I said. I was lying, though. Instantly I hated Jay, who was clearly a rat-fucker. But out loud I said, "Maybe I'll be meeting him sometime. I'll want to know."

"It's true, if there's a party this term at CC we'll certainly be here for that. He's just a guy at the Annex. I like him. He's good in bed. His penis is a little weird though."

"What?"

"Well, he has one of those banana dongs." She was tittering over it. "His dick is big but it's like, skewed. He's built very well, his body is all muscles, but his penis is *bent*. Your penis is really nice, Robert. By comparison, I mean. Your penis is really nicely formed. I told Jay that."

"You actually said that to Jay?"

"I sure did. Any girl would be happy to have it for company. Eva for instance."

I sighed. "All right, stop trying to cheer me up. So...I think it's twenty dollars a dose. At least that's what Connor paid."

"Oh, Connor's into this? I didn't know that."

"He did it with Janet. About a week ago."

"You helped him score?"

Reluctantly, I answered. I explained a little about the test, and what I went through to get the stuff. That Mike Dix was in a chemistry crew of some kind.

"So you did it? You've done it already?"

"Yes."

"I thought so! And? Is it a love drug as they say?"

"You had best come to your own conclusions. We can talk about it after."

"How about Connor and his friend?"

"Well, you could talk to him. I don't think it's a secret. But to be honest I think it's transformed him. He's a lot more open suddenly. He cried the other morning listening to Joan Baez."

Cindy laughed. "You gotta be shitting me!"

"I shit you not."

"What was the song?"

"*The Night They Drove Old Dixie Down*." I was stone-faced; but then we both broke out laughing.

I think I loved Cindy more in that moment than I ever did later. She had forgiven my sin; more than that; my sin had barely even touched on her. It left no mark. Everything that I wanted as a despicable craven, my worst and most shameful secret fantasy, was known now, and out in the open; I was naked, or worse, arrayed like a clown dressed in a suit of ridiculous clothes before her judgmental eyes; and yet she passed on it.

***

So it happened that I was able to procure some of the stuff from Mike Dix for Cindy Lou Who. Cindy of the big bent penis. But I bought three pills, not just the two. So I was still scheming. I knew it was wrong, but I just couldn't help it.

***

So now we can connect back up to the moment when I encountered Carrie Anne Kyber. You see, when I came through that front door, Cindy was with me. In fact, she was pretty high, too. I had taken her away from the Annex, we slipped out, because it turned out that Jay was not that interested in drugs. So Cindy wanted me to do it with her.

Yes, I know.

We took the pills and I suggested we should go back to the co-op. But she didn't want to go immediately. We spent some time in the kitchen and I met a few of the Annex crew. But then the drug started to come on.

'Damn,' I thought. This was a stronger rush and felt different than when I was with Terry and Mike.

Cindy was apparently coming on too. She was talkative, even voluble, which of course for her was unusual. She put her hands on her torso and felt herself here and there, finally testing her crotch. "I'm numb, Robert. I don't think this is working. Love drug? It's no such thing!"

For my part I kept blathering on about absurd things like my misplaced adoration of Osho the con-man, and my secret fantasies about the Trinity.

"What's the Trinity," she said.

"That's what I call you, Rachael, and Eva. You are the Trinity Friendship, the power trio of the Campbell Club. Or at least you were."

"Sure. I like that. Power Trio. Yes, I still hang out with them both, especially Rachael. She's got such a nice rack; did you ever see it?"

I suddenly became bashful. "Well, I—we did go skinny dipping."

"Oh, that's fantastic. You saw her in the nude, out in nature. Oh I'm so jealous. She's like a statue. Did you do more than that? Did you touch her?"

"No, no way."

"You should have. You don't realize how much she likes you. She likes you a lot, I'm sure you could fuck."

"Oh, no way!"

"Yes way. Just normalize a little. She's a bit more traditional. You could have Eva too, but you'd have to listen to her blather on for hours!" And then Cindy started laughing. "She's such a tease. But really a dance tragic. She's all black swan inside."

"And what about you? What are you like inside?"

"Oh, me? I'm just a normal person, I guess. I feel like I'm 30 years old, though. Sometimes I think other people, especially guys, are so childish, it makes me laugh. The world is so vast, life is beyond all our imaginings. Have you ever surprised an Emu mother with her babies running in the bush? Have you gone down into a cave with ancient rock art? Aboriginal stuff? You have no idea. You have no idea, Robert Sutra. It's all so deep, life is a well with no bottom. And the Campbell Club, it's deep, too. Oh Robert, all this chatter. That's not like me. I wish Jay would have been into it."

"So I'm a substitute?"

"No, no. By no means. But I'm with Jay now. We talked about this."

"I know. Old banana dong."

She laughed, then, and I started in about God and Jack Kerouac, and explained how I wanted to be a holy hermit and be free of desire and "live down on that island, you know, the one you can see from the foot bridge that goes to the Stadium. I have a recurring fantasy about it." And Cindy thought it was a great idea. "Oh definitely, I can see you doing that. Alone on your island in the middle of the stream. And then a big wave comes one day and washes you out to sea! So sad. In Sydney things like that happen. People get washed out to sea by the tide. As a child I saw that once. One of my little play friends was washed out to sea. He never came back. Never turn your back on the waves, Robert. Do you understand? Never turn your back! Hey, try to pay attention! I'm talking to you for once!" And she began laughing and hitting me, punching me like a boy. "The one time I try to talk to you, you completely zone out."

"Ouch, you're so physical!" I said.

"I am. I'm a material girl," and she laughed and sang the line from Madonna about being a material girl in a material world.

"Maybe dancing? What do you think? Not that I could do it with you, but you could move."

"Not right now, I'm in a funny place inside. This drug, it's making me feel things. Things I didn't expect."

It was clear something was happening with her. She was obviously rushing hard; her pupils were now fully dilated. Her face looked like an icon painted by Andrei

Rublev, the eyes glowing dark and sad. Perspiration glistened on her forehead; he cheeks were bright red.

"You remember, you said you wanted to trick me, to make me love you. Remember?"

"Yes. I remember."

"And now you have done it. You said it was bad but you did it anyway."

As she was talking, she reached out to me as if for support. "You thought this would do something to me. That it might change me. Didn't you? Well, I think it did. I think it did."

I didn't answer. I was suddenly broken now by the realization of what I had done. The bad thing I had schemed, that thing had eventuated, and I felt a terrible sense of guilt. The result was right in front of me. She was so obviously over the top rushing, her breathing seemed laboured and she was wheezing. It was wrong somehow. I had done this to her. It was like I had accidently shot a beautiful songbird; the bloodied remains were scattered all over the floor in front of me. Stupidly, I had killed the one thing I loved the most.

"Oh my God," I said. "I'm so sorry. I—that was so wrong of me. I'm some kind of monster. Oh my God." I was losing it. "I am really a bad person, you know? I'm a con-man." I must have stood up. I felt cold and unnatural, like a stone. I was crying suddenly, a sob came out of me. I think I was trying to leave. I was just suddenly so sad. But Cindy stopped me.

"No, no, Robert Sutra. Stop. Don't go. I do love you. I do. I really do. Come here." She was touching me now as if I were a child, pulling me away from the door; she wrapped her arms around me, like a blanket, but from the back, holding me. Not letting me leave. She spoke very softly into my ear, from behind, so that no one else could hear what she said. Because I probably have not explained but other people were present. This kind of "Experience" was going on fairly regularly and the Annex folks were almost used to this kind of absurd magic theatre. They didn't pay too much attention. Besides, there was a general sense of shared personal space and the residents at the Annex were all pretty cool. But now she was speaking very quietly; she knew this was something I would consider private and did not want to embarrass me any further.

"I do love you," she said. "I do. It has nothing to do with this drug. You did not need your plan; it was quite unnecessary. I loved you from that first day in the kitchen, you remember, back at CC, when you were acting like such an idiot and lying about being a writer, trying to impress me."

"You knew that?"

"Of course. And you remember how you used to come and just hang out in front of my room when my door was open, like a lost puppy. I used to open my door. I knew you would come. I loved you for that. But what I feel about you, it's not the kind of love you mean. It's not like that for me. I don't believe in that. But you do. For you, all those romantic ideas, it means something to you."

I wasn't sure how to react to that. But obviously, it fed into my general understanding that I knew very little about women and had a lot of prejudices and perhaps this was one of the corrections to my misshapen world view that I had to take onboard. Also, at least she did not blame me. That much got through into my seared brain. She was not angry. It seemed I was forgiven, and that was a relief.

***

After a while Cindy wanted to see Leo and Rachael for some reason. So then we started out for the co-op. I'm not even sure how we got there; perhaps someone gave us a ride. As the arc of the drug's effect accelerated, my attention was disintegrating into the overall hum of the universe. Obviously, that hum was some form of the higher power; but because I was high, because I had in a sense, illegally gained that music by cheating with a drug, it was discordant and out of tune. I could not take pleasure in it. Everything was vibrating and I was a vibration and Cindy was a vibration; we were all in motion amidst dancing light and bathed in a cacophony of sound. It all became a blur and then my next memory is we were going into the Campbell Club living room. When we got there, the door of the house was propped open, and like a breeze, we blew gently inside.

***

But I completely forgot about her. Cindy I mean. That was the remarkable thing, at least when I thought about it later. When I started interacting with Carrie Anne, there in the living room, all my attention went into her, and Cindy apparently paused for a minute and watched the encounter, or perhaps, the intervention, and then went her way into the dining room, unconcerned (because this was Cindy—she grokked that I was suddenly deep with Carrie Anne, and that was cool with her) and glided into the dining room where she started interacting with Leo and Rachael, who were having coffee and deep in a discussion about how to deal with Rob and the Deplorables. She asked them if it would be alright if she sat with them, explained she was high, and then said she wanted to take her top off. And she wanted them both to stand with her and talk about what the co-op experience had meant to them as they all looked out the dining room windows. Rachael then took her top off, too, exposing her breasts to the sunlight, and Leo undid his button down, exposing his bare chest, and they all held hands and reminisced.

So while all that was going down (and I would have killed to be there, what I have related is what Leo told me later), while that was on, I was locked eye to eye with Carrie Anne.

But Carrie Anne was delivering something that those kids could not give me; that much was clear.

I was looking into Carrie Anne's eyes and we just stood like that and I suddenly realized she was wearing a cross; that she always wore a cross.

"Are you a Christian, Carrie Anne?"

"So you noticed? Of course, silly."

"Have you ever seen a movie called *Chariots of Fire*?"

"No," she said.

"Do you mind if I tell you a story from that movie? Can we sit for a minute?"

"I guess. Go ahead."

I was going to go to a couch, because I thought I was going to pass out, but she just dragged me down to the ground and we sat on the carpet, Indian style. "OK," I said. "In this movie, there's a track and field team—it's the British Olympic track team. The year is something like 1920."

"Olympic team?"

"Yes." I thought that might engage her, and I was right. She pricked her ears right up. "There's an athlete on this team, he's a Christian, really seriously committed, and he doesn't want to run on the Sabbath—"

"Wait a minute, which denomination is he?"

"I don't know, Carrie Anne. I think he must have been an Evangelical of some kind, because his parents were missionaries."

"I see. Go on."

"And he is told he *must* run on the Sabbath, they demand he run, after has recently chided kids for playing football on Sunday. 'It is wrong to play sports on God's Day.' Does that make sense?"

"Yes. Yes, of course. It's like a test of faith."

"The day of the big foot race is fixed."

"Of course. He would not be able to change the day of the heat, if it was scheduled on a Sunday. He would not be able to run. So, what does he do?"

"Well, he finds a way to run in a different race—he refuses to run in his special event, for which he is well known, which is the 100-metre dash. This man has the reputation for being the fastest man in Scotland."

"Yes. A Sprinter."

"His friend, a team-mate, who already has a medal from a previous race, bows out of his own race, which I think is the 400 meters, so that this man, this man of god, can run in his place."

"A sacrifice! But that's not his event. How can he win? It would be impossible, I would imagine."

"Well, somehow he does. But now we get to the part of the story I wanted to tell you; the important part, at least to me. Listen carefully, Carrie Anne. You see, when this man runs, he feels the power of God inside him. And this is probably not accepted by his religion. In fact, it is basically outside of it. But that is exactly what happens to him. He *feels* God when he is running. He *feels* His pleasure. And so when he runs that race, he feels that power surging through him, and it gives him the strength to complete this incredible distance. I mean for him, the sprinter. He has the stamina, that extra something."

The expression on Carrie Anne's face was priceless. She was just kind of staring at me, stupefied, her mouth open. But she quickly rallied. "How? How did you know?"

"I want to know if this happens to you."

"But that's very personal. It's a private thing, Sutra. Like the bedroom."

"Look, I know that it might be. But I need to know if it was God who was talking just now. You know, when you intervened."

Carrie Anne stood up smoothly, her eyes still amazed, blinking like an owl.

"Help me up, Carrie Anne," I said. "My head is a little wobbly."

"Sutra. I can't lie. It's true that sometimes when I'm training I feel an inner power. That isn't me. It can't be!"

"When you were telling me about God just now— was that power doing the talking?"

She looked at me confidently. "Yes. I think so. Certainly."

"But Carrie Anne, listen. What am I supposed to do? I don't know what to do. I don't know where God is, so I can't get closer to him. You said, 'if I go closer to God, he will come closer to me.' Tell me what I am to do. You must!"

"Oh. Well that's easy, Sutra. Stop messing around and get your head together. God is in everything we do."

"But—that doesn't help me at all. I've been listening to shit like that for years."

"Everyone has something they care about," she said.

"You mean like a job?"

"Yeah but more than that. Don't you have a dream?"

I looked around, because I was starting the crash, and collapsed into the couch nearby. "I'm sorry, I can't stand up anymore. I don't think I have a dream. I'm not MLK."

"But how can that be?" Carrie Anne said, ignoring or not getting my reference. "My goal has always been there for me. I started thinking about the Olympics when I was four years old."

"Maybe you're just lucky."

"No. Everyone has this, I think. Maybe it's just hidden by, you know, your bad habits. You tell too many lies."

"Yeah."

"What is your dream, Sutra? Think!"

I sat thinking. I was still high but the rush was fading. It was like being splashed with a bucket of cold water, talking to Carrie Anne. God had spoken clearly to me, and I had to be honest. I was completely clueless how to do what had so clearly been demanded of me. I felt sick.

"I honestly don't know."

"Well, just keep thinking about it. Think hard. Not now, you're too messed up. Stop doing this stuff. This is so wrong, Sutra. God doesn't want that. You must stop."

"Yes."

"Tell me you will stop."

"I will stop."

"Good. Look, I have to go. I am already late."

"Thank you, dear Carrie Anne. Please go. I'll be fine."

She got up and walked towards the door and then looked back at me and pointed. "I'll be watching you, Mister."

I nodded. Then she left and I heard the big front door close behind her like a casket lid closing.

Part Five. In Which We Eat Pizza, Everything Comes Crashing Down, and the Green Revolution Begins.

"The butterfly's heart, confused by the colour of flowers in its dream."

—*Saigyō (1118–1190)*

I saw Napoleon Brown Jr. one last time in strange and wonderful circumstances. Leo had stayed in contact with him and had even been to his place, which was a very small, shared house over on Villard St. Napoleon had a bicycle and he often rode in the neighbourhood around Villard and East 17th. His small group of Rastafarians would picnic and nature worship in Hendrick Park. His good and kind personality manifested love all around, which translated into words of greeting and open friendship that helped the uneasy neighbours to get past his race and religion. For this is still Oregon, if you remember. One up from California, California's "younger brother," and the dumping ground for the homeless, for the map-impaired who got lost somehow and never made it home, and so ended up here.

On paper Oregon, like Washington State, and even some places in California, can feel 'progressive,' (whatever that means) but at bottom all the ugliness of America is still there, like blood on the soil that is slowly being eaten by maggots. No place is immune from the poisonous mind, from the grinding stone wheel of pain. You just have to give it a provocation, or maybe just be in the wrong place at the wrong time, and then things go off the rails.

Fall term was fast coming to an end, and Leo finished up in stages, as a man does who is dying. He gave away some of his things and did some preliminary packing, taking down objects from the plaster walls and looking at the voids that formed. He was seen talking with people who he ordinarily did not have much to say to, like Carrie Anne and Trip. He spent some time at Janet Smith house. Things like that. The only reason he had been hanging around, in truth, was to complete a largely meaningless course—ironically in music history and culture—that he needed for his degree. Then he would be a free man, a graduate. But he didn't seem so happy about it. One day I suggested we head down to Sy's New York Style and grab a pizza, and a few select people wanted to come along. Johan was going to be late but he said he'd meet us there. We walked. It was a glorious fall day and in Eugene the trees tell you the time of year. It was Leo's idea to invite Nappy, which he did by phone.

***

I should say a word or two about Sy's New York Style Pizza, which is a real restaurant (as most of the localities in this book are, or were, real). The pizza is thin crust, baked in an oven that has seen about a million pies, an oven blackened by time and use, and the sauce is about the best I've ever had. We were students, with no money, but somehow there was always a way and a time for a slice. The place itself is the proverbial hole in the wall, tiny, just a front counter with the big ovens right behind, and a few bar stools that hardly have any room, and where a mirror helps expand the space. I remember going in there and seeing sorority girls on a Friday night, observing themselves in that mirror, unbuttoning their tops by one or two buttons to reveal more skin, and checking their faces, to get ready for the night of hunting ahead. I remember the heat of the oven in the summer and the guys behind the counter, gnarled from their efforts, scorched and perspiring, as the big overhead hood fan hummed.

It's probably no longer true today, but back then, Sy's was known for sometimes accepting bud in lieu of money as payment for a pie. Please—if you are reading this, don't go into Sy's and offer to pay in weed. Oregon's 'experiment with legalization' is now over and the clampdown has returned. But I digress. We now return to our regularly scheduled programming, already in progress....

Yes, Sy's Pizza. Napoleon steps up the counter, offers a bud for a slice. "What do you say, man?"

The guy at the counter nods and says, "show me." And Napoleon quietly produces a small baggie with some very tasty looking buds and passes it over. "Have a small smell of dat." And the pizza guy is now grinning; his eyes light up. "One of these? The big one?"

"Sure, my man."

"Well, for that you get a whole pie, not just a slice. With pepperoni and pineapple."

"Leave di pepperoni, man, but I'll take di pineapple," Napoleon said, in his best Rastafarian.

"You got it."

And everything is going well and Leo and I are sitting waiting for him and quiet, we laugh, and we're all just minding our own business. But some frat boys have observed what happened at the counter, and they feel like making trouble. They stand out in the crowded little place. I see them leaving, snickering and pointing with their baseball caps on backwards, and I nod at Leo, who doesn't look. We're used to stuff like that. But these jerks go back to their frat house and one of them calls the local PD to make a complaint. "Some nigger is buying a pizza with marijuana.... Yeah, pepperoni and pineapple and everything. No. He's selling weed. No, we didn't buy any...." And we've not got too far into some of the best pizza on the west coast, when we see a squad car's lights flashing outside. The cop, who looks young, almost as young as we are (but we feel old) parks obtrusively so he's partly blocking traffic, causing problems for others just trying to go about their day, and making a scene.

Gets out his baton, because, obviously, any black kid is a threat. And his aviator glasses are kind of silly.

He comes in and has Napoleon stand up. "How'd you get that pizza?"

Napoleon says, "uh, di usual way. By ordering? Would you like me to demonstrate?"

And the cop reacts poorly, takes off his aviator sunglasses, and says "Not funny. Turn around," and proceeds to put handcuffs on him and then pat him down aggressively. Trying to get something to shake loose. But Napoleon has put the weed where the cop doesn't think to look. It's up in his cap.

"Hey, what are you doing?" says Leo.

"This is none of your business," says the cop, and marches Napoleon out onto the street. Leo and I follow. The cop says, "No, you two go back inside." I go back in, but Leo continues to ask what the problem is, and the cop starts to become belligerent. "If you don't back off, I'm going to arrest you, too."

"For what," says Leo.

"For interfering with an officer."

"That's nonsense. This is my friend; I invited him to have pizza with us. You can't just go around putting handcuffs on people without cause. You haven't even asked anyone any questions. Are you new to this job or something?"

The cop then gets on his handset and calls to his comrades, "I need back up! I need backup! Locals are obstructing."

He then puts Napoleon against the wall and tells him to stand there facing the wall and orders Leo once more back into Sy's. But he doesn't go.

At this point, stories may diverge, but what I remember is Leo getting the baton thrust into his chest. A good hard nudge, so to speak, and he's knocked back. "move!' says the cop. And this is right around the time that Johan must have come on the scene, because he saw the cop hit Leo and that put him into a cold rage. All the times he's seen cops do the wrong thing at The Riviera, or around town, everything he's read about policing in Oregon, it all seems to be confirmed now.

By this point the cop is starting to lose his cool. He's feeling he needs to gain control at all costs. He pulls Leo to the ground roughly and cuffs him, so that he's lying face down on the concrete sidewalk, pats him down, and then tries his radio again to see if he can get more cops to come and help him manage the situation he himself has created.

Suddenly the cop notices the lights on his squad car have gone out. Someone must have cut the engine. By the time the cop is up from cuffing Leo, he sees Johan standing near the car, his arms crossed. Not in the car, but nearby. And he's got a big smile on his face.

"Hey, what the hell are you doing?" says the cop.

Johan stands his ground and says, all innocent, "Nothing. Standing on a public street."

The cop is now locked out of his own squad car, and still no backup. He instinctively checks his pocket, because the car is not running—*did I turn it off?*"—and because he suddenly realizes his keys—*wait, the keys!*—are not in his possession. And at this point he does something that he probably should not have done, he draws his gun. Points it at Johan. "Put your hands up!"

Johan complies.

This is the moment when the police Sergeant pulls up in his own squad car. Stops, sees his young officer with his gun out, one suspect against the wall, one handcuffed and lying on the sidewalk, and a third, very large and formidable looking man, his hands up, standing near the squad car, which for some reason is dark. No lights, no engine, and the car is blocking traffic on the right side of the street, so traffic is beginning to congest. People observing, honking, making gestures. He opens his own squad car door and gets out, as the young officer, seeing him, lowers his gun. Johan keeps his hands high but smiles and waves at a passing car.

"What have you got here, Chalmers?"

"I got a report of a black kid selling pot. That's him over there. And this one," here he points at Leo, "was obstructing. And now that guy, he stole my keys!" The young cop almost sounded like he was going to cry.

"Calm down, Chalmers."

"The Sergeant then goes and has a talk, first with Nappy, who says, "I was just minding my own business, sir. But respect, I and I don' speak to di police."

Then the Sergeant helps Leo to his feet. "So what's your story?"

"We were just eating some pie. This officer burst in and cuffed my friend here, he had no cause to do that, we were minding our own business. If this is some frat boy complaint, well, we get that kind of harassment all the time."

"Did you obstruct Officer Chalmers? Did you touch him or get in his way, block him?"

"No," says Leo. "I did ask him repeatedly why he handcuffed my friend, and I did refuse to go back inside when instructed. But I'm not a bystander. That's my friend, we're here together. If he's done something I'd like to know what."

By now the guy working the counter from Sy's has come out. He is still wearing his apron. He says hello to the Sergeant and they have a few words. "No, I don't know what happened, these guys were just eating a slice. They're local kids. Students."

Finally the Sergeant goes and talks to Johan. "You look familiar. Aren't you Johan?"

"Yes, hello Sergeant Benson."

"You're Thomas's friend, from over at the Campbell Club, right?"

"Yes." He points at Leo. "That's Leo Johansen. He's the Campbell Club house president. And Nappy—Napoleon—used to live in the house too."

"So you're all students?"

"Yes."

"And what's this about you taking Chalmer's keys?"

"Officer Chalmers needs more training. I saw him hit my friend there, Leo, with his baton, with no provocation. And then he pointed his gun at me—threatened me with lethal force. But he has no cause. He did not see me do anything."

"You're saying you didn't turn off his squad car? You don't have his keys?"

"I'm saying he needs more training. Ask him if he *saw* me in his squad car. Ask him if he has patted me down. Did he find any keys? Do I have his keys? I think not."

The Sergeant then talks to young Officer Chalmers. "Well, what about it? You drew your gun on this fellow?"

"Yes."

"Why?"

"I felt in danger. He has my keys. He was in my squad car!"

"Was he?"

"Sure. I saw him."

"Oh. You saw him."

"Yes."

"Chalmers, this is Johan Tunz. I know him. He's a student at the University. And he's very smart. Probably smarter than me, and definitely smarter than you. So I'm going to ask again. Did you actually see him in your squad car."

"No."

"So you made a mistake. You drew your weapon by mistake."

"But he *must* have my keys! Let me prove it!" And the young Chalmers rushes over to Johan and yells, "put your hands up! Now!" and Johan complies, doesn't complain, as the cop vigorously pats him down and finds—nothing. Absolutely nothing. And steps back.

"Officer Chalmers," says the Sergeant. "Get over here. This is what you're going to do. You're going to apologize to these three. You're going to cut the black kid loose. You can bust him for pot some other time. I see him around town on his bike. He's not exactly hard to find."

"But what about my car!" wails Officer Chalmers.

"I'll see if Johan has any ideas about your car. Maybe he saw who took your keys. From *your* squad car. Which is illegally parked at the moment, the lights off, siren off, and blocking traffic."

So Chalmers goes and uncuffs Leo and Napoleon and stiffly apologizes to them, as Sergeant Benson goes back to Johan, still standing, now with his arms crossed, over by Chalmer's squad car.

"Well Johan, Chalmers is very sorry for his mistake, and he will be apologizing to you in a moment. But I wondered if you can help us with the mystery of the missing squad car keys. Any ideas?"

"I would be happy to help. Yes, I saw a guy brush past me. I didn't get a good look at him. But I think while the officer was busy beating on a University student for no reason, this strange man ran up, turned off the engine to the squad car, and took the keys, and threw them as hard as he could up in *that* general direction— onto the roof. There—" Johan now points at the roof above Sy's façade. "It may take a bit of work to get them down. It must be embarrassing to lose control of a squad car."

"It's a bad look, to be sure."

"The Officer probably needs to learn how to look after his vehicle more closely."

"I agree. And he will. Thanks for helping on this. Please say hello for me to Thomas Pincheon the next time you see him."

"Very kind of you, yes, I will do that."

***

Now, some readers may remember that the Whole Earth Catalogue (which was basically our world wide web and internet before those things were invented, for those who don't know) has an entry somewhere that describes taking the keys out of a police squad car to deflate and disempower police if they go on a rampage. But at the end, that account admits it is fictional; aspirational.

However, I assure you, my narration here was not based on the fictional story in WEC. Everything in this novel is fiction, as even I am a fiction; but what Johan did that day is based on a true story. Perhaps he was inspired by the WEC; or perhaps he was the inspiration for it. I cannot say.

***

One night, it was quite late, Cindy came to the Campbell Club. She did the unusual thing of seeking me out. I was sitting in the kitchen and reading and Leo was puttering in the kitchen, possibly making a sandwich.

"Hi Robert," she said. "Hey Leo."

We both greeted her and I proposed she join us. I thought for a second she wanted to talk to Leo, as it was just about his last day at the Campbell Club.

"No," she said. "I'm pretty tired. I wonder, could we go up to your room?"

I looked at Leo, as if to confirm he didn't mind, and he shrugged, and I said "sure, of course." And then we walked up the back stairs.

Leo said later that, after about ten minutes, Shawn XXXXX, who had lived at the house a few years back, showed up in the kitchen. He burst through the swinging doors from the dining room. "Where is Cindy Sterling?" he demanded.

Leo observed that Shawn seemed to be 'drunk or on serious drugs.' His face had that look of the drunkard, the red somewhat pickled appearance of alcoholism; and his clothes were in tatters. He seemed seriously reduced from his former state. And Leo noted one more thing: he had an enormous erection; his trousers were bulging. It would have been funny, like in Aristophanes, except that he was deadly serious.

"Where is Cindy Sterling!"

"She's not here, man."

"But where is she?"

Leo tried a different tack. "She doesn't live here. Listen, do you hear? She doesn't live here."

"But I want her! Now! I want Cindy Sterling."

"You don't live here anymore, either, man. Please go. Go!" and Leo pointed with his hand, commanding him. But it was no use.

"Not until I find her!" he shouted, and he burst through the back kitchen door, intent on searching through the house.

***

It was a 'close shave,' so to speak. We got to my room only a few minutes before, unaware (at least I was unaware) of this hungry ghost running amuck.

Connor was there doing some study at his small desk. We came in and Cindy sat down on my bed. She seemed agitated, and I knew something was wrong, but I didn't want to question it. In that moment I was just happy she was there. So I just went along as if everything was cool.

However, Connor was quick to understand something was up. "Hey Cindy. Uh, did you guys want me to leave? I could go over to Janet's for the night."

"No, no, Connor," she said. "Don't go. Please. I want you to stay. Do you mind if we lock the door? I just want to hang out here with Robert, if that's OK."

Connor and I looked at each other, and I got up and locked the door. What followed was, we just hung out, and were quiet, doing studious things, like kids at a library. We didn't even kid around. Cindy didn't want to talk. Yes, it seemed like quiet was the required thing. She had a bag, really quite small, with a few toiletries, and pulled out a book: *Winter Season*, by Toni Bentley.

After a while, when it seemed like I should give her some space, maybe go downstairs, she said, "No, Robert, come and sit here. On the bed." And she did the strange thing of putting her hand on me, and pulling me closer, almost as if I were a pillow or a stuffed animal to comfort her. From that point on she wanted to keep physical contact, a hand, a foot, on me all the time.

I was fine with all that, of course. After the Ecstasy experience I felt changed. I didn't push back with people as much as before, I was quite a bit more trusting of the intuitive, and also more silent and introspective. I put up a note to myself next to my bed, that read "*Eat less, Sleep less, Talk less,*"[4] and there was also a drawing I had attempted on the magic day I was with Cindy, the day Carrie Anne—and through her, God—spoke to me. It was a small portrait of Cindy, about 2 inches by 3 inches, in pencil, on a scrap of notepaper. I had drawn it from life; something I don't think I could do again. She noticed it, and I thought maybe she was going to cry for a minute. But she didn't say anything.

"Robert, would you mind if I stayed here tonight? Just for the night. I need a place to crash. I don't want to go downstairs."

"I think that's fine," I said. Connor was already in bed, dozing, and we had the lights off; there was just a candle at that point. "Should I blow this out?" I said, as she started to get undressed. "No, Robert. Leave it until I'm in bed. Robert, we can't do anything tonight."

"Yeah, I know. I'm not a complete dummy."

She stripped down to her underpants and stood for a moment in the candlelight. She paused and seemed to look at me. Just for a moment I was reminded of her by the firelight in the living room, where I had failed so gloriously at copulation; but that time seemed like a million years in the past or in a different incarnation;

---

[4] It's from the Qur'an.

we were different people now. I don't know what was in her mind, and she didn't speak; she might not have been (as I optimistically or perhaps ridiculously imagined) giving me a "last look." Perhaps she was simply thinking of some distant time or some completely unrelated thing she had to do; she might not have been thinking about me at all; but there was no way to find out. What was certain was that her face had changed. She was sad. It was mostly in her eyes. I realized in all the time I had known her and all the different emotions I had seen on her face that sadness was never one of them. It was like sadness was a black liquid poison, a black oil, washing over a polished white stone; there was no way for it to get into the stone; sadness washed off her like water off a lotus leaf. Her positive nature had always been joyful and energetic. But now, the rock had cracked, there was a fissure, and black poison had found its way in. Now, it had taken hold.

She got into bed and we just sort of wrapped my blanket over us both and spooned. I blew out the candle and we were in complete darkness except for the tiny blue lights on Connor's stereo, and the radium dials of his alarm clock. Connor was out like a light, and his peaceful sleep was reassuring somehow: it seemed to imply sleep was possible, not just in theory, but in actuality.

I was not certain that would be true for me. I could hear Cindy breathing. I could not hear her heart beating (as Master Po would have wanted); but I could sense her pulsing form next to me in its totality; she was alive and present and so small somehow. I marvelled at it all, and I was as timid as a hunter stalking a rabbit for fear it would dart away. She did the extraordinary thing, then, of asking me to put my arm over the top. I had not had the temerity to do that. My back was towards the wall, and she was in front with her back to me, and we were both on our right sides. Our toes were touching. "Put your hand on my breast," she said. "It's not really spooning if you don't do that. It's OK, I want you to hold me."

I was definitely not going to say no to that. So we spooned, as she said, the correct way. As far as sleep was concerned, well, I was right, that was far away, but I didn't care. It was the one and only time. I kind of knew that, somehow.

After a while she very quietly said, "Robert? Are you still awake?"

"Yes."

"Is it true, what you said that day, when we were in the hot tub?"

"I said I loved you. Or words to that effect."

"Yes, you did. Were you really telling the truth?"

I said, "Yes." I sighed. "It's true. Maybe it's karma."

"You love me? For real?"

"Yes."

"Good," she said. "That's good." And then she was silent and seemed to be more at peace.

Later, perhaps around 2 a.m., she asked the same question. "Is it true?"

I said, "Yes. It's true."

"You love me?"

"Oh yes. You have no idea." I wanted to say a lot more, to keep talking, but she had taught me not to. I learned from her about the essential; the thing that does not get said and perhaps cannot be said; the thing behind the words and actions. That 'thing' was neither good nor bad, it was beyond judgement, beyond human understanding.

***

Regarding this repeated question, if I loved her, I think she asked this question one last time, or perhaps even more than once, perhaps many times, over and over, in the darkness that night. I passed in and out of the sleep stage, like a drunk with a hang-over. Frankly I was not used to having someone that close and I flop around a lot at night, but at some stage, you just sleep because you must. In that emptiness there is bliss.

Perhaps those additional questions and the answers I gave were merely in my dream, and never actually happened. But I think they were real. I want them to have been real.

***

In the morning I woke up and my room had one less body; Cindy Sterling was gone. It was still quite early; Connor was still sawing logs. I thought, maybe she's just gone to the toilet, but no, she didn't return. Her bag was nowhere in sight. I noticed that the small portrait I had made of her was gone as well. There was a void now on the wall with some bits of tape as the defining outline. Osho was also missing in action; but I had shitcanned his picture some months back. At the time, Connor had said, "Oh my, Sutra, I kind of miss it now. Those little beady eyes looking back at me."

"Good one," I had said.

I went down to the kitchen, thinking she might be having some breakfast, still hanging around; but there was no sign of her. The paper had come but it was wet from the rain, useless. I muttered and poked around and finally went back upstairs.

I'm not going to lie; I felt a little let down. I thought I at least rated a see-you-later. But that was how things were and I told myself, 'That's just Cindy. It's never going to be different. For ever and ever and ever that is how it is going to be. Some Nietzschean eternal return bullshit. What a hard karma.' But in truth I was happy to have been in the right place at the right time. Little did I know that it was the last time.

***

A few days later I was in the dining room and someone came in and said to the room generally, "Hey, is Sutra here?"

I put up my hand and said, "Yo, Kimosabe. I answer to that name."

It was a tall, handsome fellow, with significant upper body development, his chest sporting a white oxford shirt wrapped in a seersucker blazer, and matching slacks. His sharp crew cut was etched into sandy blond hair. He came over and held out his hand. "Jay Rodgers," he said.

"Jay. Welcome to our humble co-op home."

"Can we talk for a few minutes? Sorry to interrupt your dinner."

"Did you want something? Feel free to grab a plate."

"No, I need to get going soon. But I need to talk to you."

I was none too pleased about this. I didn't really want to be friends and buddies with Jay (which is pathetic, I know). I suggested we go out on the front porch, and he followed me out there.

"So, Sutra. Listen," he said. "I don't know what you've heard—"

"Probably nothing," I said. "Tell me everything."

"Sure. So Cindy and I met at the Annex, and we've been seeing each other for a while now. You knew that?"

"Yes."

I was thinking Jay was probably a Business major with a minor in Beach Volleyball. He had the build and the tan for it.

"I need to give you some news about Cindy. You see, she's left town."

I didn't say anything so he continued.

"What happened was—maybe I have to go back a bit. Cindy said she lived here a few years back, and she had a connection with this guy, who also lived here. And that guy wouldn't leave her alone—sort of a stalker type."

I nodded. "A 'connection.' Right."

"Yeah." Jay seemed uncomfortable, but he continued. "And this guy, he was the reason she left school for a while in 1985. She went back home to Australia at that time. So, anyway, after time had passed she tries again; comes back to Eugene. And for a while everything is good. But a few days back this same guy shows up at the Annex. He's drunk and belligerent. I wasn't there, but some of the other people were. I—I don't know what happened exactly."

"Are you saying she was assaulted?"

"Well, I don't know for sure. But what I do know was that we called the cops, and they spoke with her. I'm not clear on the outcome. But she left, she bugged out after that, I think she came over here."

"Was that on Wednesday? Wednesday night?"

"Yeah, exactly."

I nodded. "She did come over here. She stayed the night at the Campbell Club." I didn't say she stayed with me. For some reason I kept that private.

"Right, exactly." he was saying. "So that morning, Thursday, she came back to the house and collected her things, just a few bags, and left. I—I was out that night myself. She left me a note. And in the note she asked me, one of the things she asked was to come over and tell you what happened, that she needed to get out of Eugene. Apparently this guy is insane. Like, physical danger."

"Yeah, it sounds like it."

I realized my attitude towards Jay up to that point was totally wrong. Obviously he was a right guy to come over and talk to me. He was doing exactly what she asked; what a legitimate boyfriend who was not me, would have done. He was even trying to be a friend. In his own way.

"I realize this might be hard for you," he said. "Cindy thinks a lot of you."

"That's cool. I mean, that makes me feel good. Thanks for saying that."

"You know, she said something funny. I don't think I should repeat it but considering the circumstances. She said you had a really great cock."

"Really?" I said. "Well, that's a compliment."

"Definitely. She said it more than once. 'My friend Sutra, he's got a great cock.'"

He didn't say, 'and I wish yours was more like his,' which I already knew, I was 100% sure she had said exactly that. Because that was Cindy. But I didn't say anything like that at all. I tried to be human, to be what was expected of a human being in this situation, as far as I understood that species. "I appreciate you saying that. So, do you know where Cindy went? How to get in touch?"

"I have some ideas, but I'm pretty sure I'm not supposed to say. I think she just wants to go dark, if you know what I mean."

"Yeah. That makes sense."

"Yeah."

He paused and looked at his watch, which was the kind that can go underwater, a surfer's watch, probably a Seiko Chronograph. Very expensive. Not a Rolex; but I was sure that a Rolex was in the cards for someday. Out loud, I said "Look, I really appreciate you coming over. If there's anything you think I should do, please let me know."

And he said much the same. And then was on his way.

Later, when Leo explained about the return of Shawn XXXXX, and his physical appearance and obvious insanity, it all made sense. I felt ashamed that earlier, that morning, I was still irritated with Cindy for leaving the Campbell Club without saying goodbye. *I'm such an idiot,* I thought, once I understood.

***

I have put off talking about what happened to Connor and Janet because I felt ashamed about it for a long time. First of all, the *Summer of Love* had turned into "*The Fall*," as in the Fall of Man, because we all kind of agreed that Ecstasy had changed us and it was having a bigger impact than anyone had predicted. And then after the break we went into the "*Winter of Our Discontent*." But that was my own moniker, I did not share it with Connor and Janet. Leo was gone, and Cindy was gone, and things were changing.

Regarding the Ecstasy, I just didn't understand about that stuff. I thought the way all drugs worked was very much like alcohol: you drink it and have fun (or not) but then the next day you are hung over and then the day after that (at least for some people) you go do it again, because the effect is temporary. Of course over a long period of time, Alcohol changes and damages the body. If you drink a few beers, it's not like that keeps you drunk forever. Nor does it normally do permanent damage.

But with Ecstasy, it seemed like one or two pills did in fact change me forever. I had a few more, but that first pill, and what happened with the second, changed my personality. It was a side-effect, this change, and not the rush people were usually looking for. But the change was tangible and there was something dramatic about that; also something terrifying about people taking a drug that powerful for kicks.

That being said, we quickly learnt that a law of diminishing returns was in effect; people who kept dosing did not change more and more; and in fact what the drug did seemed to lessen in intensity with each dose. Obviously, one developed a tolerance quickly, and I didn't understand how Mike and Terry could keep taking it. For me, one dose was plenty and in fact, should have been enough.

But of course nothing is ever enough and everyone insists on burning their particular candle down to the bare stub, down to that little metal tag at the bottom, sputtering and flickering on the edge of disaster, until the flame goes out catastrophically, leaving that person in total darkness.

Connor was not one to listen. He wanted me to buy him more. And I didn't want to. I pushed back. He thought this was a betrayal, that I was keeping access to myself and for my own special use; when in fact Terry and Mike wanted to limit access to people they trusted, in part because they didn't want to get busted and put in jail, but also because they didn't want anyone to get hurt. Their method of testing using the "Truth" game was original, perhaps unique, but the purpose behind it was not incomprehensible. And Connor never did play that game. He was only 19.

The other thing that happened which I feel shame about was that Janet had started to get a little bored with Connor. He was experiencing his first serious love affair, while for Janet, there had been many affairs, many different lovers. She was 32. So it was natural that at some point she would start to change. What happened was that the Ecstasy changed her rather abruptly. As I have said, for Connor it was fantastic and then they had both "got creative," and went into the studio. For Janet, that time in the studio (and the subsequent come-down, the after-effect of the drug, which is intense and very much like depression) helped to make certain things clear in her mind:

Connor was too young for her; Connor was too attached. Connor was not going to be in the picture that much longer.

I learned these things later because, to my shame, I had a sort of affair with her. I say "sort of" because it was only a few quick interludes. OK, well, actually it was more.... It started out very innocently, because we three all hung out and I was even taking the class and so expected to be in the studio that one term. One day someone noticed a small bird, a finch with red feathers, was inside the studio, it was stuck inside with no way out. It had flown in through the open back door and now could not find its way, and was in distress. I put down some sunflower seeds from my lunch, and it came down and I was able to catch it. I carried it gently in both hands to the door. As I got there, Janet was coming towards the door from the outside, and I emerged at that moment. I was holding the bird. I opened my hands and it flew out skyward. "Dah-dah!" I said.

"It was like a magic trick!" She said to me later. That was apparently the moment when she shifted her attentions from Connor to me. The thing was, I didn't want that. It's not that Janet was ugly, or undesirable; far from it; I just didn't want anyone other than Cindy. (Of course, Cindy was completely unavailable and with someone else, and had explicitly told me she would never, ever, be what I wanted her to be; and then later she wasn't even in country, as far as anyone knew. So that was all fairly definitive).

Janet also was physically very different from the other women who were in my life or immediate environment and I admit a level of natural curiosity. As

I have mentioned, she was a mature 'Susan Sarandon' type. That is to say, she was formidable. In *Pretty Baby*, the protagonist is infatuated and obsessed with a 12-year-old girl being raised in a brothel; but it is the mother, played by Susan Sarandon, who is the true erotic interest from the point of view of a grownup male. Janet was a grad student, respected within the program by the professors, admired by the other grad students, creative, knowledgeable, and had her own working area in the main studio which even had a door. She had been known to ride a motorcycle; there were pictures somewhere at her place to prove this. Connor claimed it was a Bugatti. Which I found unlikely.

Not quite a Faye Dunaway (I would have been lost in that case) but a delightful second-wave feminist (Just as my dear Abigail was of the first wave) who was continually challenging all my biases about women: that was Janet. Abigail had broken me, in just a two-day span, of many of those absurdities. She had proven to be a better carpenter, a better cook, and a better lover, than I probably would ever be. But Janet seemed to want to break the rest of my assumptions.

"Sutra, come in here for a minute." Reaching for my belt buckle and pulling me close, she looked at my face and smiled. "Relax. This won't take long."

Rachael and Cindy could have been called 'girls' as in 'I went to get the girls." But Janet was no girl and could never be mistaken for one. And yet, she was not old, either. But she was too old for me. And probably for Connor, too. She belonged in a Dashiell Hammett story, maybe if Hammett were writing in the fetid gloom of the 1980s about a *femme fatale* who bonks two boys in the back of a Ford Pinto and then the damn thing blows up.

***

"My body isn't what it used to be," she sighed.

That day her corner nook in the Ceramics shop smelled of clay dust mixed with hints of blueberry and pine nut and coffee, fragrant like a wine. I was just sitting there like an idiot looking at her as if under a spell, because her tits were so fantastic under that tank top, while Connor wedged a 10 pound ball of clay in the other room. I could hear him working rhythmically at it. We both could. He had his Walkman on, too. Janet was reclining on an upholstered chair, her legs akimbo. Levis on a murder machine. Just all there.

"These are getting flat," she said, and grazed her breasts. It was like an Emmanuelle movie. She wasn't wearing a bra, and she saw me looking, grokking her form, and clearly didn't mind. She just smiled in that way that she had as her nipples hardened.

"They are real," she said. "No silicone here."

My mouth was little dry now. "I don't know, Janet," I said. "Those dodgeballs look like they can still bounce."

"Oh Sutra. You're such a con-man sometimes. But I see through it. You're a bullshit artist. Like Osho."

"Honestly, I've never seen...a rack like that," I said. "You might as well be Susan Sarandon."

"But these used to stand up." She lifted her breasts from underneath like bar bells, hefting them.

"See? Now they just sag."

"You're a goddess, Janet," I said, truthfully. "Maybe even a Faye Dunaway." I was having some difficulty with my nouns and verbs. My face felt hot.

"A Bitch Goddess, I think," she said. "Sarandon, I think is right. Not Dunaway. So you want to worship all this? Start our own little religion? Isn't that what you do with a goddess? What would Osho do?"

Faintly, I tried to answer. "I would need to, well, *know you* a little better, first."

"Oh really?"

"In the biblical sense."

She laughed softly. "Right."

"But what about—" I had tilted my head. I left the question hang.

"Let's find some time for your education. Sometime soon. I want to know you, also. Been dying to since, well, you remember the little bird?"

"That I let go?"

"That's the one. That was the moment. I have a little bird you can release, too. Have you seen *The Devil in Miss Jones*? You know that one?"

"Maybe," I choked out.

***

To call her "mature" would be an absurd euphemism, but that seems to be what I am left with. At 32 she was at the height of her sexual potency. We say, "adult entertainment" and it is another euphemism for sex. But "adult" surely could mean more than that. What is emotional life like for a 32-year-old woman at the height of her physical, sexual, and mental capacities? What does she experience? How does she see her world? What does she dream and fantasize about? And why would it involve younger men, boys as it were?

I wanted to talk about things like that, to learn the inner core of the woman, but it was never possible. Either Connor was near, or she was in the mood for attention and physical stimulation and we didn't even use words. In those moments, I was weak; pathetically weak. I was drawn like a tiger leech, eyes wide closed. Her secret self was hidden to me even as her intimate self opened out. That intimacy was a mask. The truth, I suspect now, is that I never really knew Janet at all.

What I believe she wanted from me, her fantasy love scene workout, was to arrange things in such a way that she could have us both. She wanted to reenact *The Devil in Miss Jones*, the scene where Miss Jones has two men at the same time, where they can feel each other as they penetrate her in two different orifices. That sounds absurd, I know, but she made jokes about it, talked about 'three' being a magic number, and so on. Those kind of hints.

But all that was impossible. I didn't want it, and Connor couldn't have dealt with it emotionally, it would have completely destroyed him. I knew that.

So Janet ended up having to be satisfied with a few clandestine hook ups, in unusual locations such as in the back area behind the ceramics shack, kissing on a shard pile, or in her car, the horrible explode-mobile I called it, the Pinto, meetups I felt terribly guilty about, but due to my desire to please, or my craven nature, I agreed to; and it was true they seemed to pacify her needs and keep her with Connor. It kept the group together and *The Fall* was averted. And my craven desire for her bod got fulfilled as a part of the deal. I got to "know" all about it. I feel constrained not to tell the details of what we did in an explicit way. It was not great. I knew what love was by then, and this was not love. This was pornography.

***

Abigail had taught me to pay close attention to what a woman wants not with her mind, or says in words, but what her organs want, even her glands, to observe how her body reacts, her pacing, the inner heat moving through her lower chakras, and to respond accordingly, in a mode of pure acceptance and kindness, even if that something was, well, not necessarily that enjoyable (or whatever) from my own perspective. To love is to serve. And Abigail also had said I would be able to satisfy, which gave me confidence with a "real woman" of the voluptuous and adventurous type. But my heart was not in it. In those moments I tended to think about Cindy, as dumb as that sounds, Cindy who was for all I knew on the other side of the world, doing other men—no, I was absolutely certain of it, those fucking Australians, punks, surfer types, and so on, and so on, my mind went in that direction, even as I was rather quickly and perhaps too efficiently giving Janet exactly what she wanted.

***

So, how did *The Fall* occur? How did Connor find out? I'm sure you can guess: Connor found out in the worst possible way. Janet had asked me over to her place for a special "session," and didn't tell Connor. But he saw I was gone from CC and put two and two together. A guy knows. He got on that infamous ten speed and rode over in the dark of night and saw the unspeakable through her bedroom window. We had been too stupid to even close the drapes.

The next morning, when I got back, he looked at me and I had a sickening feeling. It was guilt, I guess, mixed with fear, sweat, and too many lies.

"You rotten bastard!" he shouted.

"Connor, wait!" I tried to get him to stop, which of course was absurd. He charged and hit me a few times. I didn't put up much of a defence but when I'd had enough I left as best I could.

"Is that a shiner?" said Leo.

"I ran into a freight train," I said.

"Right." Leo didn't seem too impressed. The House was generally against me anyway. In his rage Connor had smashed a bunch of dishes and pots around the co-op, stuff he had made that people really loved. And of course people wanted to know why. My name was taken in vain a few times I'm sure.

***

And this is where things really go off the rails. When it all came out, when the sordid details became known to Connor, the secrecy, the betrayal of it, he blamed me for everything. Every stage of loss swept over him: shock that 'his woman' would cheat; denial that it could be true; violent anger when he became convinced it *was* true; bargaining, trying to make what had happened go away; and finally a sullen, bitter depression. But he never got to the final stage, which is acceptance. Instead, he eventually hatched a fever dream plan of "getting the band back together." You see, he thought the drug would change her, or at least make her listen. It was a love drug after all, or so they said. He demanded I supply more MDMA, and when I refused, behind my back and without me being aware, went to Mike Dix and said he was only a messenger from Sutra. He bought six capsules, which is a lot for two people. If only he had listened to me, but I was about 1,000 miles away from him from then on. Completely out of range.

I didn't hear much from Connor after that. He didn't formally move out, his stuff was still in the room, but apparently he was staying with Janet (which surprised me).

About two weeks passed. It was early morning; the phone rang on the second floor. I wasn't about to get it. I heard a door open and feet stumble in the hallway. Then, a blood curdling scream. Karen Tamlen was at the phone booth, screaming and sobbing. "He's dead!" she kept saying. "He's dead! He's dead!"

She was screaming like a banshee.

I went over to the phone and picked up the receiver. *"Hello? Sorry, I'm Connor's roommate, could you please repeat that? Yes. What's happened? ...so he's alive? ...What?"*

Karen had got it wrong. It was not Connor who had been killed in a car crash. It was Janet.

"...he's in hospital in serious condition...OK, what hospital is he at? ...Do I know his family's info? No, but I can try to find out. ...OK, thanks for calling."

I hung up and stood there, stunned.

That day is a blur, but at some point I got Rob, who was still the SCA membership coordinator, to call Connor's family. They were based in Chicago; Rob would be able to look up the details. I heard that Connor's father was going to come out to Eugene the next day.

As Connor's roommate, and probably (sadly) his best friend in the co-op, it was my natural duty to do things. Like tell people what was going on. But I didn't do that.

It was Rachael who sensed, perhaps dimly, but with more understanding than others, what I was dealing with. She gave me a hug and asked if I needed anything, if I wanted to talk. "Not just yet," I said. "Not for me. But I wonder, do you think you or a few people could go down and see him? I can't quite bring myself to do that."

I could see she thought I was a complete chicken-shit, but I took that rap. I deserved it. And yes, she did do the noble deed and even took a few people from the house. When she returned she was unsettled. "He didn't ask about you, which is weird. Sutra, the police are asking questions. You may need to front some of those. Apparently his girlfriend died. Janet? And they say he was high at the time of the accident. He had a tox screen and it came up positive for drugs. I think he may be in serious trouble."

"Yeah."

"Uh, we may also be. I hope this doesn't blow back on the co-op. It's already in the *Register Guard*."

She was really pissed. I could see that, and I could see that I was to blame, that a lot of what was going on, which was unspoken and unknown to Rachael and others, but sensed, the way a mouse in the dark senses the presence of a cat just waiting to pounce—all of that was coming to the surface, not today, but soon.

"This sucks," she said, and stalked off. We didn't talk again for a long time.

***

That afternoon there was a knock on the door of our room. Karen opened the door. She looked frightened. Behind her was a short, balding man wearing spectacles who frowned at me over Karen's round head.

"Thanks Karen," I said. "Hi, I'm Sutra."

"Hi Sutra. I'm Fred. So, do you know what's happened?"

"I know Connor's in hospital, that there was an accident."

"Yes. He's alive, thank God."

"Can you tell me anymore about what happened?"

"Yes. But there's also some things I don't understand. I was hoping you could fill me in, actually. Because we had not heard much from Connor and as far as I was aware, everything was going really well for him. He mentioned he had a very cool roommate at the co-op."

My heart sank. It would all have been so much easier if he had hated me.

I hedged like a weasel. "I don't know if I can fill in the gaps."

"But you knew his girlfriend? You have some idea what was happening in his life?"

"Yes, I do," I said heavily. "Connor was going through a breakup. Janet was breaking up with him. But he didn't want to admit that he wanted to get things back together. I hadn't seen him in two weeks. He was staying over at her place. We...had a falling out."

"Oh? What about."

I sighed. "It was about Janet."

"Ah." Fred put the pieces together. I could see he was intelligent. It would have been foolish to hide facts from him. "This Janet, she was quite a bit older...than either of you."

"That's true."

"Do you think she bears some responsibility for what happened? I understand drugs were involved."

"I would never believe Janet would take drugs."

"Really?"

"She was a wonderful person. Very responsible."

"I see. Well thanks for sharing. Connor is in hospital. His hands are burned but otherwise he's not too bad off. Physically. They were out, it was at night, in her car—"

"Yeah, it was a Ford Pinto. Go figure."

The father didn't want to laugh; it seemed wrong to him where it seemed perfectly reasonable to me to crack a joke. Because the unthinkable had happened. The Pinto had indeed exploded. Just exactly like *Consumer Reports* said it could. There was a truth in there, a comic truth, but the father was not having it.

"They went off an embankment and hit a tree. The car burst into flames. Connor luckily was thrown free of the car because the passenger-side door handle was broken and loose. But on the driver's side, the door was jammed. He tried to pull her free from the car, burned both of his hands doing that. He was a hero. But he couldn't get her out of the car. She burned to death."

I sighed. "It was quick. That's something."

But the father, Fred, was now angry. "That's a terrible thing to say!"

"Is it?"

"You should be more compassionate for a—a god-damned Rajneeshi—" but he didn't finish.

"What? Maybe you don't understand. Janet burned to death and that would have really hurt, but it was over in a matter of minutes, perhaps even seconds. But poor Connor, now he has to have that image in his head the rest of his natural life. Death is not so hard. Living is hard."

Fred was now beside himself with anger. "That's such a crock of shit! What kind of a drug-dealing creep are you! I think you gave Connor those drugs. You've destroyed my son's life. Admit you did that!"

I took a breath. "If he was on drugs during the crash, I did not give them to him. In fact, I told him not to buy them. He went around my back. Yes, he asked for drugs. But I said no. He then went to someone else. That's the truth. You can ask him: ask him did Sutra give you those? Didn't he say, 'don't buy those?'"

"Well, I did ask him, but he can't talk very well and he's on pain meds. But he said you introduced him to that drug. I'll never forgive you for that."

"I understand."

"You admit it?" His face was mottled with anger.

"I admit that Connor—was my friend. Anything beyond that is none of your business. In case you haven't noticed, he and I are both adults."

"Well, if that's the case then I'll be on my way. Just to let you know, I'm taking Connor out of school. I'm going to med-flight him back to Illinois. My wife and I will be by to collect his things here. It would be great if you weren't here when we did that."

I nodded, and he left, his fists clenched. I thought I probably got off with him pretty easy. I had expected him to beat the crap out of me.

***

The *Winter of Our Discontent* played itself out slowly. Those were some hard weeks when no one wanted to talk to me. But I spent most of the time holed up at the various University libraries. It was a quiet time with a lot of reflection and soul searching going on. Solitude has its virtues. I was slowly, day by day, getting stronger. I rode Connor's bike, which he had left behind, out to South C. Street and looked at Abigail's place discreetly from the other side of the road. I didn't see her, but I heard gentle laughter. I realized I missed Abigail more than I had realized. Or maybe, just because I was sad, it seemed she was the solution. But that was absurd (I knew). I had an idea about the solution, though.

***

After the mirthless winter break, the Spring term of 1987 was in progress. I decided it was to be my last term at The Campbell Club. I watched the violets come up from below the thin snow in February, and the bulbs followed them in March. I was basically not going to class anymore. It just seemed so pointless.

It was about six weeks into the term, perhaps mid-April, when I approached Rachael. She was on the front porch, enjoying the fresh air in a tank top and shorts. I had heard she had a new boyfriend.

"You look amazing," I said.

She frowned at me. "Not now, Sutra."

"No really, I have something important."

"Sure."

"Do you mind if I sit for a moment?"

"It's a free country."

I sat on the old couch next to her, not too close. "Have you been down to the Urban Farm this year?" I asked.

"Not yet," she said, suspiciously.

"Look. Don't be hard on me. I'm doing my best here."

"You're *persona non grata*."

"Yeah."

"You've said absolutely nothing yet, don't beat around the bush. If this is an apology, I have to go. I have to go to class soon. Thomas Pincheon III says you haven't paid your fees. He's a bit worried."

"I haven't paid all of them. That's because I'm leaving. But I have something for you. Something big. For the Green Revolution. I need to hand that over before I go."

"Oh?"

"I wonder if you can meet me, maybe tomorrow or when it is good for you, down at the Urban Farm. It's best if it's sunny and about mid-day, and not too windy. There might be a day like that this week."

"I don't think so, Sutra. I don't want to meet up with you. And certainly not down there."

"Please?" I got down on my knees and begged like a bad actor and clawed at the air. "PLEASE?"

She laughed involuntarily. "You idiot. OK, fine. This better not be a setup. I will let you know. But tomorrow might be good. Say, 1 pm?"

***

I was already down at the Urban Farm when she arrived. A class was just finishing up. Young fresh students with fresh ideas and dreams. I was sitting near the wildflower garden, just waiting impatiently, trying to keep it together. But I felt really good, too, perhaps for the first time in a long time. The sun was shining, but the wind was fairly calm. *This is it*, I thought. *Conditions aren't going to get much better. Although it might be too early in the year.*

Rachael was on time and looked radiant. She was a Junior this term and looked the part of the experienced co-ed. What a lovely sight. She came down riding on her Schwinn Cruiser wearing a straw hat and a floral print dress, and I almost fell in love.

"God Damn, Rachael."

"Don't be like that, Sutra. Now is not the time for it. Besides, all of this is for someone else."

"Yeah, I heard that."

"Can we start over, please? Or else I'm out of here."

"Absolutely. Absolutely. Please. I'm sorry. Really. Come and sit with me."

Still suspicious, she said, "What's our itinerary?"

"I just want to talk."

"Uh-Oh."

"Please? This will be quick." I pointed to the blanket I had brought and spread out on the grass. We were near the wildflower garden, the one I had weeded that time a century before, before the Ecstasy, before Connor went off the rails. There were plenty of flowers already in bloom.

She sat. I knew I had to be serious, so I just got on with it. "The Green Revolution," I said.

"Yes? Wouldn't that be nice."

"Take a look at this. I've photocopied some of the pages. But the original book is in the University library."

"This is a description of a butterfly."

"Yes, it's called Fender's Blue. It was first described in 1931 but believed extinct because it requires a particular type of wildflower, Kincaid's Lupine, on which to feed and lay its eggs. Apparently the butterfly is supposed to hatch in spring, and it lays eggs in the fall. The larvae eat the leaves of that one plant, and no other, in fall, and spend the winter among the roots of the plant as well."

"But no one has seen this since that early work of identification. The places where the Lupine grows have been mowed over or developed over. I'm sorry Sutra, but this insect is definitely extinct."

"It's documented as being very small, only about an inch across. The exact description—see, it says 'the males of this species have an upper-side iridescent sky blue color. The females are brown. Both sexes have a black border outlined by a white fringe on the dorsal or upper side of their wings.'"

"Yes. So what?"

"Now look at this flower. Come over here. Stay low."

I had her come into the wildflower garden. "You see this?"

"Yeah. Is that?" Her eyes were puzzled.

"Yes, that's Kincaid's Lupine. Someone must have been interested in growing it. It's threatened, just like the butterfly. People at the Urban Farm might know that."

"But there's a lot of it growing in here, Sutra!"

"Yeah, it seems to be thriving. Maybe if someone were to propagate it."

"But the butterfly—it's extinct."

"Is it?"

She looked at me. I suggested we sit back down but she was getting excited. She was trying not to show it. Not wanting to give me anything.

"Patience, Grasshopper," I said to her.

It did not take very long. We sat and watched while various bugs and flying things came and went. Suddenly, she cried out. "What's that?"

It was a small brown butterfly. It had the right size and looked like the drawing—for there was nothing to go on except the drawing and the original description. But it seemed possible. Then, in a moment, it happened. The male, small but iridescent blue, settled near the brown female.

"I've got no camera! I've got no net!" she said.

"But you see it, right?"

"I see it, I see it! Holy Crap!"

She was almost crying. "Sutra, you found it."

"No," said. Actually it was this guy Connor and I met. Janet had met him first. He lives back there—" I pointed vaguely towards the river. "Back beyond there. Or at least he did. The Sheriff comes around every year and rousts him out in the Spring. But He usually winters back there in a tent. Deon is his name. Anyway. Connor and I had a survivalist training lesson from him. And he talked a lot about animals and plants and how the environment was in desperate need of more wildflowers. And I remembered him talking about this one butterfly, how it was supposedly extinct. Maybe I dreamed it. But I'm pretty sure he said he was convinced it was still here."

"I don't think you dreamed it. It's real. Sutra, this is a big deal! I mean, maybe other people have seen it. Or maybe not. But it's real! This is a discovery!"

But then her eyes narrowed. "Wait a minute. Why are you telling *me* about this?"

"You're an ecologist. I thought this would be something you can work on. You see, if it's true that the Fender's Blue is not extinct, then if we planted the Lupine, if it could be protected, then the butterfly species and the flower together could come back. Maybe one day even thrive."

"That's all very noble. But I don't trust you anymore. Sutra, I'm wet. I'm actually wet right now because of this. And this is exactly what you would do."

"What do you mean?"

"You are a schemer. You want to get me in the sack."

I sighed. "I don't deny you're lovely. You're the most—"

"Don't say that shit to me! Never say that! I'm so sick of that fucking shit from guys!"

I tried to speak calmly. And in fact I stopped talking for a minute and took a breath. I was surprised to hear Rachael swear. She must have been right on the edge of crashing out and leaving, so I just tried hard to get small and shrink down to the size of a nothing. A null. Finally, I looked at her. "I'm not scheming. This is no scheme. This is my gift to you. It's basically a going away present. I'm leaving town. I think I told you that the other day."

"But don't you see, that's exactly what guys do. Guys will say anything to get what they want. So you crafted the perfect scheme. You went to the library—you've been in the library hiding, I know all about that—and you hatched this incredible idea of the extinct butterfly, and finding it, how cool that would be. And it is. It has got me going in a big way. You have no idea what it's like to have hormones. To be a girl. Damn you. Damn you, you bastard."

I just sat and listened. I didn't even look at her; my head was down.

She was really worked up, and now I thought I would find out why.

"I am pretty sure," she spat out, "that you caused the death of that girl. Connor's father, he came and spoke to me. He yelled at me, insulted the co-op. But I couldn't say anything. I knew inside he was right."

I was going to say something, but I thought better of it.

"You have no response?"

"So you want to know?" I said. "Are you sure? Will you listen or have you already decided."

"I am listening."

One false move by me would have been it. I thought for a while, trying to take my time. "Did you ever meet Janet?"

"I think I saw her at the co-op once or twice. I'm not sure we ever spoke."

"Did you notice that she was, well, there's no word for it."

Rachael was succinct. "She was a brick shithouse. That's what Cindy would have said."

"If I said that I'd be in big trouble. You know?"

"That's right. Some things only a woman can say about another woman. You can't say things like that."

"I described her as being a Susan Sarandon, but not quite a Faye Dunaway."

"Oh, that's indescribably sexist."

"I know. Sorry. Anyway—I digress. Look, the truth is, Janet and I were lovers. Briefly."

"No! My God! That's outrageous!"

I put up my fingers here and did air quotes. "I 'cheated' on Connor. I cheated I cheated I cheated. OK? It was wrong. But not because of some bullshit morality."

"You're not making me think any higher of you, if that's what you're trying to achieve by telling me this."

"But what if I told you I didn't want to. I mean, I wanted to, because she—but the point is, she was in the driver's seat. I didn't scheme. *She* approached me."

"Not helping here," she said.

"What I'm saying is, Janet decided. I was weak. But it was her will. I think if you remember, it's what you want too, to be in control. To have it your way, hold the pickles, hold the lettuce, special orders don't upset us. Right? So I went along with Janet. I did what she wanted. She didn't want Connor to know. That's the god's honest truth. And I did not give him the drugs. He went straight to Mike Dix, our friendly in-house chemist. I told him taking more Ecstasy would hurt him. He wouldn't listen. I swear to God, I told him."

"I still don't trust you. But I do think I understand. If you are telling the truth, which I've learned is impossible for any man to do."

"That's true. You're not wrong. And if I get philosophical with you, that would just be more lies, from your point of view. But there is a reason to trust me. There is a reason why this is not an attempt by me to get into your sack. Your big beautiful sack."

She laughed then, in spite of herself. "You bastard! You made me laugh." She stood up. "Last chance."

"Because I'm leaving," I said, looking up at her. "I wrote to the Sensei of the Mountains and Rivers Order of Zen Buddhism. It's in New Zealand. It's a real monastery, Rachael. I'm going to become a monk. A real one, not a bullshit Neo-sannyasin following a con-man's teachings. The main monastery is actually in upstate New York, but I asked if I could join the order in New Zealand so as to get as far away from America as possible. You won't see me, maybe ever again, if things work out."

"I sense a deception. It's too convenient."

I had to dig out my paperwork and literally show her the correspondence and let her read it all in full. She sat and went through every letter, every response from the Sensei and from the monastery. Fortunately I understood Rachael to the extent that I knew this level of proof would probably be needed in order for her to believe me—that I was really going. "And then there's this."

Finally I produced airplane tickets routing to New Zealand dated for April 17th, which was three days away. "You see? Portland to LAX, and then on to Christchurch."

She looked closely at the tickets. "One-way," she said, uncomprehending. "One-way."

I didn't say anything for a long time.

She looked at me and just kind of let the papers drop to the blanket. Her face lost all expression and became marble. "You're going to be a monk."

I nodded.

"So, this whole thing with the Fender's Blue. You did that—did you do that for ecology? Or did you do that for me? Because if you say you did it for me, then this is just a trap."

I looked at her steadily for a long time. "Do you remember when I told you about God sending messages through human beings?"

She nodded. "Yes, I've always remembered that. It was a weird thing to say. I thought it was some bullshit spin to get you laid. It almost worked."

"I know. Well, Carrie Anne told me that I had to get my shit together. I was high, it was the same day Cindy came into the dining room and you and Leo were there."

"I remember that day."

"While you were with Cindy, Carrie Anne was giving me a message. She's very religious, did you know that? At any rate, she told me, "Each step you take towards God, He will take one step towards you." And I asked her what that meant, and she said I had to figure that out, to get on with doing what I am supposed to do. And for the longest time, I couldn't figure it out."

"But now you have."

"Yes."

"Oh, you are a bastard."

I frowned. "What did I do now?"

"It's the ultimate trap. You are the king of traps. Bullshit traps."

"I don't think I follow. I'm leaving, like in two days. We can't do jack. I'm not going to see you again; I'm leaving your life totally. The credit for finding the extinct butterfly? Well, I want no part in it. You found it, you take it to an entomologist. That scientist might just get the credit. Or you might. That's all up to you. I don't care. But the least you can do is to follow through and have a campaign. The Green Revolution! You can finally do it! And you will have that for the rest of your life! You can plant those flowers. And you can save a species. Think of it, an entire species of life, which at least in my belief system is just as valid as the human species. Just as important. I'm doing that for you. For you only! I want nothing! Nothing!"

And as if to punctuate that sentence, I leaped up and grabbed my paperwork, and ran away, I left the blanket, just bailed. I ran in the direction away from Franklin, towards the foot bridge, towards the bliss giving Willamette. I ran as fast as I could, like a complete idiot, and what for me was my top speed. I had the absurd idea to go and hide in the woods. But by the time I got to the middle of the footbridge I was winded. I stopped, bent over breathing, and looked out at the 'Island in the Stream,' where Connor and I had started our training with Deon, and I felt good that my mission had been accomplished. It was done. Like Jesus, I had done it, I had accomplished what God had asked. Jesus had been asked to save millions; I had only been asked to save myself; and thus avoid Connor's fate. But I was also asked through Deon to save a being with no defender, no friend, the littlest and least of beings, who humans had wantonly and carelessly destroyed, and that was the Fender's Blue. I had not left that work undone either. Now it was Rachael's problem to actualize or not. I washed my hands of everything. Glorious Rachael of the marble statue was now the sole heir and possessor of the secret of the discovery.

Suddenly I felt a great sense of peace and love, as if I finally, for once in my whole life, had done something right. But in the process I also understood who Rachael was, and what she was: not the "perfect woman" (which actually was true of her, but not germane) but rather, the physical and mental manifestation of the highest idealism of the age: the Green Revolution. All that was best in us, in my generation, which you scornfully call boomers, all that was necessary for the continuation of the world, the spirit of Vishnu, of Life, Love, and Everything, was contained in that one idea; and she was the incarnation of it. And just coincidentally, this is why people are attracted to the idea of the Green Revolution: no one really knows what that means, but they know they want it. That's because inside it is hope. Hope, like a hidden jewel, like a diamond clitoris, is hidden within its folds. The outward perfection of Rachael's body and mind were merely extensions of this "Green" idealism, expressions of it. Rachael, and those like her, had been sent into the world by the higher power in order to save the world from itself. That was an awe-inspiring task, a life's work. Even Carrie Anne would be impressed by such a task, I thought.

But I had to forsake her. In order to complete my own task, I had to put her behind me forever. Never would I taste her physical perfection; nor bond with her in those traditional social patterns that I always scorned, stupid things like dating and marriage. In grade school we sang "first comes love, then comes marriage; then comes baby in a baby carriage." I thought it stupid and useless to take on and repeat those obligatory gestures and endlessly suffer the tedium of a social life modelled on someone else's dreams. A job, a mortgage, a child. Bills and Christmas presents to open. But those were things that she would want—being somewhat of the traditional and even romantic type—that was the underlying spirit of the age, romance, nostalgia—and she richly deserved all of it. She deserved to be happy. I could not give her that. She was not wrong about me; I was a con-artist and would fail her. But it did not make the pain less real. Never would I make her laugh or cry with happiness as I watched our child's head crown between her spread legs while she pushed and screamed; the baby finally expelled and then laid gently upon her breast; her face radiant; never would I see her grow old and die together with me in the same bed, peacefully, as old people sometimes do.

"Hey, Sutra! Hold on! Wait up!"

Suddenly, it was Rachael. I was knocked out of my maudlin reverie. She was on her Schwinn (of course) and had easily caught up with me. She rode right up to me fast and slowed down and then stopped next to me by putting her feet out as brakes. I could hear the sound of the soles of her shoes as they pressed against the concrete. When she finally came sliding to a complete stop, her face was quite close to mine.

She looked at me and then at the ground. "OK, you win."

"What?"

"I said you win. I surrender."

"But I don't want anything."

"Oh, you are such a liar. You have wanted it forever. You have teased and played your games forever with me. But now, I want it too. I'm saying you win. I believe you. I believe that you are leaving. I believe that you have done something big, something bigger than anyone has ever done for me, and that has won my love. I know it's true because you don't care about anything else. You don't care about ecology. Butterflies? You don't give a flying fuck about butterflies. You did this whole business of the Fender's Blue *for me*. But now you frustrate my love. I'm soaking wet over here. And then you say you are leaving; you produce a plane ticket. It feels so much like the ultimate trap, the trap with the promised back door to freedom which is then shown to be impossible."

"But it's not a trap," I said. "I really am leaving. And I swear, I'm never coming back. At least not to Eugene. I mean, this is it."

"I know that now. Shit. God-damn you." She was almost in tears. "Shit, shit. Shit. You're leaving for real."

We stood on the bridge for a while and maybe she cried. I can't really remember what she was doing. But I was *definitely* crying.

***

The moment passed. She wiped her eyes and looked down at the 'Island in the Stream.'

"Did you ever make it down there?"

"Yes," I said, "that's where Deon had the first session of his survivalist training. We built a little hut down there. We even caught a fish with a, like a hook that we made. Connor was the one who made it, come to think of it. I suppose I would starve. But I loved that fucking island."

"You remember we talked about it. I thought maybe you would find a way to live there, like a mystical hermit."

Yeah. I'm not too good at actualizing things."

"I think you were just too busy staring at my breasts that day to do anything else. It would have been nice to check it out. Somehow I always pictured you out there."

In my mind I flashed back to that glorious day of skinny dipping. I could see her nude marble body floating in the sunshine, as strands of her thick blond hair spread out in the biting cold water like the snakes on a Medusa—oh yeah, I certainly remembered— which was not the right thing at that moment, and I manfully tried to keep my shit together.

"I wish it could be like that," I said. "You are—you are too good for me."

"Oh, shut up!" She seemed furious now.

"Sorry."

"You had better be. Now listen. It's good you know something about that little place," she said, "because we're going to go down there."

I looked at her, uncomprehending. She looked like a Michelangelo sculpture, not the pieta, but one of the captured slaves. Or something. Very determined.

"We're going to go down there," she repeated. "And we're going to go to the end of the island, down that end, where it's sheltered and people can't see. Like on the day we skinny dipped. Yes, I was looking at your body, too. Your dick... I was sizing you up."

"What?" I couldn't quite believe what I was hearing.

"You were nude and I looked. I wanted you. I wanted you very much. But you were too stupid and self-involved. Guys are so bad sometimes."

"But—but—" I was stunned.

"We're going, Mister. Right now. It will be like *Swept Away*, if you know anything about movies. Do you know that one?"

Of course I did. All the guys of my generation knew that one.

"Yes," I said out loud. "It's uh, very erotic."

"It is. You'll get sand up your ass by the time I'm done with you. The water will roll over us in the sunshine. And I'll be raw, with dirt up my crotch and scratches all over my body. And then when we're done, I'm back to the co-op, and if I ever see you again after the date on that ticket, well, I will probably shoot you. Because you will have tricked me, and I don't much like guys doing that. I'm fed up with it. You know, I'm from Montana. And Montana girls know how to shoot. So you better take this seriously. It's not just Cindy who knows a thing or two about the bedroom. Montana girls know all about it."

"If we're going to have sex, you can call me Robert. All the girls seem to like that."

"Sure. Anything you say, Robbie." She motioned with her head. "Get going."

"But what if I don't want to? What about staying out of your big sack?"

"It is only what I deserve after all your nonsense these last few months. You owe me something for that. You are a rotten bastard and now you owe me. That's how I see things. I've been so frustrated I just feel like I could burst. It's time for you to pay up. Think of it as a 'karmic debt' if that helps." She scoffed and wagged her finger at me. "Such a loser. And bailing out in the middle of the term when I most need good people at the co-op? Just ignoring all your responsibilities? Skipping out on your fees, even?"

"Yeah. That's pretty lame."

"Totally fucking lame. And you made me cry just now, you bastard."

"I'm sorry."

"Besides, Cindy and I talked about it."

"What?" I cried. "You talked to Cindy?"

"I asked if I could have you and she said that would be fine. I was even going to take things further with you. I had ideas, plans. I thought I could break you of your bad habits, make you into a man. That was all before I learned about this Connor thing. Before you went completely off the rails and killed someone. Yeah, Cindy. She sends her regards. We spoke on the phone. Apparently all the Australian men are terrific in bed. Of course, she used much more graphic terminology than that. She wanted me to tell you she's having a field day. Also that everything is alright, she's fine now. She sends her love."

"Oh my," I said, my heart sinking. Suddenly becoming a monk was a lot less interesting, whether it was required by God or no.

"Oh buck up," said Rachael. She was shaking her head in disgust. "My God, the things a girl has to put up with. Just get going. I don't have all day."

***

So you see, I could not exactly say no to her. I had never seen the Venus de Milo so aroused. Not like that. She was like a hungry young lioness. And I was the meat. Frankly I was terrified. And I was pretty sure she was not joking. About the Montana thing, being able to shoot. Or Cindy. Or about any of it.

And back at the Campbell Club the Green Revolution was just getting started.

About the Author

David R. Smith is an American expat. He currently lives somewhere in the mysterious bushland continent of Australia. He is happily married and has four adult children.

His pen names include David Apricot and Mia Sandalwood. He has three previous novels and a number of translations. There is a website:

https://www.metamadbooks.com/

Inquiries to the author may be directed to:

metamadbooks@gmail.com